THE TRENCH ANGEL

THE TRENCH ANGEL

Michael Keenan Gutierrez

A Novel

Leapfrog Press
Fredonia, New York

Published in 2015 in the United States by
Leapfrog Press LLC
PO Box 505
Fredonia, NY 14063
www.leapfrogpress.com

Printed in the United States of America

Distributed in the United States by
Consortium Book Sales and Distribution
St. Paul, Minnesota 55114
www.cbsd.com

Portions of this book were published in *Scarab* and *Crossborder*.

Author photo courtesy of Rebecca Ames

First Edition

Library of Congress Cataloging-in-Publication Data

Gutierrez, Michael Keenan.
The trench angel / by Michael Keenan Gutierrez.
pages cm
ISBN 978-1-935248-71-2 (paperback)
1. Photographers--Fiction. 2. Interracial marriage--Fiction.
3. Colorado--Fiction. 4. Mystery fiction. I. Title.
PS3607.U8175T74 2015
813'.6--dc23
2015008777

For Jessica

The piano played a slow funeral tune,
And the town was lit up by a cold Christmas moon,
The parents they cried and the miners they moaned,
"See what your greed for money has done."
—Woody Guthrie

CONTENTS

PART ONE

The Anarchist's Son

THE SOMME RIVER VALLEY

The men lined up for their pictures before they died. It was
an orderly, single-file queue snaking through the trench,
no pushing or shoving, none of that childhood hokum, because, after all, they were Englishman. Each held a letter addressed to his mum or sweetheart, brother or father,
mostly commenting on the poorness of the weather or the
morale of the men or even razzing the queer ways of the
French, but they didn't have any words for the war. How
could you remember all of this and put it down on paper?
When their turn arrived, they handed the letter to me, the
Yank, and I raised my camera, the indestructible Miss Constance, then fired. The pose never changed—head tilted
a smidge left, eyes wide—the same picture over and over
again like a broken projector. You went through that death
line enough times it became rote. Still, if I could go back,
if I could somehow reenter the mind of my younger self,
I'd have kept those photos, every last one of them, and I'd
have put them all together in a book without a title because
no pithy phrase could sum up those stares. When you're
young you never think you'll forget anything let alone all
of it. After a while, you forget all you've forgotten. Or you
write it down.

Richard McDowell was next. He had a dark birthmark
on his Adam's apple and skin shaded like boiled egg yolks.
It was McDowell who taught us to keep the lit end of the
cigarette *inside* our mouths. The first couple times burned,
but, afterward, it got so you liked the heat, the fire right
beneath your brain. He passed me a letter addressed to his

wife, June McDowell of Manchester, and I slipped it into my back pocket, between two dozen others, and then raised Miss Constance.

"Thank you," McDowell said. They were like that, grateful.

The night before, McDowell confessed that he'd lost his memory of color. He could no longer remember the color of his mother's flowers, the blues, greens, and reds that bloomed behind her house each spring. He'd forgotten the color of his wife's eyes and his father's beard. Even in the present, when he looked at his own hands, searching them by firelight, he couldn't say their pigment.

"Brown," I told him. "Your hands are brown like the rest of us."

At the end of the line stood George Worthington. He'd been missing the top half of his left ear for a good year and he'd written nine different goodbye notes to his wife. He passed me the tenth.

"Don't bother delivering my letter by hand," he said. "She's too pretty to bother with an American."

"I'm married," I said. This was true for another hour.

For Worthington, the war erased his conception of time. Moments from his childhood happened just last week. Sometimes, he said, he'd been stuck in France since Napoleon's reign. A lot of men were like that, exiled in history, some as far back as the days of Nero, and one corporal could even recount tales of Babel. Before retreating to his own section of trench, Worthington told me, "And don't sell the damn picture. I don't want you to make a single bloody pence off me."

I stepped away, stunned. Of course I'd never sell it. No one bought pictures of dead men anymore. Not since 1915. This was just a damned courtesy, or, as they liked to tell me, a courtesy for the damned. In any case, the remark reminded me of my father, the old anarchist, who had believed photographs stole a man's right to his own time. He figured that if you could capture moment, print it, and profit from it, you made time just another commodity like coal, guns, or boots. You brought humanity that much closer to enslavement. That was the idea, at least.

I didn't believe him, not when I was a kid and not that last morning on the Somme. But then again, I didn't believe much of anything by then. Like a lot of men without experience, I'd held a devout faith in the power of ideas, but that was before the war, before I'd raised my camera to my first corpse and recorded my first death, back when I'd been a photographer of faces, rather than a chronicler of boots. Those ideas—the perfectibility of man, the progress of history, and the war that brought peace—lost their meaning on some marble orchard between Paris and Verdun. Yet, I wasn't entirely faithless. I still trusted the reliability of memory, the photograph as truth, and the written word as meaningful. But the cause? Thinking about it in my soiled trench, my mud-crusted charnel house among the lice and vermin running the maze of spent shells, I struggled to find any inspiration that wasn't propaganda. The armies marched behind liars and fools and, yes, I'd been complicit in the spreading of those lies, the propping of those fools. The whole lot of them—Haig, Falkenhayn, Joffre—could kill each other into the next year, the next decade, hell the next century, as far as I cared. By the time I took Worthington's picture, I knew this was my last day on the Western Front.

Neal Stephens was quitting the Great War.

The guns fired, again. A thousand British cannons rained munitions upon the sopping German trenches. The men looked east, studying the ladders they'd soon mount. I turned west: there was nothing left to photograph. The landscape had returned to its original volcanic state—a sea of steaming sand rolling along the Earth's crust—only a lone chimney teetering in no-man's-land remained of civilization. It was like the view from my childhood home, where the Rocky Mountains, jagged and primeval, filled the bright horizon, teaching me that we were all just one plague away from returning to cave life. At the time, I thought I'd never return to Colorado. I'd told my wife that lie. But in that trench, during that first Great War, I believed myself honest because I was going to get her out of France, off the gray front, to a place where white men could live in matrimony with black women without fear of the hanging tree. That place was Lisbon.

The mines detonated and the ground shook like San Francisco. I, ever brave, quaked against a sandbag.

Imagine if they'd all gone off.

Most of them didn't. They just went thud, a failure of European manufacturing. It could have been so much worse if all the ammo worked. I've heard you can go back to that same place along the Somme and see the trench and walk through a field where no-man's-land used to be, and some say you can hear the whispers of the dead, but it's really the wind through the wheat and if you're not careful, if you don't watch your step, you're liable to trip over some unused shell, some unexploded mine, and then you too get to be whispering to the living in that field. That's what they say.

A mess sergeant, James O'Keefe, poured me hot coffee with a lashing of rum. He was the dandy of the bunch, with a freshly trimmed moustache and slick hair coifed beneath his steel helmet that glimmered with a polished sheen, like a target. Next to him, Roland Reynolds, encrusted in mud, coated in lice, shuffled through his pack, making sure he had everything, and he had *everything*: a rifle fixed with bayonet, goggles, a shovel, two flares, a message book, a mess tin, a ground sheet, a water bottle, field dressings, spare socks, a shaving kit, a hand grenade, a gas helmet, a towel, an iron ration, wire cutters, some dry rations, and the collected works of Goethe in the original German, just in case. He also had the sledgehammer. Every tenth man got handed a sledgehammer and Reynolds drew the dime. If they'd taken the German trench, who knows, maybe they would have needed that sledgehammer.

From the twin rivers, a band of mist swept across the earth, but it wasn't cover or camouflage. The sky was too clear. Once up top, a soldier could see clear to the Germans and the Germans could see clear to him. Rain fell a few hours earlier, but not much rain, just enough to give the mud a fresh sheen. If Eskimos have a hundred words for snow, and Americans have a dozen words for indifference, then trench soldiers had a thousand words for mud: mire, sludge, bogland, cunt-clay, blood-soil, death marsh, cock-slough. The morning rain turned the dirt into a heavy, clumpy mire that caked their uniforms, weighing down their seventy-pound packs another pound or two, but what was another pound or two when you were going to die?

They all died by the way. I should have said that before. Every last one of them died.

I crouched on the duckboard, and then drew Lorraine's letter from my coat, unfolding it—*I love you, Snowball and I'm here to bring you home.* I'd read it near a dozen times that morning, going over each word like it was code, as if counting the syllables might illuminate some secret Masonic message, but she was honest and forthright and it was I who played games with language. I would read that letter a thousand times after that day, until one wet night in 1928 when I sat in a phone booth on the Negro side of Chicago and her letter crumbled in my fingers like a hieroglyphic scroll, and it was then that I knew I'd never remember what her face looked like again, but that was still a long ways away. In that moment, in that trench, my wife, my Lorraine, was still alive, safe in a Red Cross tent barely a mile away. I'd make things right with her. We'd get to Lisbon.

But of course it didn't work out that way. It's strange, now, to think about how those things I wanted so much when I was young, those places that I would have done anything to get to, are now, years later, the things that scare me the most. Lisbon's like that for me. You couldn't pay me enough to go there.

When the guns stopped, the absence of noise, the air empty of fire, made me dizzy. My boots sunk into the kind of mud that didn't exist in America. I looked to the chimney, to my magnetic north, and settled myself. This spell, like something out of an antebellum romance, hit me whenever it got quiet. Soon now—ten minutes, a sergeant said. Orders arrived. Soldiers were not to assist the wounded. As an officer yelled for the men to stand ready, I pressed against the back of the trench, away from the condemned with a loaded Miss Constance. The Sergeants fixed trench ladders in place. Soldiers partnered up—taking turns affixing tin triangles to each other's packs—making sure they shined for those watching the war play out through binoculars. There were no cries. This wasn't the time for sentimentality. No maudlin speeches of camaraderie. Let the Germans weep.

I checked Miss Constance a third, a fourth time, then stepped back from the soldiers and raised her, hoping to get off one last shot, because, after all, it was nearly time for the dénouement.

The Captain opened his watch, the slow tick louder than Big Ben. Rats jostled over boots. Roaches burrowed into the mud. Everyone inhaled.

At seven-thirty, on the last tick, the Captain lipped the whistle, then blew. A half a million men sighed.

The unit commanders climbed first, then helped their men over the top, like they'd planned. Forward on, don't stop. Even when the Germans opened their machine guns, even when their cannons filled the air with fire, the soldiers filed up the ladders like mourners entering a chapel. When the final officer went over, I was alone, the last man on Earth.

Two steps up the ladder, Miss Constance mounted on her dirt tripod, I squinted through the viewfinder. Brown boots on brown ground, at first in motion, then still, only the tread visible on film. I should have gone up with them, stood in the line of fire, and really gotten a good shot off, but that's the thing with war photography: if I wanted to get a good picture I'd have to be willing to take a bullet.

A shell exploded, sending me to the dirt, my helmet riddled with metal fragments. I scurried along the duckboard with the rats, checking my fingers, my limbs, looking for a tunnel to hide in. My eyes burned and I breathed smoke and mud. When I stopped moving, when I tried to cough, I couldn't smell anything, so I touched my face, wiping mud across it, relieved I still had a nose and a jaw because to me, then, the only thing worse than death was disfigurement.

I found myself sitting on the duckboard, my back to the war, lit a cigarette, and then watched the mud rain into the trench. Had my father been this scared? That's what I asked myself. I was a stray bullet away from heaven, and I couldn't think of anything more profound than the anarchist Jesse Stephens. He had that way about him, an ability to creep into the recesses of your memory, only to emerge unscathed when you'd been sure you'd gotten rid of him. Had all of the blood horrified him? Did it confirm all he'd believed about the corruption of governments? They said it was anarchists who brought this war upon us. It was an anarchist who sent me here.

On my feet, I looked through Miss Constance's lens. More boots, just the treads showing. The Germans kept shooting, their Gatling guns firing round after round like a telegraph ticker. Even though it looked like the war was over and the Germans had won, I hoped to get off one more shot, something I could take to Lorraine, but I was always missing the point. Hell, if I'd had a better camera, one with a stronger lens, I might have seen past those boots, beyond the shell casings and the mine craters and the barbed wire, right up to those Germans manning that cannon aimed straight at me.

Maybe it was because of the cannon's poor quality, or the soldiers' miscalculations, that the shell sailed over the boots of dead Brits, over the barbed wire, over the trenches, and over me as I abandoned my trench and ran west toward the Red Cross tent, toward Lorraine.

The shell screeched over me in a colorless fire, incinerating my dual belief in the infallibility of truth and the reliability of memory just as solidly as if the damned thing had detonated square on my skull.

—I—

I heard the train long before I saw it, a march of steel
charging along a stone embankment. It shook my boots
and I raised my hat and let the rumble course my skin.
The steam came next, a black plume hissing into the wind,
followed shortly by the profile of the locomotive rolling
through the white sagebrush, charging head-on toward
me. From New Sligo, it would abandon the plains and cut
due west, slipping through the shadows of Rocky Mountain
canyons until it reached the Mormon desert and then speed
toward the dark waters of San Francisco. From there, I
could board a ship going just about anywhere.

Like most mornings, I had ended up watching the trains
come and go. Back then New Sligo didn't have a recog-
nizable railway station, just a lean-to, along with a small
radio room and a clock tower which was always a couple
minutes behind, but that day it seemed like the whole town
had come out to see the train. It was nearing midday and
scores lined up to board and more would be here tomorrow
and the day after that until New Sligo was just another
ghost town: merchants with means sending their families
to Eastern relatives; bankers with brass-plated steam-
er trunks taking long autumn holidays; even out-of-work
miners, down to their last nickels, lolled about, hoping to
jump an open freight. The few remaining employees tried
to keep order, but their hearts weren't in it. As the train
slowed, the crowd hushed. This is why we'd all come.

"The Spirit of '49 is now arriving," a Negro porter said.
"Please ready your luggage."

The wind, foreshadowing snow, blew down the white-lit mountain. Dust flew into my eyes and then settled on my skin. A pair of cows wandered out onto the tracks and the conductor got off the locomotive and shooed them with his coal shovel. Boarding passengers stood a safe distance from the clock tower, where, beside me, lay a dark cluster of war gimps, those breathing memorials, limbless in battered army uniforms with tin cups outstretched, moaning at different pitches like a deaf a cappella troupe. In my coat I found a bottle marked "Maple Syrup" and took a swig of something that resembled rye, before I offered it to a nearby cripple, a man I called Eli, but that wasn't his real name. Eli shook his head no.

"You sure?" I said. "It might make your legs grow back."

A boy came by with a stack of the *New Sligo Eagle*. The headline: Strike Talks Break Down from Red Menace.

It was horseshit.

"Nickel for the *Eagle*, Mr. Stephens," the boy said. "Best paper in town." Only paper in town he should have said.

"Trade you a drink." I offered the bottle.

The boy looked at me like I'd just propositioned his mother. "You got a nickel Mr. Stephens?"

"No, do you?"

The boy swore under his breath, afraid to say anything lest he found himself out of his ripe paper job and inside a mineshaft just like the rest of his family. He lowered his head, sulked away.

I shimmied up the steel supporting post, and then slid Miss Constance from her bag. She found Eli, legless and sober. "Don't move, corporal."

Eli turned and looked right at Miss Constance. Within that flinty face, Eli managed to open his mouth and expose a few charred teeth.

"Christ," I said. "Act natural, will you?"

But Eli kept it up. A picture of a smiling cripple—no matter how horrifying a smile it may be—was no good to me back then. It was staged and it was phony and I wasn't some damn portrait artist like Curtis with his Indians. No,

I'd sooner trust Miss Constance to a band of gypsies.

I went over to the radio room and looked in at the operator, a myopic man named Anderson, while he gave orders to the train conductor. It was a small job, not much dough in it. A couple of miles outside the station, the radio went dead and you entered this space outside the modern world.

The Negro porter stopped beside me. I'd seen him a dozen times, but I didn't know his name. We both leaned against a wall littered by wanted posters with my father's picture on it.

"They're all going," I said. I turned and spit. "Shame, them shitting themselves over a little strike like this."

"If I may say, Mr. Stephens, they're the smart ones."

—2—

Because it was nearly noon, I drove across town to Mc-
Guffey's, the greatest tavern in the Western world. I should
have been at work—all hands on deck during a strike—
but I figured Roosevelt Robinson, the editor of the *Eagle*,
would find me if I was needed. Besides, there was no better
place to find rest and companionship than McGuffey's.

Established in the last century as the town's Ne-
gro-friendly saloon, McGuffey's was New Sligo's lone tavern to survive prohibition, partly because it was hidden
in the basement beneath O'Clair's Butchery, but mostly
because it was the joint favored by Jacob Bailey, the town's
police detective. On Friday nights, the crowd of miners,
newspapermen, and cowboys swelled to nearly a hundred,
with a line ten deep at the bar, while everyone else min-
gled alongside the dozen tables in the back. It was not,
you could say, a tavern frequented by the genteel. Cigarette smoke fogged the underground bar, camouflaging the
smell of iron and the darker, rancid odors beneath it. Animal blood occasionally dripped through the ceiling cracks,
filling the ashtrays and coating the tables. Even in the
dead of summer, everyone wore one of the black slickers
hanging on the coat rack. Near festivals or holidays, when
Old Man O'Clair really hacked away, when each cut of his
cleaver rattled the light fixtures, blood pooled on the dirt
floor and seeped through your boots. Without windows,
without natural light, with only candles illuminating the
path your hand took to your drink, time's normal constraints evaporated like river water. If I reach back into

the recesses of my memory, I can still feel the blood of lambs on my fingertips.

I was halfway through my second beer when the old Negro barkeep, the indomitable Lazy Eye Norris, hung up the phone and turned to me and winked with his good eye.

"That was Jacob," Lazy Eye said. "Someone plugged O'Leary. They found him stiffening up at the jailhouse."

"Clyde O'Leary, the Sheriff?"

Lazy Eye spit. "No, his dead daddy rose from the grave, went to the jailhouse and someone shot him. Who do you fucking think?"

I looked at my beer, a foul elixir, and then drank it down. His death meant nothing but grief for me. To say Clyde O'Leary and I shared a history understates the depth of our long and violent association. A lot had happened between us—after all we'd grown up together and tangled in numerous ways—but our entire relationship was shaded by the simple fact that my father killed his father. The other problems—and there were many—all rested under the shadow of that lone fact.

Meanwhile, as I reconciled myself to Clyde's murder, Lazy Eye hit the cowbell behind the bar, usually a sign of trouble. The crowd quieted.

"Someone just murdered O'Leary," he said.

I swiveled my stool toward the sad lot of cripples and miners in the back. Their faces contorted, comprehending the news. Men turned to old friends, exchanging expressions of stunned good fortune, the kind rarely begotten in the hours before a strike. They didn't know how to take the news.

Lazy Eye did it for them, raising a mug, then bellowing, "To O'Leary's murderer. May they bronze his likeness in the town square, so the generations can admire a true goddamn hero."

The mass of men, bone-tired and hunched, soot-stained and soused on this Monday morning, raised their heads from their drinks and collectively cheered as though the soprano had just finished her encore. They stomped their boots and hugged their fellow man. In retrospect, it was kind of touching.

But I didn't see it that way at the time. As the celebration died down, the men turned to me and I knew what they were thinking.

"I've got to blow town," I said. "No need for me to see this out. I ain't brave."

"Why? You plug him?" Lazy Eye's smile disappeared. "What you going to say when they ask where you were early this morning?"

"This morning?"

"That's what I said, ain't it? O'Leary was colder than a cripple's cunt."

"Home," I said. "I was home."

"Too bad," Lazy Eye said. "I was hoping it was you."

"What did I do?"

"Nothing. You ain't ever done a goddamn thing you pasty little cocksucker." He leaned in and then whispered, "They ain't gonna hang you, not like these mealy-eyed fucks."

He was right. I looked around at a bunch of men who didn't stand a chance against the law. It was a shame: Clyde couldn't even die honest. He had to go ruin another man's life from the grave. It reminded me of the time before our fathers went O.K. Corral on each other, when Clyde and I were just children in the old, violent days of the West, and Clyde confessed that he was destined to die before thirty because God had it out for him. Sweet Clyde O'Leary, sickly and weak, believed he'd catch diphtheria like his sister. But he was wrong. He caught a bullet, just like his father.

"You think your old man did it?" Lazy Eye said. "He cooled Big Hank."

"He's in Europe." I stomped my boots against the boggy floor. "Been gone fifteen years now."

"You keep telling yourself that."

I dropped a match in a blood-pooled ashtray. A plume of smoke rose out of it. Above the shelves stock full of whiskey bottles hung a sign that read, "If Killed on Premises, Will Pay for Burial." It was near a poster of Big Hank O'Leary, the old head of the coal miner's union, wearing a Christ-like robe with a halo above his head: the union man as martyr.

Beside me, a slow wheeze drifted from Sam Bailey, the old pastor, who hunched over the bar gripping its rails like he was making sure it didn't fly off the floor. Poor bastard. At fifty-five, Sam wasn't long for this world. He was like a building caving in on itself one floor at a time. It was only a matter of waiting out the slowing tick of his liver's clock, until Sam got his wish and died on his barstool.

"How you doing, Neal?" Sam's lips were white like he'd been walking in the desert without water. "I'm real sorry about your Mama."

"Thanks, Sam." She'd been gone ten years.

Sam sipped the foam from his beer like a child with a cup of milk. When he pulled himself upright, beer dripped from his sagging chin. "And your father, Neal," Sam said. "Your father has returned?"

I sighed at Sam's spindly shadow. His hair had fallen away, his jowls hung from his face like a bulldog, and lint collected in the dark folds of his hands.

"Because if he was, I'd have to lynch him," Sam said. "Yes, I'd hang him in Pioneer Square. Wouldn't I, Nigger Norris?"

"Be quiet, Sam," Lazy Eye said. "Let the man drink his fill."

"I'm just saying that the Stephens' and the O'Leary's got a blood feud. Been going on for near twenty years now. That's all I'm saying," Sam said. "And you know what else I'm saying? No, well let me tell you two gentlemen that the older O'Leary was killed just like the younger one. In cold Devil's blood."

"Stop it Sam," I said. "Everyone knows Big Hank was armed."

"Not when he died he wasn't."

"Yes, he was." I grabbed Sam's thigh and I could almost feel down to the bone. "And my father is in Europe and I know a hundred people who've been itching to kill Clyde, so let's ease off on the rumors, please."

"Blood feud," Sam said. "Like the Hatfields and Mc-Coys."

The phone rang and Lazy Eye retreated. Sam smiled. "I've been thinking, Neal. We should, I mean you, your sister and me should go down to the Lutheran church together sometime. It do you good in these trying times."

"You know I don't go to church and Tillie don't believe in God."

"Just like your Daddy. Just like that Jesse Stephens."

When Lazy Eye returned, he tapped my mug. "Finish up, kid."

"You kicking me out?"

Lazy Eye nodded. My editor, Roosevelt, had called: O'Leary's murder was my story. I took the last of my drink, and then turned to the rabble, hoping they might wake me. Their faces were familiar, like I'd photographed them once upon a time, but it wasn't the same as recognition. It was different for them; they knew where I'd been born, where I'd gone to college, and that my wife was dead. They nodded my way and held the door, but it wasn't entirely friendly because my uncle owned the mines and my father shot their leader and I worked for the company paper and those facts were all that mattered.

"Take a nice a picture of O'Leary's bullet holes for me," Lazy Eye said. "Least you could do you son of a bitch."

The masses cheered, again. A man wearing a blue trench coat raised his glass and began singing an old union song.

> *It is we who plowed the prairies; built the cities*
> *   where they trade;*
> *Dug the mines and built the workshops; endless*
> *   miles of railroad laid.*
> *Now we stand outcast and starving, 'midst the*
> *   wonders we have made;*
> *But the Union makes us strong*
> *For the Union makes us strong.*

Lazy Eye took my mug. "Before you go," he said, "you mind searching old Sam's pocket for his billfold?"

I tapped Sam, but the old preacher didn't stir. Inside Sam's coat, I found his wallet. There was only a dollar, but Lazy Eye took it.

"Man has got to pay for his bed," Lazy Eye said. "Has to pay for it."

—3—

I drove out to the jailhouse, taking a right on Garivogue, then a left on Fourteenth, along the town's thoroughfare with its three-story fronts, ornamental brick sidewalks, and twenty-foot high telephone poles running wires alongside electric streetlamps illuminating the boulevard for window shoppers. The town had changed since I'd gone to Europe, and even after three years back in New Sligo, I was still amazed at the pace of growth, the rapidness of the modern world encroaching upon the frontier. There were two new car barns replacing the livery stables, a couple of ornate picture shows, and you could even buy honest to goodness Parisian summer shoes if that was your taste. My uncle hoped travelers saw *that* New Sligo, rather than the *other* New Sligo, the New Sligo of Lazy Eye and Sam. We did our best to hide our refuse, our Mexican migrants, war cripples, and flu orphans, concealing them on the other side of the railroad tracks, or, if they insisted, inside McGuffey's. It was better that way, my uncle said: you don't need to show your houseguests your underwear drawer, and to an extent, I understood. We needed to make money. Yet, during that drive to the jailhouse, I got the nagging feeling that the town's sordid skivvies were about to be put on display at the National Museum.

As I drove, I tried not thinking on Clyde's murder, but I couldn't help it. Like I said, we'd been friends once, as boys, long before the war took me away, but that all changed on one black day in 1904, when Clyde's father walked into my father's office and never walked out. Back then, my father had been a normal man, running Rahill Coal & Electric, alongside my uncle Seamus, my mother's brother. There was a strike on, but then there always seemed to be a strike on. Yet that one was somehow different. Not too long after Big Hank died, my father disappeared, eventually showing up in Europe as a leading anarchist, one prone to violence and melee. For a long time, I'd been able push my father out of my mind, almost as if he was dead, but with Clyde's murder, it all came rushing back.

By the time he died, Clyde had been Sheriff for two years, elected with 90 percent of the vote, mostly because his opponent, the incumbent Sheriff, Michael Corrigan, dropped out at the last minute. Some say O'Leary threatened Corrigan's children, others thought it was simply blackmail, a type of crime Clyde had special deftness with. In any case, Clyde was the youngest Sheriff in New Sligo's history, and our first Sheriff who only had one working eye, a result of mining accident when Clyde was thirteen. Sure, Clyde was cruel and corrupt, but they all were. Back then democracy was a bit more rough and tumble. We'd only just gotten the secret ballot and a lot of our elected class was owned by either the union or the company. However, O'Leary was different: he didn't owe anyone. We were all scared of him.

I turned right on Seventh Street, then slowed to cross beneath the Union Pacific rail trestle. Here, the paved avenue ended and the gravel strip through Germantown began, with its windy, abandoned roads scarred by deep gullies that had been left unfilled since the war broke out. Fragments of broken window glass littered the roads, sparkling like a dry salt bed. Most of the homes were gone, burned to the ground with only their tin roofs remaining like industrial headstones. Stray dogs wandered the roadside, looking for their long-dead owners. Further on, I came upon a sandy strip of barren land, eventually passing Chinktown, which lay nearly dormant, just a few cooking fires burning inside oil drums, the smoke funneling into the blackening air. And a little past there, I found myself across the road from Rahillville, where several thousand miners and their families endured in identical two-room shanties, a ghetto owned and operated by Rahill Coal & Electric. It seemed like the sort of place where someone cried, real loud, all night long, so that it kept you awake until the dawn.

When I reached the jailhouse, I parked, and then saw, just over a crest about a hundred yards west of the road, a pair of prairie dogs standing on their hind legs, scouting me. I shivered. Nasty creatures, the type of animal best suited for Clyde's company. I got out and looked around but didn't see Jacob. Just outside the front door, surrounded by a half dozen milk crates, an old oak tree towered thirty feet into the air, with a single limb pointing west. Black burn marks ran unevenly spaced along the limb, counting, like shamed tree rings, the number of nooses that had been fixed to it.

I went inside, stepping into the shadow cutting across the jailhouse floor, and my feet sunk into a puddle of dark, drying blood sloughed beneath the doorway. The blood swept into the room like a mop stroke, coming to an abrupt halt at O'Leary's bare feet.

"Huh," I said. "That's odd."

O'Leary, plainly dead, sat bound and naked, his body bent against the desk, his wrists roped and knotted to his feet, his head slumped in repose, the back of his skull open and breathing. Sunlight shot through the high window bars, spotlighting his bloody forehead, which looked like it had collided with a blackjack. I lifted O'Leary's chin: he'd been shot in the mouth. His eye patch was his only clothing. I got close and photographed his profile, taking care to focus on the eye patch.

I searched the jailhouse, scouring the makeshift kitchen and the toilet for any telling detail worth photographing, only coming to a halt at a cell where a rope lay knotted to the bottom of one of the bars like a dog had been tied to it. It had bound something, wrists perhaps, and then been severed with a knife. I snapped a picture. I went to the desk and pulled open the drawers. They held forms and other assorted police supplies, along with the usual sorts of interrogation devices found in any backwoods Western jail:

knives, handcuffs, pliers, hatchets, kerosene, matches, and salt. There was a camera empty of film, some photographic paper, but no file with my name on it.

I wanted to keep searching, but I stopped when I heard footsteps and saw a great flop of a detective eclipsing the doorway, his corpulent frame a miracle in a town so familiar with starvation. Jacob was the son of Sam Bailey and carried the weight of his father's life like a millstone around his throat. He was gluttonous, corruptible, and cranky, and if you'd asked most people about him, they'd say he was a worthless son of a bitch, but he was also my oldest friend and you look past certain foibles when you've shared so much history with a man.

"What you doing?"

I raised Miss Constance and snapped one last photograph—*O'Leary in Repose.* "Searching for something to mourn."

"Find anything?" He took off his hat, put it to his heart. "Because I sure as hell can't. Christ knows what I'll say if the preacher asks me for a eulogy."

"His mother loved him."

"Some time ago, maybe. Hasn't let him eat at home in a long time."

Like me, Jacob had run with O'Leary in the old days. But Jacob was never prone to sentimentalizing the dead.

"He'd have been a good man," Jacob went on. "If someone shot him twenty years ago."

Sunlight spread across Jacob's patent leather shoes, which were tattered like old bandages. "Got to ask where were you last night between the hours of two and six?"

"Bored and frigging myself blind," I said. "Why? You find my fingerprints?"

"No just saw there's blood on your shoes and a little on your tie. Fresh blood at that and you smell like cigarettes and booze like you've been seeking solace for a sin, and most damningly, the rope around O'Leary's wrists is a bowline and I remember the day your father taught us to tie that very knot."

"Nice work, but it all proves is that I was in McGuffey's this morning and that the killer might have worked on a ranch."

"Strange Roosevelt sent you, seeing as you and O'Leary had a history."

"Hardly knew the man."

"Except that your pa killed his pa."

"Except that," I said. "Where's my uncle? I figured he'd be here."

"Church," Jacob said. "Wanted God to forgive O'Leary's soul."

"He'll be a while. He say anything else?"

"Said O'Leary was a waste of the Lord's mud and even in death he couldn't serve the world. But don't write that. You know, for his ma."

We wandered out into the dirt lot and I could still smell Clyde on my shirt.

"Why's he naked?" I took out my notebook and pen.

"Can't figure that out. Doesn't look like he was raped."

"I'm gathering he was knocked on the head at the door, then dragged inside."

"Then disrobed, tied up, and shot," Jacob said. "In that order."

"Prisoners gone?"

"Yeah, Seamus' horse thieves." Jacob said.

A week earlier a pair of Seamus' prized Appaloosas went missing. Clyde arrested a family of Mexican migrants, even though they didn't have any horses with them.

I fanned myself with my hat, and then coughed. The coal smoke turned the sky colorless like dull wet gravel that smelled of sulfur and filled our lungs with a tar worse than tobacco. Toward the west, dark storm clouds climbed over the top of the mountains. They always seemed to be there, struggling, stopping, and then evaporating. But once in a while they made it down to New Sligo. When they did, it could snow for days.

"One man." Jacob pointed at a set of footprints leading in from the cornfields. "Know what people are going to say. Seamus even mentioned him."

"He's in Europe, you know?" I tapped my notebook. "Was O'Leary drunk?"

"Very, but don't write that down either. His ma and all."

I stepped beneath the hanging tree, fanned myself with my notebook.

"Do you think it really was a jailbreak?" I said. "What if they were here for O'Leary?"

"Doesn't winnow things much," Jacob said. "Range would be endless. Mexicans, Negroes, Jews—"

"Women, children, livestock."

"I know," he said. "But easy enough to narrow down."

"How you figure?"

"Hate to break it to you like this, but Clyde wasn't the most honest Sheriff New Sligo County's ever had." Jacob grinned. "Blackmailing half the town. Had files on all you rich folk, but then you already knew that, didn't you?"

He'd found a ledger out behind the jakes with names, dates, and dollar amounts. He read off the highlights: Roosevelt, Lazy Eye, Forest, Tillie, and me.

"Quite a list," Jacob said.

He smiled back at me in that sort of way they teach you in cop school, a smile that makes you soil yourself. "But I don't think you did it. You're not much of a shot. Am curious what you're hiding though?"

"Bedded a German girl during the war," I said. "Treasonous what I did to her."

"You keep to that story, because I got to imagine that it has to be an awful secret for you to give a goddamn what anyone thinks. You ain't easily shamed."

I thought for a moment of my sister. I wasn't surprised her name was in there. She was a doctor and brilliant, but she practiced the sort of medicine, helping out the sort of girls whom the town's pious thought shameful.

"Wasn't Tillie either," I said. "No way she could get the drop on Clyde."

"Whatever you say."

We went out to the road when we heard the roll of wheels on gravel and saw a brand new black Ford galloping toward us.

"Christ," I said. "I thought he'd be a while."

"Just glad I'm not related to you two."

When my uncle emerged from the dark of his car, he slid his revolver into his holster and put on his derby and it felt like the wind shifted from west to east and the air was suddenly full of brimstone and the Holy Spirit, but I might be imagining that. He wasn't a bad man, not in any classical way. And he didn't hate me, though it may have seemed like it later on. No, Seamus Rahill loved me, almost as much as he loved God, but not nearly as much as he loved money.

My uncle came to us, light on his feet like some evangelical hoofer, his long gray beard framing his pink Irish face, making him appear, if you didn't know better, like a gentle country preacher. But it was his Colt '45 that gave him the menace of an ordained mercenary.

"Mr. Rahill," Jacob said, removing his hat. "How are you?"

"A looming strike, a dead Sheriff, and an anarchist on the loose," he said. "Just one disaster after another, but I know the Lord wagered on me."

"My father isn't back," I said. "That's crazy talk."

He touched my shoulder like he was blessing it and looked at me with those gray eyes that made me feel small and forgettable. "You're at the edge of the cliff, Neal."

"I'm fine."

"Well, we define that term differently, I imagine," he said. "I'm surprised to see you out here."

"Wouldn't miss seeing O'Leary's corpse for the world."

He smiled. "On that we can agree."

"Almost done in there, Mr. Rahill," Jacob said. "Know more in a few hours."

"Any theories?"

Jacob told him about the ledger, about who was in there, including Tillie and me. I had to expect it. Jacob and I went back a long ways, but he wasn't going to put himself between my uncle and me.

"Blackmailing a dozen people," Seamus said. "That boy

demonstrated industry, you have to credit him for that. It's a holy miracle no one shot him sooner."

He turned to me, sizing me up. "And your offering to the young O'Leary was awful decadent."

"Misbegotten youth," I said. "Figured you'd appreciate the discretion."

"That I do. That I do,' Seamus said. "There is no shock about your sister."

"She's still family."

"I know what she is."

He told me to head back to the *Eagle*. "Roosevelt knows how to handle this sort of thing. We have to put it to the people delicately, so they understand the truth of the matter. Otherwise, they get confused.

"And Neal," my uncle said. "If you see your father, do the honorable thing."

My uncle lived in the wrong century. No one talked of honor anymore, not after the war, but what could you say about the war to a man costumed in a Derby and a Colt?

"You'll be the first man I call," I said. "But he's not coming back."

My uncle smiled: I wasn't sure if it was assent or just recognition. He wandered over to the jailhouse, whistling a bar from Wagner, thinking in anachronisms.

—4—

When I got back to the *Eagle*, I left my film with the art
editor, and then found my desk and wrote up my story as
fast as I could. I went through my mail, mostly outraged
letters from readers. They called me my uncle's lackey and
they were right. At the bottom of the pile, I found a letter
with no return address, just a name: Miss Esther. It was a
joke of O'Leary's, a memory from our shared childhood.
Every month on the first, I sent O'Leary a check, and every month, after that check cleared, I received an envelope
containing another piece of evidence from the file he kept
on me. Usually, it was a government document of some sort
like Lorraine's birth certificate or our wedding license. Yet,
O'Leary did have some sense of fairness. He promised that
after he'd sent me the last piece of evidence—a photograph
of Lorraine and me—our business was done with.

So when I opened the letter, I expected to find a legal document, something like Lorraine's death certificate, but this
time was different: a check for five thousand dollars made
out to Henry O'Leary, dated June 18, 1904, the day he died.

Signed, Jesse Stephens.

The check confused me. Clyde had mailed it to me just
a day before his murder and he hadn't included a letter
explaining why I was paying for this. I figured it was just
another part of the file he had on me, just another piece of
blackmail.

I didn't consider it for long. Instead, I went to Roosevelt's door, knocked, and when no one answered, I walked
inside. Roosevelt was dictating his editorial to a copy girl.

"It is the opinion of the *Eagle*," Roosevelt said, "that any man who wishes to assume the position of labor organizer has forsaken his right to American citizenship because he has chosen treason over patriotism, slavery over liberty, vengeance—no—madness over justice, and, therefore, we call upon the great people of our Republic to strike down Godless labor, burning the likes of Debs and Kaslovsky in a pyre of their heathen pamphlets. End editorial."

The girl put down her pen, and then repeated back what he'd just said.

I glanced at the typewriter bound to his desk, which rested beside a dozen file folders, a stapler, a pair of scissors, a trimming board, a box of Roebuck dry plates, photo paste, a bundle of pens, and a six-shot revolver. A lot of people wanted to kill Roosevelt, mostly union men like Forest Kaslovsky, the head of the New Sligo local. They had their reasons. Roosevelt had accused the union of every sort of crime imaginable: prostituting their own daughters, complicity with the Germans, and, most recently, spreading the Spanish flu amongst the townspeople.

When the girl finished reading, Roosevelt smiled and touched the tip of his incredible moustache. "What do you think?"

I shrugged and lit a cigarette.

The girl smiled. It was forced and if I remember right, she had some kin who dug coal. "Very nice, sir."

"Thank you, dear. Now, would you mind taking that to Norman and telling him to run it on page one above the fold?"

He stood, and then hobbled over to the liquor cabinet, pouring himself a whiskey. It helped ease the pain in his polioed hips.

"How's O'Leary?" he asked.

"Dead."

"You're a born storyteller. Crane hasn't got a damn thing on you."

He glanced at the copy on his desk, and then shook his head. "It's an article on why Jesus hates unions. Something that pansy Marcus came up with. Got a priest to say that the disciples' real mission was to obey. What do you think?"

It was a big question. "Well that seems to be a matter of faith, not—"

"On the strike, genius. The strike."

That wasn't complicated. I *knew* it was a fool's errand. Forest and the rest of the union would be lucky to hold out through the week, but that's not what Roosevelt was asking. He didn't care about my political insights. He wanted my feelings. I told him the truth.

"I don't care," I said. "It's just a story."

"Good man. That's the company attitude. Take pictures, get quotes, and type. Let H.L.-I've-got-a-Goddamn-flag-pole-up-my-ass-Mencken have opinions. Real newspapermen don't need them. By the way, I hear that Miss Ida is putting up a show of your pictures tonight. What a fucking racket."

"I take it you're not coming."

"Of course not. Your pictures are the art of a born charlatan, especially that hack job you call *The Trench Angel*. I don't know what you did, but I'll figure it out Stephens."

"Believe whatever—"

"And besides Miss Ida and I are no longer on speaking terms."

"Heard you gave her the clap."

"The consequences of a well-lived life." He pulled from his desk a bottle of mercury pills. "Your sister was kind enough to help an old bastard out."

Tillie doctored all sort of ailments.

"That reminds me," I said. "Jacob found O'Leary's ledger. Your name is in it."

"Of course it is. O'Leary broke his blackmail cherry on me."

"Means you're a suspect."

He tapped his awful cane against the linoleum. The handle was bronzed and molded into an image of his own face. It made him look like a demigod.

"Who else?"

"Me and Tillie."

"I'd have been shocked if you two weren't." He laughed. "Forest?"

"Yeah," I said. "For one hundred a month."

Roosevelt whistled. "That's enough to pop the little weasel in his weasely mouth."

"Come on," I said. "We don't know that."

"You just accused me."

"You're a son of a bitch. Forest has principles."

"Principles? They're damn excuses, justifications for a crime against America and the principles we were—"

"Stop it. You don't care about the strike."

"I care about keeping your uncle happy," he said. "Let's see your shit story."

Roosevelt took out a gold pen—a gift from my uncle—then, with increasing force, crossed out half my sentences.

"You write like a goddamn fairy," he said. "No real man uses colons, dashes, and semicolons like this."

"What do you want me to change?"

He handed the story back to me. I read it aloud:

"Sheriff Clyde O'Leary, 29, was gruesomely murdered last night while bravely protecting the New Sligo Jailhouse. The Sheriff's office believes union leader Forest Kaslovsky, along with his accomplice Jesse Stephens, the notorious anarchist, murdered the valiant O'Leary in order to incite discord and fear in the hearts of patriotic New Sligoans."

I looked it over one more time. "This is horseshit."

"It has a symmetry that would give Dickens a half-stock."

"I don't care."

"Fair enough, Stephens. You know you're not the worst hack I've got on staff, just the laziest. I'll give you a peace offering for helping send your daddy to the gallows."

He wanted me to photograph tomorrow night's debate between Seamus and Forest. It was ostensibly a forum for debating ideas, but we all knew it was no such thing: Seamus was telling the town the consequences of the strike.

"I'll take it," I said.

At the time I believed that I wanted to hear what Forest

had to say, perhaps the man's last public words before the strike blew up in his face, but now I know it wasn't my only reason. There was too much going on to simply hang around and watch from a distance. With a dead sheriff, I figured there was something happening beneath the surface and it had something to do with me. But even without that gut feeling I would have wanted in, because out on the prairie there was a file with my name on it and I needed to find it before my uncle got a hold of it.

—Paris—

Others have written about the night the *Rite of Spring* debuted. Historians have chronicled how the crowd booed the dancers, throwing oranges and cursing mothers, and how the night represented the end of the *fin-de-siècle*, a foreshadowing of the bloodshed to come. Those theories might be true, but those people are part of another old man's memory. What I saw was this: the lights outside the *Théâter Champs-Élysées* illuminating the rain falling upon my alpaca suit, while Miss Trixie, a generous camera, waited beneath an awning, safe and dry. It was a young man's mistake.

An ancient, hunchbacked woman materialized from the dark rain. She wore a bandana and a patchwork skirt and no teeth. Most people saw her as nothing more than a beggar, but there seemed something romantic about her, something specifically Parisian. Perhaps it was the child she held.

She swung the infant from her hip in such a careless way that I was sure she'd drop it and I'd have to watch a child die. Instead, she laid it in a puddle of rainwater.

"What are you doing?" I asked in English, of course. "Don't do that."

The old woman bowed, and then lifted her skirt above her ankles. She danced.

"Hell." I wiped the rain from my eyes.

She splashed her toes through the water and spun beneath the streetlight.

I pointed at the child. The water seemed to be rising. "Baby."

The woman bobbed and weaved.

"Baby," I said. "Baby. *Merci*. See voo play."

She danced: trotting, tapping, and careening. She waltzed through puddles, jigged on stone. Her eyes smiled like she was remembering a long-ago love, a soldier who never returned.

"Son of a bitch. Get the damn baby."

The woman spun, her hand on her head, light-toed like Diaghilev's ballerinas.

"Enough."

I picked up the child, fearful of letting it drown.

"You have no sense," I said, tapping my forehead. "Nothing."

The show let out and the gypsy and the child dissolved into the herd of tuxedos and gowns stampeding from the theater, and because I was caught up in the mayhem, trapped in a scene that seemed telling, it took me a moment to realize Miss Trixie had vanished. I pushed through the crowd of assaulting bow ties and gouging parasols to reach the spot where I'd left her, but of course the gypsy had stolen her and I knew I was a fool.

But, like a lot of young men, I hadn't yet developed a sense of humor, so I kicked the garbage pail. A rat jumped, hissing. It ran beneath the crowd's feet. And then they were gone and the ushers shut the lights and I was alone in the dark, but the darkness no longer mattered because I had no camera in need of light. I took stock. Back at my room, I had an extra suit and an open-ended return ticket to America. I quickly came to the conclusion that my noble adventure was a failure, and I was knocked out. And I reacted as such—

"Shit, shit, shit." I fell square in a puddle that soaked through my pants and I sobbed into my hands. It wasn't that I hadn't thought of failing. Everyone predicted it. It was just I'd expected to hold out a year before failure commenced, but I hadn't lasted two weeks.

And I thought: this never would have happened to Jesse Stephens.

"Oh, God."

A woman stopped in front of me. She wore black, pain-fully pointed heels that seemed specially made for her dainty feet. I took a moment to stare.

The rain stopped. It all seemed silent, as though the whole city had fallen asleep and the strange woman and I were the only two awake.

I wiped the rain from my forehead, my eyes. My hat felt heavy, soaked through.

"You cuss like an American. It's sweet to hear," she said, her voice warm, nearly southern.

"You got troubles?" she said. "You look as pale as a snowball."

I shut my eyes. "I have no money."

I stayed sitting and she kicked me in the leg hard enough to remember it.

"I'm not out here muffing it," she said. "I get by fine without turning a dime for strangers."

I dropped my hands, tilting toward her, and knew right away she was the most beautiful woman in the entire me-tropolis of Paris, if not all of France, and perhaps, even, Western Europe. She was luscious, taut, and curvy: she owned all of the adjectives of a beautiful woman, but it was her Negro face that made her special. It was jagged with a cutting nose and rigid cheeks and impossibly wide eyes, the ideal of cubism, but it wasn't grotesque, not at all. It was strangely balanced, fitting in some complicated man-ner I've never been able to explain. Hers was a face worth warring over. It was a face too complex for a camera, but apt for a poet. But, of course, I can't remember what she looked like anymore.

"That's not what I meant," I said. "I'm sorry."

Leftover rain trickled over the brim of my hat onto the plain of my nose. She held the umbrella above me and I lowered my head, bowing, because I thought it was the only proper way to apologize.

"I'm Lorraine."

"What are you doing here, Lorraine?"

"Walking. You?"

"Crying."

"This your crying spot?"

"Tonight it is."

"Why you crying tonight?"

"It hasn't stopped raining since I got here."

She looked around the street, the sidewalk. "You'd think with all that rain they'd have more trees. Back home, all you see is trees. Trees galore."

"Not where I'm from," I said. "It could take all day to find a spot of shade."

"You homesick or something?"

I didn't know what I was. I didn't want to return home, not yet. When I went back, I wanted to be hailed. Not like this: a wet, camera-less photographer.

I looked across at her shoes. "You've got beautiful feet."

"You been drinking?"

"No."

"You want to?"

"Yes."

I scooted up the wall until we were eye-to-eye. Lorraine was taller than me in heels and she held her head straight even as I looked her up and down in a way that wasn't quite gentlemanly. She was so solid. It was like she'd been constructed, not born. Manufactured, not conceived. I could squeeze her as hard as I could manage and she wouldn't give, not even a little.

"What?" she said. "Have you never seen a Negro before?"

"Yeah, no. I mean, of course I have. Why?"

"You're looking at me like I come from another world."

I smiled. "I'm just shy."

"What do you do back home?"

"I'm a photographer."

"You want to take my picture sometime?"

"No camera."

"A photographer without a camera is like a cowboy without a horse."

We stood beneath her umbrella. She smelled like roses

46

and sunflowers and baby powder. I closed my eyes, crying.

"You're in a sorry state," she said. "That's why the Lord invented wine."

"You smell," I said, choking up. "So lovely."

"In that case, I'll buy."

Later, when I got back to my flat, I took out my return ticket and slid it into my Bible. And as young men are apt to do when they fall in love, I stopped writing home.

—5—

It was nightfall by the time I reached Rochelle Street and Miss Ida's Gallery of Fine and Exotic Arts and Crafts. There was a sign outside the second floor entrance with my name on it, but no one paid attention when I walked in. It was still early—the gallery had only opened an hour before—and while the room was fairly filled, I didn't know too many people, not the ladies with dead animals draping their shoulders or the men with top hats fastened to their heads.

Miss Ida—spinster and sometime mistress to Roosevelt— had done up the shabby room with a flourish, drenching it in a Greek Revival style fashionable with the kind of people who thought the modern world stank. Eight-foot-high white columns stood beside stone pedestals displaying marble sculptures of milky, bare-chested Greek gods. It was coarse and tacky, but at least it made the event feel less common, less sad. And it was sad. My pictures hung in crummy pinewood frames in a sort of haphazard way, with no attention paid to thematic integrity. The primitive lighting turned them into shadowy specters. From any vantage point in the room, no matter the sight line, there was only one word to describe them: cheap.

When Miss Ida spotted me, she performed an overdone sigh, and then dragged me to the middle of the room, where she announced my arrival.

"And please give a hearty cheer for our town's greatest artist, Mr. Neal Stephens."

I bowed and then tried to slink back to the corner, because

even if I was vain enough to like the idea of recognition, I'd never been one to enjoy the center of attention, but Miss Ida held on, whispering, "I understand if you're not well enough. We could have pushed this off until next week. Everyone would have understood."

"What are you talking about?"

"That's the spirit," she said. "Live each day like it's your last."

"Have you been drinking? Where you hiding it?"

"Oh Neal," she said. "You're such a gas."

She was the type to get maudlin on me, so I slid through the gallery taking quick, furtive glances at my photos, and, most important, as any artist worth his salt will tell you, their prices:

> *Boots on the Somme: $50*
> *Terrier Impaled on British Bayonet: $70*
> *Amputated Toe (Self-Portrait): $80*
> *Dead Women in Vegetable Garden: $120*
> *The Trench Angel: $150*

It seemed like a lot of money for pictures I couldn't remember taking. Of course, I knew the photos were mine. But after a while they seemed to create their own memory, as though through some sort of parlor trick the celluloid replaced my remembered image with the material one. It was becoming that way for a lot of us: our memories of the war altered by movies filmed on California back lots.

Everyone left me alone, until some brave lady with too much powder on her face came up to me and said she liked my pictures. "They're quite surreal. Were you influenced by Picasso?"

"No," I told her. "They're entirely literal."

She got the hint and ran off.

Eventually, I found myself at the window, staring across the street at the guard circling the New Sligo History Museum, which my uncle had built during the war. While the city owned it, the old man chaired the museum's board, and he ran it like a business, counting every penny, firing men at will. People put up with him, partly because of his money, but also because of his theocratic manner. Everyone, for the most part, followed his orders, including me.

The museum's name was a misnomer, though. It has nothing to do with New Sligo's history, probably owing to the fact that the town was just fifty years old and there isn't a whole lot of historical interest in coal mining and cow shit. No, this museum was stocked with the sort of stuff only an addicted anglophile found fascinating, and my uncle was certainly one of those. There was some medieval armor, jewels from a forgotten duchess, and even a first-edition King James Bible, signed by John Donne, that later turned out to be a forgery. Not only that, but any day now they were taking possession of an original 1613 Shakespeare quarto featuring one of the first copies of *Hamlet*. It was all pretentious horseshit. For some reason, my uncle, the "great" Seamus Rahill, the most Irish-looking son-of-a-bitch west of Galway, loved the English so much he'd have worn stockings and a crown if he could have gotten away with it. He believed the museum was his crowning achievement, the idea that put New Sligo on the map. The old man didn't know how silly he sounded; New Sligo was a backwater coal town and no amount of faux-British austerity would change that.

As the crowd filled out, an older woman, maybe fifty or so, came by looking like she wanted to save me. Her loose black dress, laced at the breast, was the kind popular with the co-eds down in Denver who smoked in public and argued in cafés about contraceptives. She gripped a glass of what looked like juice with her full palm as if she feared the slippery hand of a waiter would pinch it before her final sip. I'd noticed her earlier, partly because of the dress and partly because of the scar that ran across her cheek, one she came by from either a knife or a piece of glass. Still, I thought this conversation would be like the others: unpleasant.

I was wrong.

"I snuck in a flask," she said. "Want a sniff?"

"Yes, ma'am."

"It's Madeira straight off the boat from Lisbon," she said. "Did you know the congress drank over fifty bottles of it after signing the Declaration of Independence? Seems positively un-American for your Mr. Wilson to break it up."

She turned to the crowd. "Christ almighty, it looks like someone got sick and spewed Plato all over the room. I'm gathering she never finished *Symposium*."

I liked her right off. "You're not from around here, are you?"

"I know," she said. "The altitude does wonders for the skin."

I pointed at her glass. "It also gets you drunk quicker."

"Thank God for small miracles."

"You didn't say where you're from?"

"Sweden, the dangerous part."

"I didn't know there was such a place in Sweden."

"Oh yes, Stockholm can be terribly frightening. Have you ever been attacked with a frozen herring? Quite harrowing."

"Your English is near perfect."

"It's an old story, really." She hiccupped. "I was young and innocent. He was an American with an impressive wallet. The English helped with the courting, if you follow? I'm sorry, I'm such a silly old bat—I'm Alma Lind, soprano."

We shook hands and I directed her smile toward the crowd. "Which gentleman is lucky enough to be yours?"

"None, but I've only been here for a few minutes," she said. "I was married once, a long time ago. That's the truth. Now, I make my living singing opera."

"You're killed on a nightly basis." There was the familiar grimness that Lorraine detested.

Alma didn't seem to notice. "Exactly. I've died a thousand times in a dozen different ways: poison, avalanche, strangled, saber, dagger, hanging, guillotine, poisoned lips, consumption, syphilis, burned at the stake, and of course trampled underfoot by a runaway carriage."

"It will be a Packard soon enough."

"Oh, don't be so modern. It doesn't suit you. Play the melancholy and misunderstood artist in all his disheveled glory. It makes your eyes sparkle."

My face felt warm. "Well—"

"Do you see that man there?" She pointed at some blanket ass with a bushy moustache and thin-rimmed spectacles. He'd said something to me earlier about the evils of Portuguese colonialism and I'd told him I didn't know Portugal was a colony.

"He's one of those fashionable revolutionaries," she said. "The kind that sends money to Ireland and Russia and German Jews, yet he lives off his mother's inheritance and has hands as soft as silk. Christ, what a slew of bores.

"I'm sorry," she went on. "I'm not talking about your father."

Frankly, I hadn't even thought of that because there was nothing "pseudo" about my father, for he was the genuine article, a godforsaken, no-doubt-about-it, blowing-up-buildings anarchist.

"In fact that's one of the reasons I've introduced myself," she said. "Your sister helped me garner a month performing in New Sligo."

"Which one?"

"*The Beggar's Opera.*"

I smiled but I didn't know a thing about opera. Yet she reminded me of Tillie and I looked around the room, searching for my sister in vain, knowing by then that she wasn't going to show because she wasn't the type. Alma seemed to sense that I was upset, so she took me by the arm. "Give me a tour," she said. "It's not often you get the artist as guide."

She pointed to a nearby photograph, the last I took during the war: *Dead Women in Vegetable Garden.* In it, a mother and daughter, each shot in the head, lay fetal in a garden in front of their own home. At the time, I thought this picture was a metaphor for German brutality, a sort of symbol of their imperial cruelty, but now I know it was just a sad story, a domestic tragedy of pride.

"That had to be horrifying," she said. "They look so scared."

"I don't remember much about it."

She drifted toward the next frame. "And this one," she said. "I've seen it somewhere. You took it?"

The photograph—my most famous—showed a human figure levitating, arms outstretched like wings, body on fire: *The Trench Angel*. A fiction. It was neither in the trenches, nor an angel as far as I knew. As with the others, I couldn't really remember taking the photograph: it just materialized on my camera and made me famous during that dark autumn of 1916. Yet it was different than the others. With them, I recognized my style, my eye in the photos. I knew I had taken those. But *The Trench Angel* was abstract, without a clear sense of focus or my specific angle of vision, and it was even shot with the wrong light. It was like someone painted it on to the film. Pictures like this didn't just show up out of nowhere. It needed a story.

"You must have made a lot of money off this one."

"I did okay," I told her.

I did better than that. The War Department paid me an obscene fee for it and then plastered the photo across the country as a recruiting pitch. Boys who couldn't yet grow a beard lined up to fight Germans because of my photo. For a brief summer, I was bigger than Uncle Sam.

"I read somewhere," Alma said, "that it's your wife."

"I said I believed it was."

"What did she look like?"

I didn't have to think about my answer because I had performed this bit so many times before.

"Blonde with a willowy figure and a beautiful smile." Then I laid it on thick. "Angelic. What you'd imagine the Holy Virgin would have been like if she'd been raised in America."

"They say she died in front of you."

"I was at the front, and all the men had gone over the top, and everyone was dying and there was nothing I could do, and I could see the shells closing in on her tent, and I had to get her and I ran as fast as I could and I was nearly there. I could see the tent. It felt like I could almost reach it, but—"

"Boom," Alma said. "I'm sorry, that was rude. I joke when I'm sad."

For some reason, I began laughing and I couldn't stop.

I turned from her and noticed that folks were watching me, staring at me. A group of young women, probably from the land-grant school, smiled. Alma noticed too.

"Don't worry," she said. "They just fancy you."

"No, they're talking about my father."

"So your father's an anarchist? Big deal. Mine was a drunk and a gambler and pretty poor at both."

"No, it's not just that."

"Do tell."

"It's just that time of year," I went on.

"What time is that?"

"The time when everyone thinks my father's come back," I told her. "You can count on it like the leaves changing."

Alma had no answer and I shouldn't have expected one. We watched the crowd mingle in the dark of the white room. They ate their cakes and sausages and drank their Coca Cola and bubbly water and felt so sophisticated for going to a gallery, for remaining above the fray. I hated all of them.

Just as I was about to leave, someone called my name from across the room.

"Neal Stephens."

An egg of a man in a white wool suit and red tie waved from beyond the cheese table, then waddled over, tipping his drink onto his fine shoes, and swearing to himself. I'd seen his picture in the paper.

"Son of a bitch," I said. "That—"

"You, Stephens," he hollered. "Neal Stephens, I need to talk to you."

"Absolute bores," Alma said. "But this might be interesting. Maybe you made love to his wife?"

"No," I said. "It's not that."

Roland Matheson had made a killing selling crummy boots to Europe's armies, black boots made of twice-worn leather, sewn with cheap Alabama thread. My toes ached just looking at the piss-ant. He operated out of Denver. Why he'd driven fifty miles north, I couldn't say.

"I've been meaning to talk to you all night long."

"Well, here I am, sir," I said. "You want—"

"Don't sir me. I'm a boot man. I've been getting my hands dirty since before you were born."

"I know who you are, sir. So why don't you get on with what you were going to say and I'll get on with what I was going to say and we'll see how it turns out."

I reached into my pocket, but I never carried a weapon.

"Oh, so you know me. So did your father and that's why we need to talk. I want to talk to him."

"So do I. But we'll have to go to France or Italy to find him." The words arrived slurred, a little drunk. I leaned against a statue. Dionysus. Of course it was Dionysus.

"Papers been saying different lately, saying he's here. Don't you think I can read?"

Alma pushed in between us—I tried to stop her—I didn't want saving anymore. "I don't think you can read," she said. "But you sure can afford to have others do it for you."

Matheson eyeballed her. "Aren't you a little old for that getup?"

"Leave her be," I said. "You come to my showing and you'll show good manners. Now say what you're going to say so I can go back to doing what I was doing."

"You're your father's son and that's what I'm here about. By my count you owe me $98,346."

"What? Are you mad?"

"You heard me. Jesse Stephens dynamited my factory and I want it paid back in cash. Wouldn't take a check from no Stephens."

The crowd shoved in closer, anticipating a scrap, a real-life western fist-to-cuffs. I got the sense the smart money was on Matheson, and, if I'd had the chance, I'd have bet against me too.

"Good for him."

"What do you by that mean, boy?"

"A lot of men lost a lot of toes and feet because of your boots, mister, including me."

I wasn't cowing but even a bit drunk, I knew I was over-matched. While he looked ridiculous, the mass of him up close revealed me as the featherweight I was. Yet there's a certain point you reach in an argument when it's better to get clocked than run away. At least, you believe that before you've been clocked enough times.

"I only got nine toes now cause of you and I still miss that toe," I went on. "It was my toe and it's your fault it's gone and I'm not forgiving you and I'd sooner cut off the rest of my toes than toss a goddamn nickel your way."

I reached for my boot, but stumbled, then steadied myself against Dionysus. Using the pedestal as leverage, I yanked off my boot, revealing that I'd once again forgotten to wash my socks. Alma tried to grab hold of me, but I shook her off. She should have known better. You never stop a man midway through humiliating himself.

"It was a pretty toe," I said. "My wife loved it. Said it was her favorite. She married me for that fucking toe. It was in our vows."

It was then, for the climax of my performance, that I pulled off my sock, tearing away the garters, revealing four fine toes, one scarred stump, and a dirty, rarely washed foot.

"You see, see," I said. "You took my damn toe and made a lot of money off it, so why don't we call it even, because if I had that much money I'd love to buy my toe back."

Matheson wiped his monocle on his tie. "Stop it, son."

I held up my boot to the crowd. "You see this boot? You see it? You see how the threads don't fray and the heel's still set and there are no holes leaking trench water into it? Yeah. This is a fucking well-made boot. Real craftsmanship. Had it three years, now. Yours didn't last three damn months before I got trench foot."

For a moment, I was proud of myself. I'd made my point

and I believed I'd showed the world what type of man Matheson was. If only I could have seen myself, if only I'd stepped out of my body and watched this act play out, well, I'd have known what was coming.

"You're just like your father," he said.

"You fucking cocksucker." I swung my boot, thinking I'd knock him cold, but because I only had one boot on, I couldn't balance myself right, and, in the end, I softly clipped Matheson's pillowy neck.

The shoe man didn't flinch.

Matheson dropped his right shoulder and then swung. I fell back into the pedestal. Dionysus hit the floor, breaking in three.

I woke up sober, looking at Matheson's Italian loafers.

"Nice shoes there," I said. "Quality."

He kicked me in the ribs.

"Apologize, boy," he told me. "Or the next one breaks your nose."

Alma helped me to my feet, my jaw stinging like a horse had bucked me.

"Is it your turn to punch him?" she asked. "That's how it works in America, right?"

I was done.

Alma led me past a horrified Miss Ida and down the stairwell, where I crouched, pulling on my boot. It wasn't until later that I remembered that my sock was beneath the remains of Dionysius.

"Does it hurt?"

"Yes."

"Come on, Jack Johnson," she said. "We should get you home before you cold cock Athena."

We headed toward quiet, elm-lined Rochelle Avenue, and I was thinking that I needed a long drive, and, after this strike was over, maybe I'd head south to Santa Fe for a week or two, but then I paused, examining the dark, empty space where I thought I'd left my car. I was mostly sober when I parked it there. This wasn't a mistake.

"Son of a bitch."

"What is it?"

I wiped my forehead with my handkerchief, and felt sweat rolling down my back even though it was near freezing. In the dark of the space, I saw that the thief had left a note beneath a rock.

"Someone stole it. Someone took my car."

"You sure you didn't misplace it? You seem like the type."

"He left me a note."

She looked it over, frowning.

> "There once was a man drunk in the west
> Who most folks called Neal the mess
> He took lots of pictures
> Drank too many pitchers
> Boy, just go ahead now and confess.
> *¿En qué pararán estes misas, Garatuza?*
> *El Guapo.*"

"This is cute," Alma said. "Jack Johnson has a secret."

Did I ever, but she didn't ask and I didn't feel like confessing. Instead, I thanked her and told her I'd like to walk off my beating, and, with a bit of reluctance, she went her separate way.

Finally alone, I looked around and saw it was cold and dark. I walked up Rochelle and across Garivogue and I considered stopping into McGuffey's for a drink, but I couldn't stand seeing anyone familiar, so I meandered home, keeping the same staggered pace even as the rain fell and filled my boots with water, and it reminded me, at the time, of Lorraine and the trenches because the two were forever connected.

—6—

By the time I reached my porch it was past midnight and I was wet and cold and all I could think of was sleep, but when I opened my door, Gertie Williams, my uncle's pet Pinkerton detective, was perched on my sofa, looking very much like a cat. Her nose, straight like a rifle, was flattened at the tip as if she'd banged into too many walls, and her heavy green eyes fluttered and sagged like she was a much older, seedier Mary Pickford. She was the last person I wanted to see. Over the past three years, we'd had a few run-ins, mostly over stories I'd written in the *New Sligo Eagle*, and these run-ins never failed to unnerve me.

But I wasn't going to be chased from my own house. I sat on the piano bench and saw she was barefooted and had probably been through my things hours ago, and I'm sure she pitied me because I didn't own much that you couldn't either drink or fix a camera with.

"I took my shoes off. It's a sign of respect and I do respect you, Neal. You know that about Gertie, don't you?"

I grabbed the bottle from the table—one she'd pilfered from my pantry—and took a sip.

"Haven't seen you around in a while," I said. "Thought Pinkertons had steady work."

"Gertie's been wandering this great Earth, chasing ghosts."

"And anarchists?"

"Very good, Neal. There's a reason we all call you the Prince of New Sligo."

"Nobody calls me that."

She yawned. "You know how I think your father is such a fascinating creature. I'm just trying to meet him and I searched and searched and lo and behold I think he's come back to this old dusty town. Ain't that wonderfully ironic."

She had an unconventional face, sunken and battered, but still pretty, the sort of pretty that came from years of lean living, the type of face I used to like photographing. She didn't give anything away.

"Can I take your picture? You've got the perfect face for it."

Usually, women smiled when I asked, but not Gertie. She hid behind her enormous purse, a bag that could easily carry a wallet, lipstick, and a gun.

"I'm awful shy."

"Okay, no immortality for you."

"You are silly." She laid her hand on mine—she was the kind of person who enjoyed touching strangers—then massaged it. "You're a very silly man."

"Because I want to take your picture?"

"Maybe," she said. "But I think that's just a symptom of your silliness."

"I've always thought of myself as rather stoic."

She changed tactics. "Have you ever skinned a buffalo? I have. When I was a little girl, my daddy took me and my brothers to the Badlands, and they have a park up there, where all the buffalo roam, like the song.

"We were hungry. You understand?" She brushed her hand through her hair, and then looked down at me with her practiced, serious gaze. "So hungry, in fact, we ate all sorts of creatures. Ate rats and ate field mice and ate opossums and ate raccoons and even ate a prairie dog once and that tasted worst of all because they're cute little rodents and they got families and no one likes to think that they're eating someone's mother. My mother was so hungry she died of it. Have you ever been hungry?"

I took off my boots and socks and sock garters, taking care not to look at my feet.

"But of course you have," she said. "You were in the war,

in the early years, the really lean years when all those boys were eating nothing but shoelaces."

"Can we talk about something else?"

"I'm sorry. Are you getting weepy?"

"If you don't play nice, I'll have the cops put you in handcuffs."

She fluttered her eyes again, then leaned toward me, and ran her tongue up the side of my cheek. I grabbed the armrest.

"O'Leary. O'Leary. O'Leary," she said. "See, I said it three times fast."

I crumpled my empty pack of cigarettes, and then reached for a fresh one.

"Which one?" I asked. "Pretty sure they're both still dead."

"Oh, sweet, dearly departed Clyde. Such a tragedy."

"He was a son of a bitch."

"No need to bite off my nose," Gertie said. "I was just being polite."

"What's he got to do with me?" I asked.

Gertie laughed. "It's sad. You really are a narcissist. If you died tomorrow, would we all cease to exist? Men. You all think your cocks keep the world rotating. You fool, O'Leary telegraphed saying he'd seen your father. Sent it just a couple of days before he went and swallowed that bullet."

At first, I couldn't make sense of it. Why would O'Leary do that? But then I understood: if O'Leary was telegraphing the Pinkertons, I began figuring, it meant O'Leary was most likely a Pinkerton.

"Ain't that a gem," she said. "You can see the wheels in your head turning. Not moving too fast, but you're still a growing boy."

"Why was O'Leary working with you? My uncle hates him."

"You know dear Clyde would have sold his poor mama to the Kaiser if the price was right. Well, there I was enjoying that beautiful lake in Chicago, just having a good old time, when I get this funny little telegraph from Clyde saying he needs help catching your father. Gertie's help. That's why I stopped in to see you. To see if you knew where your father was. But, darling, you really think he's in Europe, don't you? You adorable little sap. If I didn't find you so cute, I'd rub it in your face."

Of course I thought he was in Europe. There was no reason for him to return, not if he liked breathing. My uncle had promised to shoot him on sight. And as far as I was concerned, he could go to hell.

"Why would he come back? Nothing for him here."

"Let's talk about something else. We could talk about you," she said. "You're fascinating in a morbid sort of way."

"The strike. Is he here because of the strike?"

"No. Well, perhaps a little. To stick it to your uncle."

"How?"

"Bang, bang."

"Kill him?"

"And make his museum go boom."

"You've got to be kidding," I said. "You know how much dynamite—"

"I know, I know," she said. "But he blew up that bank in Budapest, which was nearly the same size. What country is Budapest in now? I can't remember. These anarchists: silly little things. I imagine he's got it in his pretty little head that there is a sort of symbolism involved."

"Of course, my father would have to be here to do this."

"You're boring Gertie. Now let's hear about you. It's been too long, Neal. You know I've always fancied you, just a teeny-weeny bit. You have those sad, blue eyes and soft, nimble hands. I'm almost blushing from shyness."

She leaned toward me and I could still feel the dew from her last lick. It was pretty clear to me, despite my headache, that we were nearing the endgame.

"Why me?" I asked. "I'm just a poor photographer who got lucky on a few pictures."

"Oh, you're much more than that. You're an artist. Look at me." She slapped the table. "Gertie said look at her. You're a great man. Maybe, some day you'll be even one of *the* great men of your generation. Who had that theory?"

"Carlyle."

"Right, Carlyle. I may have been a poor vagabond's daughter but I'm an autodidact. Do you know what that means?"

"Yes."

"I'm a researcher of the world, curious of man and machine. I pick up a little here, a little there. Just little nuggets that I stick in my mouth, swish around a bit, then swallow. For instance, the first time I saw your pictures, I all of sudden got this flash across my pretty little eyes and I then understood the importance of boots in the war. All those men always on their feet, just a sole separating them from the dirt, from outright savagery. You did that Neal Stephens. You made shoes interesting."

"I have my moments."

"And this all from an anarchist's son."

"I don't know what you're talking about."

The Lady of San Francisco approached, rattling the picture frames and floorboards. We sat silently, until the locomotive passed into the dark of the prairie.

"You're a liar," she said. "You know exactly what I mean. I can see it all over that swollen mug of yours. People look at you funny because of your daddy. It hurts, I know."

"I don't want to talk about it."

She took a cigarette from me, lighting it. She was pausing to inhale, for effect. If she'd been born to better circumstances, with better luck, she'd have had her name in lights.

"But your father, Neal. Your father's returned and everyone knows it and everyone's scared and they all think you're in on it, but you're not, because your daddy doesn't love you enough to come see you, not after all these years and that has to hurt your feelings."

I went to the fireplace and pushed some newspapers under a log and lit it, and then I put my boots beside the grate to dry. It was going to be a cold night again and I hadn't bought coal for the furnace in weeks. That was the sort of careless thing I let myself get away with back then: pretty soon folks would be stripping old buildings to their last splinter.

"I'm sorry," she said. "Fathers can be cruel. But the rest of your family, they're proud of you, Neal. They just don't understand what the war did to that brain of yours."

"I'm fine," I said.

"Your uncle, he's proud of you."

"No."

"Oh, that's troubling. I imagine if you two sorted through your differences, you'd be, what's the word, simpatico."

"Not likely."

"Oh, don't be so hard on him, Neal. He just wants the best for you."

"And what's best for me?"

"Don't get cross. Let me help. Gertie has an idea. And you know why you should trust Gertie?"

"I haven't a clue."

She reached into her bag and pulled out a small, two-shot Derringer with an ivory handle. She laid it on the table. I think she expected gratitude.

"Take out the bullets," she said. "Go ahead and do it."

I did as she asked, and, afterwards, she slid the pistol into her purse.

"Good," she said. "Now, do you trust Gertie?"

"Are you kidding?"

"I understand," she said. "You feel powerless like the Indians looking at big bad Christopher Columbus. Well, Gertie can make you powerful."

"How?"

"It's so simple, Neal. Just tell Gertie what to do. I'm your genie in the bottle. Just a quick rub and the world is yours."

If I'd been right of mind, I'd gone to sleep on a street corner with the other war cripples.

"Take off your stockings."

"Yes, Neal."

Gertie hiked up her skirt, wiggling it up her hips, and

then, like a Parisian burlesque dancer I'd once applauded, she stretched out her legs, one at a time, and gloriously unfastened her stockings, rolling them off her heel and onto the table. She put them in her bag, in the buttoned compartment where she kept her gun.

"Can't be too careful," she said. "They tear easily."

"Don't talk."

She nodded.

It took time: skirt, blouse, slip, brassiere, corset, garters, and underwear. After I shed my own suit, I led her to the bedroom, where we paused in the dark and I lifted her against the door.

"You can talk, now."

She bit my ear.

"Your blood tastes like taffy."

It happened quickly. I pulled her on top in a graceful, Douglas Fairbanks motion that seemed suave and experienced, but then I fumbled in the dark, and she laughed.

"A girl needs petting."

"You'll manage."

"Right-o."

Her body felt musty and alien, and after a while, as she tugged and clawed, I yielded. I closed my eyes and tried thinking of frivolities—airplanes and moving pictures and Mary Jane's—but only saw Lorraine's Negro face haunting me. She was the antithesis of Gertie, with fuller breasts and shyer hands, softer skin and politer sounds, a lady with no hint of violence. After a while, I felt Lorraine as well. Gertie's concave hips rounded out and her broomstick hair curled: for a moment, I was peaceful.

After she went to sleep, I snuck down to the basement, to my darkroom, and I went to work on the pictures I'd taken that day. There was nothing special in them—just a couple of cripples—but once in a while photographs show up and surprise me. *The Trench Angel* had. Sometimes they just appear and I have art on my hands and that is the miracle that keeps me going because something mysterious happens in the darkroom, something that echoed in my chest, masking the shame I was feeling most nights back then. There was a purpose in the darkroom, a task I could feel in my fingers. Without it, I'd just float. On those nights when the wind howled through the house and whiskey flooded my head, I found myself content amongst the chemicals and the paper and the still images of the recent past. There, you could forget the war, with its images of men lining up to die, and of wives, burnt alive, in Red Cross tents.

—7—

When I got out of bed, I found Gertie sitting on my sofa, wearing my shirt, drinking my rye, and flipping through a book of my most recent photos.

"You don't have any food."

"Been meaning to take care of that." I sat beside her, lit a cigarette.

"You have a lot of tree pictures here."

I shrugged. "Metaphors of something."

"And cripples. Actually is that the same cripple over and over again?"

"Might be."

"And these ones." She pointed at a picture full of strangers. "Don't people mind that you take pictures when they ain't looking?"

"Imagine they do."

"So why do it?"

"Pictures need taking. Can't help it if the subject looks away."

"I guess, but it seems dirty."

Her Pinkerton face was serious.

"Christ."

"You know you shouldn't talk that way," she said. "I go to church sometimes."

"No, you don't."

She shrugged. "You know Neal, when I find your father."

Her attention wandered to a photo of my uncle's appaloosas drinking from a trough. "These look familiar."

"You steal them?"

"Might have," she said. "They've been stolen?"

I told her about the escaped prisoners, the Mexicans arrested without proof.

"Just horses," she said. "What are they worth now?"

"Two grand a piece."

She whistled. "I could get a nag for five bucks these days."

Not one of those. My uncle bought their sire from an old Nez Perce Indian right before Big Hank died. The stallion, Sherman, was a direct blood relation to one of Chief Joseph's horses, most of which had been shot by the army after the tribe surrendered.

"My father?" I said. "You were saying about my father?"

"Yes, sorry. I'm hoping, you know, that when I finally find him, I'll get to shoot him in his face."

My chest felt hard and I didn't want another drink.

"It's not personal," Gertie said. "Just work. You know I've always liked you, but times are hard for a girl like me. By the way, you look terrible. Did I do that to your pretty face?"

In the bathroom mirror, I saw that my jaw was dark and swollen and my eyes red like the hot end of a cigarette.

A knock at the door sent me to the bedroom for a shirt.

"Someone's here," Gertie called out. "You want me to get it?"

"No."

"You sure? I don't mind."

"I'm coming."

I dressed and splashed some water on my face, but still my eyes cried sin. When I went to the living room, I saw my sister Tillie and I felt meek.

"I still can't believe you're twins," Gertie said. "You two don't look identical."

"Why is she here?" Tillie asked.

"I'm right here," Gertie said. "I can answer—"

"She's here to kill our father," I said.

My sister took off her hat—red hair plastered to her skull—and looked for a place to sit, but the sofa and chair were covered with Gertie's undergarments, wares that looked much more sordid in the light of my sister's presence.

"You should have called."

"I didn't think I had to make an appointment to see my brother," she said. "Besides, I called all day yesterday and you didn't pick up."

"I was out covering Clyde's death."

Her expression didn't change.

"Besides," I said. "My car's gone."

She looked toward the kitchen and I could tell my distance, my reluctance to spend time with her, hurt her feelings.

"What do you need, Tillie? Is something wrong?"

She paused, perhaps looking for the right tack. It didn't come easy for her because she had a sledgehammer for a mouth. "I was making sure you were healthy."

She showed me the morning's *Eagle*. The headline: Boot Baron Boots Boot Boob! There was a file photo of me beneath it.

She handed me two pills; I swallowed them.

"I wanted to make sure he didn't knock loose the working parts of your brain," she said.

Gertie coughed. She was suddenly dressed, shoes on. "I'm leaving."

She came over, closed her eyes, and leaned in like an addled starlet, kissing me on the mouth, her tongue, somehow, making its way behind my teeth. It felt like she'd stolen something from me.

When she left, Tillie went on to the porch. "It smells in there."

"Like what?"

"Syphilis."

I put on my brown suit, brushed off my hat, then went to the kitchen and gurgled soap and water. I found Miss Constance's case beneath the dining table and slung her over my shoulder, and then walked outside, locking the door. It felt like winter in the porch shade, and I wanted to fetch my coat, but didn't because I'd look weak.

When I stepped into the sunlight, it felt like summer. I loosened my tie, took off my hat and got in the car, readying myself. While most of the town just laughed off my antics, my sister found nothing I did amusing.

"What kind of flowers do you want at your service?" she asked. "I think daisies. They're appropriate for ne'er do wells. Hearty, resilient, but ultimately just a weed, something that could have been beautiful, but—"

"Stop it."

"Or do you want an Irish wake? McGuffey's could host it. We'll prop you on the bar, spill whiskey along your corpse, cry and sing songs of the homeland. We could feed you to the hogs afterward."

"Stop it," I said. "I'm fine."

"Neal, you've got the screwiest definition of fine I've ever seen. Now get out and crank the engine, will you? What use is it having a brother if he won't do that for me?"

I did as she asked.

As Tillie drove toward town at the same controlled, strict pace with which she did everything, I waited for her to say something.

Finally, "Have you seen our father?"

I was surprised she went for such nonsense. I told her so.

"The town's not going mad," she said. "There's no collective insanity happening. You've been reading too many books."

That certainly wasn't the case. I didn't even look at the *Eagle*.

"So you think he's coming back?" I asked. "I bet you think he shot Clyde."

"Would you care?"

"I don't know."

It seemed unusually quiet for a Monday, but then again, the union's contract was ending at midnight: that was why no one walked the streets on one those last warm autumn days; it was why the Victorian homes, remnants of the town's late 19th century building boom, had shuddered windows, like a big snow was coming.

"You should probably take a trip," I said. "Maybe head back east to see some old friends."

"Our father doesn't scare me," she said. "If he thinks about me at all, it's only fleeting."

"I wasn't talking about him."

"Forest doesn't scare me either."

She was Seamus Rahill's niece, and, according to the town, a practitioner of an ungodly profession who was also probably one of the leading suspects in Clyde's murder. She should have been scared.

"Are you scared?" she asked.

I thought about it for a second, running through all the scenarios I could imagine, but I wasn't an imaginative guy. "No."

When she turned down Tenth Street, I opened the paper and saw, just below the fold, an obituary for Old Padraig Kavanaugh, one of the original New Sligo settlers who'd come over from Western Ireland back in the 1870s. He'd lived on the town's southern outskirts since I was a boy. It wasn't by choice. At first, he'd had a wife and family in town, but then he'd fallen in love with a Chinese woman, fathering a pair of children. The town chose to ignore it until he moved out of his wife's home to live in common law with his mistress. That couldn't be condoned: a mob hanged the Chinese woman and her family and then beat Old Padraig with a branding iron before exiling him.

I pointed out the article. "You used to doctor him, right?"

"Not much I could do for insanity."

"Didn't know he was crazy."

"What he did—well—can only be diagnosed as a mental illness," she said.

Despite her medical objections, Tillie drove me to McGuffey's. It was the kind of medicine I needed. McGuffey's didn't change. McGuffey's didn't break into my house, and then make love to me afterwards. McGuffey's didn't keep a ledger. McGuffey's didn't write limericks hinting at blackmail, and then steal my car. McGuffey's just existed. It loved all men equally—black and white, young and old, rich and poor. Blood dripped from the ceiling and smoke soaked the skin so that it seemed like you had to douse yourself in lye to erase the smell, but no matter color or creed, Lazy Eye Norris greeted you with a bottle.

"You sound like your old man, just ranting and raving like a damn dope head," Lazy Eye said. "People been asking for him."

"What kind of people?" Blood splattered against my slicker; it ran down my back like rain. "Paranoids?"

"All kinds of people. Mostly Pinkertons." Lazy Eye dried a mug, and then pointed at me. "I don't like them cocksuckers coming around here. Gonna have to shoot one of them and then I got to clean up dead Pinkerton."

"I haven't seen him since the day he rode off into the mountains," I said. "Decades, since before McKinley got himself shot."

"You hardly decades old and McKinley been dead years before Jesse left. I know my chronology."

"Fifteen years. I haven't seen the great Jesse Stephens in fifteen fucking years."

"Fine." Lazy Eye threw his rag at me, and then kicked

the garbage can like it was a mean dog. "Believe what you want, but you don't have to be cussing at me. You ain't the only one here with troubles, Pinkertons or otherwise. And you know what else? Your troubles are bullshit. You know what a real gyp is? No, let me tell you. My father got sold. Hear me? Sold. As a little boy. They took him from his mama and sold him to some cracker down in Alabama. And you know what else? I only got one good eye. And you know what else? I got to look through that one eye at crying drunks like you and Sam and put up with pigs like him."

"Thanks," Jacob said. "Thought we were friends."

Lazy Eye was right. Sure, I had some troubles. No, not even troubles—quandaries. Yet, on the bright side, I had a whiskey in front of me. And Sam Bailey. How much worse did Sam Bailey have it? Just look at him. Poor Sam slumped at the end of the bar trying his damnedest to get a sentence out between sips.

"How you doing, Neal?"

"Fine, Sam. Fine."

Sam's eyes lit up like the Holy Spirit suddenly flowed through him. "Won't be for long. You got a lynching party coming for your red bottom. Yes, you do."

"Leave it alone, Pop," Jacob said. "Bad enough he got beat up by an old man and no one bought his pictures last night. Sorry, Neal. But he don't need a pickled preacher riding him."

"Whores, all of them." Sam swept his arm across the bar like he was exorcising the devil, but instead knocked over his beer. "No. No. No."

"I got you, Sam," Lazy Eye said. "I got you."

The group of us sat quietly for a long time, the dripping of calf blood serenading us. Sam started to say something—I think about the toils of Job—but then he lost his words in his beer. We were mostly alone, the bar empty save for Swift Mickey sleeping at a back table, his surviving leg twitching against his crutches. All of us, for one reason or another, often sought McGuffey's for its silence. It might seem lonesome, but we were just mourning together.

I ordered another drink and then went down the hall and out to the jakes. When I returned, I found Sam and Jacob engaged in a familiar debate: *how* my father killed Big Hank.

"Stop it, Pop," Jacob said. "Not how it happened."

"And how did it happen, Mr. Detective?" Sam said. "You get yourself a shiny badge and you think you know more than the rest of us good praying folk."

Jacob spit his snuff into an ashtray, and then took a sip from his gin.

"Well, here's what I heard," Jacob said.

"Christ, do you have to?" I asked. "I'm sick of hearing it."

"Man challenged me," Jacob said. "What can I do?"

Jacob recounted how old Sheriff Corrigan believed it was suicide. In this version, Big Hank entered Seamus' office begging for mercy, crying that his children would go hungry, but my uncle and father weren't feeling magnanimous. Distraught, Big Hank shot Seamus then shot himself. I'd heard this version before, just another tale among the glut of fables told about that day, some mentioning a gambling debt, others alluding to a woman or a horse. Even fifteen years later, people never got tired of hearing it. Except me.

"If that so," Lazy Eye snorted. "Why the story?"

Jacob shrugged. "Jesse felt guilty over it. Wanted to be sure Big Hank got buried in a Catholic way."

"Nice story," Lazy Eye said. "Except I knew Jesse Stephens and that bastard wasn't noble for shit. And besides, how's someone shoot themselves in the back of the head? That's insane man shit."

"Didn't say it was my own particular belief. Personally I think Seamus plugged Big Hank. Hear me out, Neal."

He went over the evidence: the bullet in Big Hank's head went up through his skull. It meant that he was shot by a shorter man, a man like Seamus. Jesse was six feet three inches or even taller in boots. Moreover, there were no signs of struggle: no blood on Jesse, no knocked-over furniture, no sounds heard from the office until the shots rang out.

So, according to Jacob, the shooting happened like this: Big Hank comes to the office bearing blackmail; Seamus and my father agree; as Big Hank goes to leave, Seamus shoots him in the back of the skull; and my father takes the blame, because, as the stronger man, it's logical that he was the one who killed Big Hank.

I'd heard this one too, but like the others, I didn't buy it. It had to be the way the newspapers reported it. Everyone was always looking for a reason why my father went crazy, and they all thought it had to do with Big Hank's killing, that it had bent him funny, but it wasn't like that. He wanted another life, another woman.

"Seamus was also shot," I said. "Don't forget that."

"In the shoulder, conveniently," Jacob said. "No, Jesse shoots Seamus where he's likely to survive, then plants a gun on Big Hank. A cover-up. Seamus was never in any real danger."

To my thinking at the time, it was just another conspiracy created by a paranoid town.

"Hooey," Sam said. "Should lynch all you Stephens. Rid the world of them."

Lazy Eye turned to me. "He's just drunk."

"No, no, no. He's back. And you know how I know? Because I got witnesses." Sam hit his chest in a display of Lutheran bravado. "You know Old Virgin McSweeney? She saw your father last week. No kidding. Took her cow. Stole it, raped it, cut out its innards, then slept in its carcass. Foul, but true. And tragic. It's hard to get a good milking cow these days."

"Is the Old Virgin still speaking to Lincoln every night?" I said. "Still telling him they have to wait until her daddy gives consent?"

"Yep."

"And she saw my father have relations with her bovine?"

"Yep."

"Sam," said Lazy Eye. "Don't be making trouble."

Sam touched his heart. "Apologies, Nigger Norris. Apologies, Neal Stephens. It's not just the Virgin who saw. The greaser family over near the golfing club said it was your daddy who broke into the jail yesterday and killed the dastardly O'Leary. And that's two."

"You been goin' around for months blaming Jesse Stephens for everything," Lazy Eye said. "Bet you blaming him for getting that Jessup girl in a family way."

"I have heard rumors to that effect, yes," Sam said.

"Shit, Pop," Jacob said. "Lay off, will you, or I'll haul you down to the drunk tank."

"Apologies Nigger Norris. Apologies Neal Stephens," Sam said. "It's just Betty. I miss my Betty."

Sam turned to his son, his old preacher's eyes drooping like a canteen. "I don't know why your mama left me. I don't know why she couldn't stay."

Jacob had nothing to say about his disappearing mother. It was like staring into the sun.

"Perhaps," Lazy Eye said, pouring Sam another beer. "Because you're my best customer."

But Sam wasn't listening. His head lay on the bar, his snores a hymn. I handed Sam's wallet to Lazy Eye.

"For the bed," Lazy Eye said. "Got to charge him for the bed."

The door opened from the alley and a clatter of boot steps descended into McGuffey's. Three fat men with coal miner hands and no necks stopped at the coat rack. The first man, the largest, wore a black city suit and carried a silver pocket watch chain off his coat that glistened in the candlelight. He stank of wealth, but it was all a ruse—the man wore each day he'd worked underground across his face like a tattoo.

He raised three dented fingers at Lazy Eye. "Whiskey," he said. "And follow it with three more, quick as you can, boy."

Jacob leaned toward me. "Union men here to keep an eye on Forest."

On a nearby table rested the head of Swift Mickey, his back moving in tandem with his snores, his missing leg buried in some Flemish field. At one time he'd been the best baseball player in all of New Sligo, spending every afternoon manning third base on the Normal School's diamond. Now, he couldn't walk ninety feet without leaning against a wall because the crutches cut into his arms so bad they blistered. He'd only been home a year, but it seemed like he was fixed to that table like the stars to the night sky.

We sat near him and Jacob raised his glass. "To O'Leary," he said. "Cocksucker, had it coming."

He had, but even though he was blackmailing me, all I could think of were the ways O'Leary could have turned out all right, maybe gotten a job in Denver or taken the train to California, anything but staying in New Sligo haunted by his father's ghost.

Then I did something funny. I guess it had just been on my mind and I hadn't thought of it consciously, but things just slip out once in a while when you least consider them.

"A Pinkerton."

"What?" Jacob reached for his gun. "Where?"

"No, I fucked a Pinkerton last night."

"He get you drunk at least?"

"No, it was Gertie. Seamus' Gertie. You remember her?"

He groaned, disappointed like a cuckolded husband. "Yeah, remember her alright."

He pulled a small revolver from his ankle holster and laid it on the table.

"Here. Try not to shoot your cock off."

The revolver reminded me of the last gun I'd owned, a French pistol I'd taken off a dead Belgian.

"I don't want it," I said. "Can't fit it in Miss Constance's case."

It was a lie, but neither of us felt like having a talk over it. Instead, we listened to the snores of Sam Bailey, the snorts of Lazy Eye Norris, the machinations of the union men, the cleaver of O'Clair. Swift Mickey stirred, knocking over an ashtray.

I wondered if he dreamed about his missing leg.

—9—

It was late in the afternoon by the time I exhumed myself from McGuffey's. I still had an hour until the debate and I needed to walk off my drunk so I slipped through the center of town and into Pioneer Park, which, lately, had begun to look more like an English estate than a piece of the American frontier. My uncle had brought in tulips, daffodils, and other European flora to give it a more royal feeling, but I missed the old sage grass and cottonwoods and Colorado clay. Still, he couldn't get rid of all the town's Americaness: the gravel pathway was glazed in yellow maple leaves, the air smelling sweet and musty like boiled pumpkins as the sun hovered over the Rocky peaks, shading the mountain snow like a bruise. The evening wind cut down the path, kicking up leaves into small funnels. I buttoned my coat, then pulled down my hat and found a bench to sleep on, but before I could doze off, I heard a miner's wet cough from down the trail, and looked up to find a giant Jew slouching toward me.

When he was a boy, Forest Kaslovsky had come to New Sligo from some ghetto outside of Warsaw. His real name wasn't Forest, but something Polish and unpronounceable and long forgotten—he'd taken on "Forest" because it was the first word he'd learned in English. He took work in our mines and rose up quickly to become a union leader because of his steadiness, his strength, and his eagerness to cripple a scab. I'd known him since I was a boy and while I can't say we were ever friends, we did have an understanding that kept us from being enemies. He stopped before me, towering like a Semitic Visigoth, and stuck his hands in his pockets before surveying the park. A dark shadow cut across his chest, sawing him in half. He looked worried.

"You being spied on?"

"Stephens, is that you?"

"Who else?"

"Shit, I figured you for some train tramp until I saw that shit camera of yours."

"Do I look that bad?"

He didn't say anything and I didn't expect him to. He was nearly fifty years old, a man of my father and uncle's generation, and thus they had been raised on street fights and knife wounds. He wasn't the type to whisper even a gentle insult unless he was there to bloody you.

"Sit," I said. "Please."

Just being near him, I could feel the weight on his shoulders, like he was holding up an entire mine shaft on his back. While this wasn't his first strike, it was the first since his wife passed from the flu. I couldn't tell how it changed him, not then, but everyone sensed that he wasn't the same man. There was something quieter about him, which, maybe not accidentally, made him seem more dangerous.

"What are you doing here?" I said. "If you don't mind me asking?"

He pointed toward a dark wooded area, and behind an oak stood a man in a black suit with a starched white shirt and black tie and long, curled moustache. He looked like an old photo of John Wilkes Booth, but of course it was just another Pinkerton.

"They're like flies on shit," he said. "And I'm smelling awful rank."

"He's a lousy spy," I said. "Seems like they'd put someone better on your trail."

"He knows I see him. That's the point. Supposed to make me nervous. You'd think that your uncle would have learned by now that I don't scare easy."

"You'd think." I raised Miss Constance at Pinkerton Booth, and then fired, but the man didn't flinch.

"I'm sorry about O'Leary," I said.

"No you're not. No one is."

"He was Big Hank's kid."

"Don't make him good," Forest said. "Truth is that boy was always mean."

I didn't remember him that way.

"Clyde used to shoot prairie dogs for sport."

"A lot of people do that," I said.

"He aimed for their legs. Wanted to cripple them, watch them drag themselves back to their holes so their families could watch them bleed to death. He was only eight when I caught him doing it, long before your father orphaned him."

He went on. "Saw you're pinning his killing on me. Front page this morning, not that I read that shit paper of yours. Telling everyone me and your father done that shit."

"You know Roosevelt," I said. "If it wasn't you—"

"Your name under the headline."

"No one reads the paper anyway."

"You gonna ask?"

"What?"

"What O'Leary had on me?" He looked hard at me, the folds beneath his eyes, the caverns on his forehead, illustrating each mine collapse, each moment mourned for his wife.

"I don't care," I said.

"You're the worst scribbler there ever was," he said. "Don't you care about nothing? Anything you might give a shit enough about to try hard on, to sacrifice for?"

"Lucky I'm pretty," I said. "Otherwise I'd be in some real trouble."

He stood and asked for a cigarette and I gave him one and he inhaled and coughed, a hard sopping cough. "Haven't had one since before I got married. Used to love them but Rachel said it was bad enough breathing coal all day that she didn't need this shit stinking up her linens."

His eyes drifted toward the woods, toward Pinkerton Booth.

"Why now?" I asked.

"Now, you got a question."

"Blackmail's regular. Happens all the time. You picking up a new vice this late in the day is odd. There's the difference."

"Guess you start wondering what things you would have changed had you not done something. Don't know if that makes sense? Figure, if I'd kept smoking, things might have gone another way. You understand?"

"No use revising what's already happened."

"So you never—"

"Shit," I said. "I do it all day long, but do you want to start looking like me?"

He laughed and I felt my back relax. I'd been more nervous then I thought.

"That's the kindest thing you've ever said to me. I'll remember it the next time I pick up the paper and think of blackjacking you."

"I appreciate it."

He turned toward town while I leaned against the bench and looked at the clouds hovering over their mountains, threatening us with a week of snow, until, out of the corner of my eye, I saw in the woods, behind that oak, Pinkerton Booth staring right at me.

PARIS

A couple of months after our first meeting, Lorraine and I sat on a fading bench beside the Seine River eating stale bread with warm cheese, drinking wine with coffee, as men marched to work and women chased their children, as barges ferried coal downriver and painters revealed their empty canvases. It was right after sunrise and Lorraine had just finished cleaning a clerk's office.

"I won't go to bed with you," she said. "I told you why."

After a night pushing a mop, her face glistened and her eyes waltzed to a silent song.

"All I asked is if you wanted to go to the ocean some time before it gets cold," I said. "Who mentioned bed?"

She chewed. She didn't talk when she chewed and she ate all the time so our friendship, and that's all it was at that moment, was punctuated by long silences. She took another bite into her bread.

Down by the river, an old man fished. He must have been near ninety. Slumped and pained, the man had been born before Andrew Jackson was President. He'd been a boy when Robert E. Lee was at West Point. He'd been too old to fight in the Civil War. Back then, I ordered the world like that. Lorraine said it was a sickness needing curing, because if I wasn't in America, I was no longer American.

"Frenchmen are always French," she'd said, in a tone I took as insulting. "Chinamen are always Chinese. Americans are renters."

"But I'm not a Frenchman," I said. "So what am I?"

"A little boy."

That was our first blowout, a fight that had lasted days. After my hangover eased, I found myself, through no fault of my own, pining for Lorraine, seeking her forgiveness.

That morning along the Seine, I'd concocted a plan to get her out of Paris, to a place where we'd be forced to share a room, a bed. Like any woman with half a brain, she'd seen right through it.

"What do you think would happen if we went to the ocean together?"

"Swimming."

"Now you're being fresh with me." She broke the bread, putting it to her mouth. She chewed.

"We take a train to the ocean," she said. "We have to stay overnight. We drink some wine. We share a room. What happens then?"

"We sleep."

She picked up my arm and then bit my wrist. It hurt. She'd done it before and I was fine with it because it meant I was getting somewhere. At first, she hadn't even allowed me hold her hand, but, after a few weeks, she'd let me kiss her and feel under her blouse, yet that was as far as she'd take it. I knew why.

"What happens to me when you go back to America and I'm stuck with your child?"

The old fisherman wasn't having much luck, his line bobbing in the brown, flat river.

She punched my arm. "Answer me. I let you make love to me and I get stuck with a white man's child while you're off telling your friends about some colored girl you bedded. What use do I have for a white man's baby?"

"It's not like that," I said. "There are ways so you won't be with child."

"See," she said. "I knew it."

She went to the riverbank to think over the water. I let her stew instead of assuaging her, which had made her angrier because she thought I was just passing out token platitudes. I'd feared she'd stop talking to me if she got angry enough, but it was never like that. She was always happy to see me. It would have been easy to dismiss me as a cad and I probably was at first but this unconsummated affair had turned into something else for both of us.

After the old fisherman had taken his bait home, Lorraine returned from the banks and sat beside me and rested her head on my shoulder and she felt warm and fitting and I wanted to tell her I loved her but I was still too afraid she'd think I was lying so I said nothing.

"You said you brought scotch," she said. "Pour me one."

It went on like this for months. I'd bring her breakfast and we'd go to her apartment to play around until she fell asleep.

Afterward, I walked the city alone, looking at faces I'd have photographed if I'd had a camera. Months after the *Rite of Spring* debacle, and I still hadn't replaced Miss Trixie. She'd been a good camera, but bulky with heavy glass plates and I'd had to lug her and the flash pan along and it all felt artificial. I'd tried a few cameras on, but none had fit my eye. I guess I was waiting for inspiration or desperation and neither had arrived at my door.

I walked the entirety of the city that winter, the dark, icy alleys full of tramps and the bright, snowy boulevards of the bourgeoisie and I talked with other exiles about the possible war and I got excited about following soldiers into battle and I knew that when the war came I'd be a part of it because everyone agreed that it was going to be one short, glorious battle.

During that winter in Paris I met all sorts of people and I felt like a part of history rather than a victim of it. I'd meet French and English girls, who, somehow sensing the coming disaster, offered themselves to me, but I always turned them away because I was in love with Lorraine. I couldn't push her into bed. I just had to wait.

One morning in February, I arrived at her door covered in sleet, desperate to declare my love for her because it was a burden and I needed her to understand. I was nervous that she wouldn't believe me.

"You're crying again, Snowball."

She led me into the house and pulled off my wet boots and laid my feet near the coal furnace.

She looked over me, confused. "What's wrong with you?"

"I'm awful taken by you."

"You need to stop drinking in the morning."

When the first day of spring arrived on a Saturday, it felt hot enough to melt wax, Lorraine said. She didn't have an office to clean, so we picnicked in a park and read English newspapers, and then stayed out late in a café. I walked her back to her apartment.

"You want some tea?" she asked.

I followed her inside and stood in the middle of her room for a long time before I noticed she wasn't making tea but gazing toward the bed where a new camera lay wrapped in a red bow. Even from ten feet away, I could tell it was an Eastman Kodak Folding Pocket Brownie. A few months earlier, I'd shown it to her in catalog, but she'd misunderstood me. It was a tourist's camera, something you gave to a mother to photograph her children. It was nothing a serious photographer would carry. Yet, I can't remember thinking that when I saw it on her bed.

"It's good, right?"

I wanted to chastise her. I could buy a hundred such cameras and still survive the summer, whereas she must have skipped meals, but I didn't scold her because she was so proud of it. She waited, her arms crossed.

"Say something."

"Miss Constance."

"What?" she asked. "Who's Miss Constance?"

"My seventh grade teacher."

I sat on the bed and held the camera above me.

"She was sturdy with a wide bosom and I was horribly in love with her."

She kneeled beside me and rubbed my calves, then took my boots off, sighing at my blackened feet.

"You need to wash these."

She fetched a bucket and filled it with water. When she returned, she took hold of my feet, but I stopped her, running my hand through her hair.

"I'm not leaving," I said. "I'll never go back to America."

She rested her head on my thigh.

"How can you be so sure?"

"I promise. I'll never go back."

The night before our wedding, I stayed in my own flat. I packed my clothes into satchels and my books into crates. I flipped through Thoreau's *Walden*, my father's copy and his favorite book. In the margins, I saw the words "yes" or "why?" I placed it beside my mother's *King James Bible*. I opened the Bible where I found, bookmarking a page in Matthew, my return ticket to New York. I'd forgotten it but when I looked at it again, I knew I should throw it away and I did and it stayed in the trash for a few minutes before I put it back in the Bible because I thought, "What harm is it?" At the very least I could sell it to some poor refugee when the time came. I wasn't going back to America. No one believes me, but I never intended to ever go home.

But it's the day after our wedding I remember best, our last day of peace before the battlefields and their trenches, before the brief leaves and rushed goodbyes. It was the day the boots marched east, the day the war ignited on its fast burn toward standstill.

The boots, brand new Normandy-manufactured leather boots, slammed in a two-beat rhythm through the city, toward Belgium. They were beautiful boots, black and stiff, freshly laced and fitted with two healthy feet living in them. I counted those boots from our bed.

Lorraine slept on my chest, her hair draped across my neck, her hand locked with mine, our wedding bands welded together. I rolled her over. She pressed the pillow over her eyes. She dreamt, I imagined, of some home we'd not yet built. I went to the window. Beneath the rows of electric lights, a crowd cheered on the soldiers, singing the Marseilles and lighting effigies of the Kaiser.

This was the third day of the nationalist demonstration. Fireworks smoke drenched the sky and the streets were stained from spilled wine. The people who spoke English were convinced they'd see soldiers celebrating victory by Christmas, and I agreed, unable to imagine another ending, not with our collective idealism, not with our technology. It would be our new guns, our new engines that would make us victors in this first and only great battle of the new century.

But I didn't know the truth then. What I knew was this: the war was my moment to become an artist of the people, a man who could illuminate the last days of the grotesque through his camera, so that later, after the war cleaned away the filth of society and erased men like my father from our shores and sidewalks, I could display evidence of the past's disgracefulness to a purer mankind.

Lorraine thought I was mad. She'd spent her summers working on her grandmother's chicken farm in southern Missouri near old slave quarters, ones disintegrating from summer storms and winter wind. One summer, her grandmother paid a man to photograph her in front of her old slave home. Lorraine asked why she'd wanted something like that, something best forgotten. Her grandmother smiled, then said, "So your own granddaughters believe you."

I just *knew* she was wrong. Yet I was grateful to her. She'd given me Miss Constance and she'd given me herself, and her trust. I aimed Miss Constance at Lorraine, the last sun falling across her face—*Woman after Day of Marriage*.

Another lost photograph.

She threw her pillow at me and then I crawled in beside her and kissed her and she took my hand and examined our wedding bands, one's she'd picked. Silver symbolized a shield, she'd said. It withstood fire and brimstone.

I buried my face in her hair. She rolled atop me, then laid a breast atop my eye, and pressed.

"Evening," she said. "You from around here, stranger?"

"If I'm ever blinded, and God help us if I have to learn a new profession, I hope to be blinded by your beautiful bosom." I rolled onto her in one romantic, ill-conceived gesture that threw her into the wall, shaking a framed photograph of the prairie outside New Sligo.

"Clumsy bastard." She kissed my forehead and pressed

against me. Her breath was warm and sweet and smelled of mint and wine.

"I see you were playing with Miss Constance, earlier," I said. "Shame on you."

"How can you tell?"

"A man always remembers the exact position he places his camera before he takes a women to bed."

"Even if that woman is his wife?"

"Especially then," I said. "Whores might steal a camera, but they're rarely jealous of it. Now a wife might find my relationship with Miss Constance unseemly."

"I do." She picked up the camera. "I don't understand how you can love a thing."

"Thing, hardly." I said. "This is a truth machine, cheaper than liquor and more reliable than morphine. With it I can capture the essence of any given moment in time. All I have to do is aim and fire. Don't look at me like I'm telling a tale. I'm quite serious. This here, this is power. While a gun might kill a man, a camera can save him."

"Now you're talking nonsense," she said. "Damn thing can't stop a bullet."

"Not literally, but it can make a man not want to fire it off in the first place."

"Look here." She pulled the frame from the wall. "What do you see?"

"Home, hearth, health. I see my mother and sister picking flowers. I see cornbread and warm cider."

"I see loneliness and people who will never like me."

"I like you." I kissed her. "A whole lot."

"I know," she said. "Just don't try stopping a bullet with that camera."

"Of course not," I said. "I'm not brave. I come from a long line of cowards. That's why the Stephens have persevered for so long."

"Don't lie to me."

"I would never. Not Neal Stephens. Never lied to a woman in his life. Besides, I got too much to live for now. All those men, those heroes, they had nothing. The Light Brigade,

Custer, Pickett, they had miserable shrews to return to, women as frigid as nuns and as limber as corpses. Me, I like my wife."

She went to the window. "It's bright out there," she said. "Flaring like a fire before it dies."

"Don't be so grim."

She turned, naked, silhouetted by the street lamps. "Not grim. Scared. I'm more scared then I've ever been in my life. Almost."

"Almost?"

She nodded. "Almost."

"It'll work out."

"We should run. Run as far from here as we can get. Run and hide."

"We'll be fine."

"You're wrong, Neal. You're more wrong than you can possibly know." She took my hand to her chest. "If something happens. If it all goes wrong. Go to the sea. Go north. You'll find me there."

And what did I do? I laughed. I called her Lady Macbeth and I called her Jenny Lind. I teased her until she laughed then we made love again. Then we slept.

But that wasn't the whole story.

In the morning I packed: clothes, film, Miss Constance, a pocketknife, a raincoat, spare boots, and my Bible.

—IO—

St. Nicholas' stood on the western edge of Pioneer Square and there isn't much to say about it except that it was built of granite and bare of ornamentation and seemed like the type of place preferred by men like Jonathan Edwards, Oliver Cromwell, or other blowhards of their ilk. It was positively Protestant, eschewing stained glass and the sort of ostentation the men from Rome preferred. But my uncle loved it.

Across the street, I leaned against the pedestal propping up the statue of Gerard Rahill, my long-dead grandfather, the town's founder and the source of the town's creation myth. Like all Rahill men, Gerard was a notorious jackass, and the statue observed this familial trait: Gerard held a rifle while standing on top of a dead Indian, with the old pioneer glaring triumphantly west as if he was seeking worthier adversaries. Even worse, the statue was like a marble daguerreotype of my face. Gerard shared my short nose and wide jaw. His eyes shined an inherited conceitedness, a reminder that I was forever a Rahill.

I pulled out a flask and then ducked into the shadow of the pedestal. When I rose, my sister stood before me, sunset draping her eyes, and she was holding herself impatiently like I'd stood her up for a date.

"Where have you been all afternoon?" she asked.

"Around town," I told her.

She reached toward me, stealing my handkerchief, smelling it. Her face contorted like she'd fallen into a manure heap. "How long were you at McGuffey's?"

"Not long," I said. "Mostly I was out talking to Forest or avoiding Pinkertons."

"I know," she said. "A Neanderthal in a black suit called on me and asked if I had murdered Clyde."

"What did you say?"

"I simply smiled and asked if he'd like to donate his brain to medicine, so, once and for all, we can prove that phrenology is nothing more than a Victorian pseudo-science."

"He must have been confused."

"It proved my point," she said.

The crowd swelled around St. Nicholas': mostly miners in their dark church suits and their wives and children holding close by.

"They can't possibly believe I was the culprit," she said. "I don't even own a gun."

"Clyde was blackmailing you."

"He was blackmailing you, too." She gave me a sort of crooked wink that made me step back. More than anyone in town save my uncle, I didn't want Tillie knowing about Lorraine. My sister's ideas about the world—her science—couldn't reconcile with the facts of my marriage. "I can only imagine about what. You must have done something incredibly dumb." She took a second look around, then whispered, "Did Seamus hire them?"

I didn't bother answering because we both knew it was a silly question. If my relationship with Seamus was often strained, it was nothing in comparison to Tillie's. They'd hardly spoken in five years, ever since Tillie returned from college to open her pharmacy, a practice Seamus thought was the devil's work.

"You should be flattered."

"Why? I don't believe the Pinkerton fancied me."

"No," I said. "They're treating you like any other man—shitty."

"You are a constant source of hope, a proverbial optimist in these days of cynicism."

I took her arm and walked her across the street, past the

miners, stopping at the entrance, where I saw, carved into a granite cornerstone, my mother's name. It had been put there ten years earlier, yet the granite was still polished, still shined in the leftover sun.

"Neal, please," Tillie said.

We went inside, where I led her up front, to the only open pews, because most had chosen to sit in back in case something awful happened.

Tillie slid into the pew. "How do I look? Tired?"

She looked brittle and powdered.

"You're lovely."

A racket erupted in the back and I turned to find a stampede crashing through the doors, Forest at the head. They chanted, "We don't need Rahill! Rahill needs us!"

I thought of raising Miss Constance, but the evening light was already too dim.

"Not quite Shakespearean, is it?" Tillie said.

"Don't be like that."

"You and your lost causes." She shook her head, and then smoothed out her dress. "We can't let them run themselves. They'll burn it all to the ground like children with matches. It's our job to care for them."

"Be careful. You might be my next lost cause."

"I'm innocent. Don't you know me better than that?"

"Just stay here," I told her.

"Fine, but at least have the decency to take your hat off."

She was right; I'd forgotten. But I wasn't the only one. The managers, the town elders, and even the tradesmen held their hats in the laps, but most of the miners, save a few of the more pious folk, kept their bowlers and flatcaps on. It made sense to me because the pews were divided like some sort of industrial wedding: management—along with Tillie and I—on the right, miners on the left, each solidly aligned with the bride or groom. Most of the coal diggers hadn't been inside this church in years, and maybe they didn't believe it as sacred as they once had.

I found Jacob near the doors, ostensibly standing guard, but mostly trying to stay out of the way.

"Why are you sending the Pinkertons after Tillie?" I asked. "If you want to ask her something, then ask."

He looked at me like I'd accused him of infidelity. "Just shut up, would you?" he said. "Haven't seen any Pinkertons and didn't send any after Tillie. You ought to know better."

"Why are you mad at me?"

"If you don't know then I ain't saying."

"Did we get married today? We didn't drink that much at McGuffey's."

"Finally got drunk enough to read that shit paper of yours. See you're saying Forest and your pa plugged O'Leary," he said. "That isn't what I think and I'll bust your jaw if you keep on saying it. If people think I sold Forest out and—"

"Why do you care?"

"I don't. Just got to walk through Rahillville without getting blackjacked. You know that. Besides, it's a lie and if you keep on saying I—"

"Stop it," I said. "No one's going to think you're pinning it on Forest. They'll think it's me or my uncle and if anyone asks I'll say you think my father killed O'Leary on his own."

"You'll do that?"

"I promise," I said. "Just promise me you won't let no one railroad Tillie."

"Guess I'll see what can be done, though can't imagine your uncle being screwy enough to send his own niece up, even if he don't like her."

"Sorry," I said. "For hurting your feelings."

"Didn't make me cry or nothing."

I made my way back toward Tillie as a slow murmur of awe and disgust filled the room. I turned to find my gray-beard uncle striding down the aisle carrying a briefcase and his derby, while his revolver remained visible beneath his coat, a corporate gunslinger. As he approached the front, I noticed a young woman by the old man's side—Gertie.

It was a sight that would make you cry mercy, like a

wife and a mistress striking an unexpected friendship. I figured she wouldn't mention anything, but the thought of it still scared me, especially since the two looked, in Gertie's word, simpatico. As she passed, she held out her hand and brushed my shirt with her fingertips.

"Nice girl," I said. "Quite sharp."

"You're a fool," Tillie said. "Your loins are going to ruin the lot of us."

"What do you mean?"

"I just don't understand you, Neal."

On the stage, Seamus and Forest stood like two pugilists listening to their coaches. I went to them, camera in tow. There was a spot, near the west end of the stage, where a stream of sunset broke through the windows.

"Would you two mind stepping over here, please?" I asked.

Both gave me the sort of annoyed look, like I was begging for a nickel.

"Is this necessary?" Seamus asked. "It's getting late."

"He's your kin, Mr. Rahill," Forest said.

"Roosevelt's orders," I said. "Now, just step into the light."

They did so, reluctantly, almost feeling like they had no choice.

"Just stand near each other and hold still, please," I said. "I'm not asking you two to dance."

They remained about a foot apart, while the middle of the frame was filled in by the wall. I thought it was going to be a bad shot: it would look like some metaphorical shadow between them and maybe that was more honest, but it wouldn't *look* right.

"Okay, like that," I said.

Seamus and Forest stood still as corpses for nearly thirty seconds as Miss Constance sucked in the dying light. You do this for enough years, you get a feel for how long a picture will take. Back then, you took long exposures or you used a flash pan, and if you used a flash pan, it looked like you'd drawn the men on the paper. It made the subject look frightened. That's why Riis was a genius and a liar: it was the flash rather than the squalor that made those poor folks look so scared. That's what I believed back then. It wasn't until much later, when I looked back at my work during those last few days in New Sligo that I saw in that picture of Seamus and Forest the origins of my new style. Both men looked right at the lens, appearing just as they wanted to be perceived: tough, tired, and ready to die.

"Thank you," I said. The men slipped away, not even passing a look to the other. I went back to Tillie, who sat, politely, listening to Gertie speak. I wanted to find a hole to crawl down.

"Your sister was just telling me that you two returned to New Sligo around the same time," Gertie said. "Isn't that wonderfully ironic?"

"How so?"

"She's confusing irony and coincidence," Tillie said. "Because she's a masterpiece of inbreeding."

"No one likes a shrew," Gertie said. "It's unchristian."

I smiled at Gertie and pointed to the stage, where Seamus looked like he was ready to begin.

"I'm not staying for the festivities," Gertie said. "Fixed fights are dull."

She kissed me on the cheek. I was simply grateful that she'd decided St. Nicholas' wasn't an appropriate place for a lick. "I'll be going, but I'm sure we'll see each other soon."

I hid in my hands.

"I'm done for."

"You have no idea," Tillie said.

"What do you mean?"

Tillie put her finger over her lips. "Shush."

Seamus stood at the podium, a strand of gray hair falling along his long forehead. He smoothed out his coat and cleared his throat, before hitting the gavel three times. Like an old Dickensian schoolmaster, he expected his wards' silence, attention.

"Thank you," Seamus said. "According to the bylaws of our constitution, we'll commence now."

Forest stepped to the podium, raising his hands in his best Jennings Bryan impression.

"Unite."

Like a magician who'd hypnotized the crowd, half the audience stood and repeated Forest's call. The Generals of France and England should have been so lucky.

Forest leaned back, coughing a coal miner's hack, a deep sodden expulsion of wet soot, which made the genteel cover their ears. No miner took notice.

"There are few times"—Forest paused, then hit his chest. "There are few times in a man's life when he sees the change. When he realizes a fork is ahead and the path he picks is his last. Fifteen years ago, my brothers, I saw that change. I had a friend. A brother. A man I loved like kin. His name was Henry O'Leary and he took me in and taught me that the world is a whole lot bigger than my own home, that the future was greater than my own needs. Big Hank believed we'd once been men, but had lost our way, our freedom sold away like Negroes, but one day we'd take it back. We would once again look upon our sons without shame.

"He believed those words. He died for those words. When I shoveled dirt upon his coffin, I saw that fork. Two paths were ahead of me. The first was the slave path, the Rahill path. I wanted that path. Thought hard on it. I had a wife who wanted a home without being scared of the Pinkerton man coming through the window. But the second path, Big Hank's path, held greater riches than any I'd seen before. Those riches weren't of gold or silver or emeralds or rubies. No, it was riches only a free man can enjoy. We only ask for what is ours and what is right. We ain't out for greed, only justice. I ain't no machine, no spinner, no plow and let me tell you, my brothers, I will not die that way and you shan't either because tomorrow we stand as men and take back what is ours."

Forest raised his hands and the soot-stained and the

coughing, the crippled and the ill, the widowed and the orphaned, rose and cheered. Seamus took back the podium. "That's enough of that."

"It's so dramatic," Tillie said. "It's just like his people."

"Leave him alone," I said.

It was Seamus' turn. He put on his spectacles then unrolled his handwritten speech like a Caesar. The crowd turned to their hands and feet, as scared folks will, and they let Seamus' words drift past them.

"We have gathered here today in the hall my father erected, in the great metropolis he founded two and one-half score ago to speak of the evils infecting our Christian society. The lies of communism. The ills of socialism. The violence of anarchy. You, ladies and gentlemen, are descendants of a great race and it is in you our legacy shall either live or die. My family hath bequeathed to you a noble world, an honorable legacy, but I fear that you shall destroy it from your fear of faith. I stand before you steadfast in my belief that our greatest battle lies before us. A battle so grave, so perilous that our entire nation is at stake. It is upon your shoulders that our nation lives and dies, on your adjudication. And that is why I so fear it. You have been shameful progeny. Our great land has been invaded by men intent on destroying the economic and political system we hold dear. I shall not stand for it and will give my last dying breath to protect it."

I was bored and couldn't stand another sentence and had no reason to be there since I'd already taken my picture.

"I'm leaving," I whispered to Tillie.

"Enjoy your drink."

When my uncle paused for a sip of water, I slunk through the shadows of the church and dashed out the back door and into the dim autumn light.

Outside, I found Alma Lind seemingly standing guard on the staircase, once again appearing like some sort of knife-scarred guardian angel. She looked out at the square with a calm, easy expression as if she were waiting on a familiar man. I put on my hat and stepped down beside her.

"Good evening, soprano?"

"What are you doing?" she said. "Shouldn't you be inside? The speech is still going on."

"It's dull."

"Yes, but he's your uncle and you can't expect family to entertain, otherwise who would we have to pit ourselves against? Everyone needs a nemesis. I think Montaigne said that."

"What are you doing out here? I'd think you'd have—"

"You want to get a drink? I'll buy."

I thought about it, but there was always the chance some sort of melee might break out, and while it was too dark for Miss Constance to be of any use, my pen, at the very least, might be needed.

"So you're staying right here?"

"Yep," I said. "Got to be able to hear through the door."

She searched my face for, I think, honesty. I figured this was her first strike and the first time is always the worst.

"You're awful serious today. Don't get so wound up. It'll all be over soon enough."

"I'm just old," she said. "And it's not getting any better."

"Go get your drink. Tell lies to some stranger you'll never see again."

After she walked away, I listened to the intermittent howls of my uncle through the shut doors, while gazing at the near empty square. The dark wind blew west from the mountains and out on to the prairie. Across the street a Pinkerton wearing a porkpie hat waited beside the courthouse, and I figured there must be a dozen of them lurking around town. I lit a cigarette and took out a flask, figuring that this would all be over soon.

Seamus pounded his fist into the podium. "Have I not given you work? Have I not given you shelter? Have I not given you food?"

A flock of geese squawked overhead, passing from north to south, abandoning the coming cold, toward Denver, toward Santa Fe, toward Juarez. When I looked back at the courthouse, Pinkerton Porkpie was gone.

The wind shuffled my coat and I heard the miners' sighs and my uncle's howls. "There will be no toleration for disobedience. There will be no forgiveness for sedition. You are my children and I love you."

A squirrel, fattened from the fall harvest, stopped at the bottom stairs and chewed an acorn. Its gnawing teeth uttered a screech that made me shiver. The wind blew dirt up from the flowerbed and I covered my eyes.

"From the bottom of my soul," Seamus bellowed. "I tell you that I will destroy every last one of you in order to save the whole, in order to preserve the greater good."

When the wind abated, I heard heavy loafers slapping pavement. A man with long blonde hair and wearing a brown suit ran in front of me, his head turned away, toward the statue. While his suit was well tailored, his boots were ratty, like he'd walked from New York in them. I didn't know the man, but the way he dashed, the manner he swung his arms, the way his boots landed seemed familiar. He disappeared behind the Mayor's office.

I took another drink and saw the squirrel had vanished, abandoning his acorn to the street. I leaned over the banister, but he wasn't beneath the stairs either.

"There will be consequences. Swift and severe."

Something made the air feel rotten. I searched the square for people, but I didn't see any, and it was then that I realized I was nervous, like those moments just before the sergeant blew the whistle. The wind returned and I lowered my hat, and saw, out of the side of my eye, Pinkerton Porkpie walking across the street, toward the statue.

"Like a gangrenous limb, I will amputate the sick to save the healthy."

A gust sent Porkpie after his hat, which tumbled toward the pedestal. I stepped onto the sidewalk to watch the Chaplin reel play out. When his hat came to rest against the pedestal, Porkpie picked it up and paused, a strange look of surprise, then recognition passing over his face. He stepped back, then took out his gun.

I stopped in the street, Miss Constance by my side.

"Like the Lord did to Sodom and to Gomorrah, I shall do unto you."

More footsteps.

"Duck, Cowboy. Duck."

Like a magician's dove, Gerard Rahill vanished. From his void a light materialized as bright as any I'd seen in Belgium, propelling into the square like an exploding star. My voice disappeared, my breath sucked from my lungs, my cry muted.

I shut my eyes thinking that this was how death arrived.

—11—

When the light bored through my eyelids, I rolled over, unable to hear the feet running past me, just a high drumming in my ears. A woman with short red hair crouched above, her mouth moving eerie and false like a mime. She laid her head against my chest. I hollered, but she couldn't hear me. The light dissolved, again, and when it returned it seemed like every dog in New Sligo howled.

I screamed.

The woman pushed me to the ground and I felt another pair of hands holding my shoulders. The Pinkertons coming for me I figured, so I pushed the woman to the ground, but the other hands, the mystery hands, were too strong for me, so I abandoned the fight.

"Calm," said the woman, who only then I recognized as Tillie. The mystery hands relaxed and I saw Jacob.

"Miss Constance," I said. "Miss Constance."

"Right here," Jacob said. "She's safe."

I cradled the camera case, and then looked inside it and saw she hadn't been damaged and everything would be fine.

"What happened?" Jacob's voice cloudy like the pauses between stutters. "Who did this?"

Who? I rubbed my eyes. They felt dry and burned. I shook my head, thinking that if I shook long enough, the howls might go away. I felt sick because it smelled like Belgium, like nitroglycerin and burnt flesh.

One of the thick union men from Pennsylvania came over, holding a hat. "Here you go," he said. "Found it over there."

I took the hat, which was crimped and burnt at the top, and then returned it to the union man. "It's not mine," I said. "It was the Pinkerton's. He died."

"We know," Jacob said.

A deputy went to Jacob, and then said, "That lady over there with the flowers says she saw Jesse Stephens."

Jacob spit. "Course she did."

Sometimes, when I walked out into the prairie, miles from cars and lights, and I stood still on those plains while the grass bent around me, I could hear the wind whispering my name over and over again like a lover haunting you from beyond the grave. In that dark square surrounded by a crowd of miners and managers all looking like they were ready to brawl, I heard that same whisper, but it wasn't calling out to me.

Jesse Stephens. Jesse Stephens. Jesse Stephens.

"I didn't see anybody," I said. "Just the Pinkerton, but I don't think he did it."

"It's alright."

I looked past Tillie and Jacob, past the crowd of miners and saw the hole in the earth where there once had been an image of myself carved in stone. I still felt foggy, dizzy, like the light was intermittent, like my eyes were failing, but then I realized my uncle was standing above, his body eclipsing the sunset.

He took my hand. "He tried to kill you, Neal. He'll pay."

I now know that he was talking about my father, but in the square, my ears keening like a widow, I didn't understand whom he was talking about.

Tillie touched my shoulder. "Lay down," she said. "Trust me, Neal."

—12—

I walked home.

The night smelled like coal fires. Snow began to fall and my feet felt cold and I realized I hadn't done a wash in weeks and my suit smelled like dead Pinkerton and Mc-Guffey's. I thought maybe I'd buy a new suit tomorrow, some socks. As I thought on this, I came upon my house, stopping at the gate to examine the front window. The lights were on.

I went to the porch and picked up a large rock I'd used as a doorstop. I figured it was probably Gertie, but if it wasn't, if it was another Pinkerton or a union goon upset with my articles, I didn't like my chances: if I couldn't land a punch against a fat man like Matheson, what were my odds against someone much younger and better armed? I leaned against the door. My burglar was playing my piano and playing it well. It was a familiar song, a slave tune, one where the master is overthrown and redemption is just around the corner. It was a song from before the war, one played by a schoolteacher. No, it wasn't a schoolteacher. It was someone else.

When I swung open the door, I raised the rock, hesitating, because at the table sat the man with the brown suit I'd seen before the explosion, and it was, as you've already figured out, my father, the old anarchist, and next to his feet rested my own severed head. I dropped the rock on my boot.

"Son of a bitch," I said.

Off on the prairie, the *Admiral's Express* rolled along her tracks, blaring her long horn into the night. Cups clattered in the cupboards. I sat on the floor.

"It's been a long time, Cowboy," my father said. On the wall, behind my father, hung a reproduction of *The Trench Angel*, the copy from Miss Ida's gallery. "You didn't really figure I'd never come back, did you?"

No, I hadn't.

"You got anything to drink here? And not them damn soft drinks everyone's been peddling." The old anarchist looked up at my kitchen cabinets. "I know you haven't gone dry like the rest of this fool state. I leave for a couple of years and look what happens."

It felt like I'd been asleep for years, a western Rip Van Winkle. Jesse Stephens was in my home, and no amount of rationalization could undo that.

"Fifteen years," I said. "You've been gone fifteen years, since Chester Arthur was president."

"You got shit brains for chronology, Cowboy. You weren't even alive during the Arthur years."

"Who cares?"

"Well, a lot of people did. He was a bad man. Real bad, Cowboy," he said. "Did awful things to the Negro and Chinaman. He had this sort of abominable depravity that only despots possess. Crimes that make a man ashamed of his country."

My father's hands rested on the piano keys. His long, blonde hair curled down his nape, and, beneath his coat, inside a shoulder holster, slept a silver revolver. His boots were covered in mud and he'd tracked filth all over my home. I pointed at the severed head resting against his boots.

"Oh, this." He held up the head, and then stuck his tongue out like a child. "After the explosion, it just rolled over to me. I got to tell you Cowboy, I screamed like a little girl thinking it was real, thinking it was you, but then I saw that it was old Gerard's likeness, that reptilian industrial dog, and I thought, wouldn't it be a damn shame to let such a priceless piece of memorabilia go to waste in the scrapheap of history."

"You killed a Pinkerton."

"Not my fault, Cowboy. I got him to chase me before I set it off, keep him out of the way because I'm no murderer, but he wasn't no good as a man or detective. Got himself lost and ended up pointing his gun at the dynamite. Still can't figure that one out. Not as if a bullet going to stop a bomb, but they never did give no reading test at Pinkerton school. Besides, why are you angry at me? I told you to duck, but you didn't listen. You've never listened, not even as a child."

I pulled Miss Constance's bag to my chest. "You didn't have to set it off in the first place. What do you think is going to happen now?"

"Probably get a shovel out there. Scrape dead Pinkerton off the street. You know, the usual works of a soulless bureaucracy."

"No, you, you damned jackass."

"Oh, you mean why did I blow it up in the first place? That's easy. It was dishonest art, Cowboy. The worst kind. Can corrupt a man's soul. Figured no art was better than art of the mendacious kind. Besides, why are you so worked up? Pinkertons aren't real people. They're minions for Satan, you know, if I believed in that hokum. I probably saved a dozen lives by ending that man's. He was a despotic tool."

At that moment, I knew my father was mad. I reached over to the side table, picking up the telephone. "You're going to jail, old man. I'm not your patsy."

I raised the receiver, waiting for the operator, but the line was dead. My father grinned.

"You know how hard it is to get someone up here to fix that?" I said. "Takes months."

"You can afford it, Cowboy, considering the coin I passed for this photo." He pointed to the photo on the wall. "It's my gift to you. A lot of missed birthdays, I realize, but I thought you'd want to hold on to it."

"You paid for it?"

"Eh, let's say I left a donation as I went out the window. How'd you come across this shot anyhow?"

I didn't want to talk about *The Trench Angel*, not with him. Instead, I just stared at him, quietly thinking about how to protect my sister and myself. You know, everyone thinks I must have been scared. The big bad Jesse Stephens had broken into my home and cut my phone line and was carrying a gun and I should have been scared, but I could see in his face that he meant me no harm. No, I wasn't scared that *he* was going to hurt me. But if anyone found me harboring the anarchist, townsfolk with pitchforks and Pinkertons with cleavers would be knocking down my door.

"What do you want?"

"You're surprised to see me. I know it's been—"

"No, I wasn't surprised at all. People have been seeing you all week."

"But they didn't know it was me." Jesse rose. "No chance in hell did they know. They been seeing me for fifteen years. They see me every time something goes bad. They can't tell their reality from their fictions, seeing as how they're trapped in the yoke of their own oppression. No, they only thought it was me."

"You killed the cow?"

"Not how they been saying."

"The girl?"

"I didn't touch no virgin," he said. "Hell, Cowboy, I'm no barbarian. Just because a man holds certain convictions that are contrary to the prevailing convictions of some dominant order set up by tyrants don't mean he wants to overthrow all of them. Just because I disagree with the economic raping, doesn't mean I'll stick my pecker in places it shouldn't go. Those deeds are reserved for politicians and others who've been mentally handicapped by capitalism's corrupting influences."

"Christ, old man. What do you want?"

"Whiskey."

I found a bottle beneath the sofa, and then fetched some glasses. It was only then that I saw my house had been ransacked: pillows torn, bed undone, closet evacuated, bureau turned turtle. A box of safes and a couple of unchristian calendars lay scattered along my bedroom floor.

"Jesus—"

"I prefer Jesse if you don't mind, or Pa if you're feeling some sort of sentiment."

"Why couldn't you have done it more delicately? I hate cleaning."

"No kidding." He glanced at the calendars. "Been lonely lately?"

"Not lonely enough."

My father sipped his whiskey, letting it linger on his tongue, before swallowing. "Ahh. That is a fine, fine elixir for a foggy head. Not quite Laphroaig, but it does clear the ringing in my head. I ever tell you about the summer I hid out in the highlands?"

"You didn't kill O'Leary, did you? Please say you didn't."

"It was 1911 and I'd just blown up the Central Bank of Edinburgh," he said slow and wistful. "Three-legged Abe and Banjo Sarah were with me and then it all went terribly wrong."

"I don't remember 1911 and I don't remember you being such a raving jackass."

"Poor Abe. Repressed personalities like Dr. Freud said. I don't care for alienists, but that Austrian's all right by me. Met him that summer he toured the states."

"O'Leary? Clyde O'Leary got shot in the head, you know?"

"Right, right, right." Jesse refilled his glass, then his eyes turned toward Miss Constance's bag. "That the same one I got you as a boy? The camera. You named it. What was that camera's name?"

"Miss Esther."

"Right, right," Jesse said. "Why you always got to go and personify the inanimate? Just another distasteful materialist trend. I didn't teach you that, did I?"

I'm sure my mouth was agape and I looked like I was talking to a madman, which I was. My father, I started to realize, had no idea what he was doing. I knew I had to get a hold of my uncle. If Seamus found I was hiding my father, he might not be so forgiving of me.

"What are you going to do?" I asked.

"About what?"

"About the fact everyone wants to hang you?"

"You think?"

"The town burns you in effigy every year."

"I'm doing Guy Fawkes proud."

"You're mad, aren't you? Everyone thinks you're the damn devil and they'll string you up first chance they get and you're sitting here drinking like none of it's happening. What are you planning?"

"Honestly, Cowboy. I don't really know." He waved his cigar, the smoke forming into some sort of anarchist apparition. "Got some ideas, some theories, but nothing to worry over because the best of it's planned on the fly."

"Did you kill Clyde O'Leary?"

"Swear I didn't, Cowboy."

"He was a Pinkerton."

"Makes no difference."

"You just killed a Pinkerton."

"Just lucky, I guess."

He kicked his boots up onto the table.

"What are you doing here?" I asked.

"You know why."

"I haven't an inkling."

"Need to get into Seamus' office. That old bastard's got something of mine."

Gertie's voice rang in my head: my father hadn't come home to see me at all because he didn't care. I'm pretty sure disappointment washed across my eyes. "That's it?"

"Well—"

"After all these years, you just want help breaking into Seamus' office?"

"Don't be so maudlin, Cowboy. I didn't mean nothing by it."

"You son of a bitch." I hurled the bottle across the room, glass shattering against the back wall, whiskey raining to the ground, through the floorboards, into the basement.

"Get out."

When he didn't move, I went for his throat, yanking his collar, but he was leaden, rooted to the chair. After a while, when this struggle became embarrassing to both father and son, he did me the favor of twisting my arm behind my back and putting me on the ground, yet another old man whipping my ass.

"Why you got to go and throw a perfectly good bottle of bootleg like that? For Christ's sake, what's come over you?"

"She's dead. Mom's dead."

"I know, Cowboy. I know."

"She called for you until the day you died, you know that?"

"I'm awful sorry about that."

"It was another woman, wasn't it?"

"You already know the answer."

If it's not about money, then it has to be another woman. In my father's case, her name was Mattie Longstreet. No one knew what she looked like, or at least the papers didn't. It was she who made him leave, become an anarchist. The papers said so. They said she helped him with all his acts right up until the day he got her killed.

After Jesse got up, I pulled my knees to my chest, my boots scraping against the floor.

"Have you seen Tillie?"

"Yeah, I've seen her."

I couldn't believe she hadn't told me. "Stay away from her."

"Okay, Cowboy. Okay."

A truck passed down the road, shaking the dining table. Jesse palmed his gun, and we stayed silent until the truck passed out of earshot. Soon enough, another truck passed by, then another. I went to the window. An army caravan passed down my street, sneaking into town in the dead of the night.

"The militia," Jesse said. "They're invading."

"They're coming for you," I said. "You'd better go."

"Pay attention, cowboy. I ain't got a lot of time and you don't have a lot of sense. I'm not looking to start a war here. The violence will be mild. I'm going after the big boys. I'm going after your uncle where it hurts. He's got this holy devotion to the material and I plan on taking some of that material away. The equalization of fortunes, you could call it. Seamus, that sheep fucker, has—"

"No."

I went to door, pointing to the road. It was snowing hard.

Jesse touched my shoulder before stepping on to the porch. He lowered his hat and looked out to the road.

"Careful, Cowboy. No one cares you were Pearl's son anymore. It ain't the old days. They'll hang you just like me. Don't forget that."

After he disappeared into the snow, I shut the light and went to the sofa, sitting in the dark for a long while, thinking of things you think about when you've had an awful day and you hope something profound comes to you, but it never does, not for a lot of years.

I walked outside into the cold air, carrying my marble doppelganger. Snow fell like ash as I walked past the row houses lit and heated by the last of their rationed coals, then strode up a hill, stopping at the summit. Most of the town lay asleep, the houses as dark as the empty prairie. Even the lamps along Seventh Street had gone black. To the west, scattered electric lights lit the outlying homes of the shopkeepers and coal executives, while to the east oil lamps and coal fires burned in the homes of Rahillville during their last night of peace.

The town had changed. It had grown out from the center like a fat man, gluttonous and greedy, consuming the surrounding prairie like a magnificent banquet. Aqueducts pocked the edge of the town, while canals shimmied out of the Platte and the Cache la Poudre rivers, crisscrossing like stretch marks. I imagined the new immigrants and the expanding families would keep growing south as far as Denver, devouring the coal, slurping the water. It was one of my few prescient moments during that long week of false prophecies. I dropped the marble head on the top of the hill and turned back down the hill.

When I got home, the light was on and I figured my father had returned for Gerard's head. So when I opened the door, I was surprised to find a rotund detective sitting on my sofa.

"You're not much for cleaning," Jacob said, flipping through one of my calendars. "Hell, neither am I."

He took a bottle from his coat and gave me a swig.

"You seen your father?" he asked. "Careful with your answer."

"You just missed him by a few minutes."

"How was the reunion?"

I pointed at the broken bottle, the turned over chair.

"You going to tell my uncle? I won't blame you if you did."

"Yeah, about that," he started. "Just arrested Tillie for Clyde's murder. She's sleeping at the jailhouse tonight. Thought it best to come here and give you the news."

You could say my heart sank or my stomach turned, but I really just felt numb. Somehow, I always knew it would come to this: my uncle would turn against us, our faces forever reminding him of our father, and mother.

"She do it?" I asked. "You think she—"

"Hell if I know." He went to the window, but I couldn't tell what he was looking for. "Seamus thinks it'll draw your Pa out into the open. Thinks he'll turn himself in for his daughter."

"That isn't the only reason."

"No," Jacob said. "Seamus been wanting to run her out of town for a long time. She's been down in Rahillville doctoring miners and the Pinkertons got pictures of it now, but you knew all that, didn't you?"

I nodded.

"Might be best if you both left," he went on. "If you get the chance, I mean, and I'm not sure you will."

"This my friend's advice or the detective's advice?"

He turned and I could see in the hollows of his eyes that he wanted to get out of town along with us.

"Look, the Pinkertons found Clyde's files in her house. Almost all of them, we think. Whether she killed Clyde or not, I don't know and don't much care, but somehow she cleaned out the jailhouse."

"Mine in there?"

He turned to his boots, not wanting to look up at me.

"Yep."

"You read it?"

"Seamus read it first, but yeah, I read it."

"Got any questions about—?" I couldn't even say her name.

"Can't fault you for the story you told. Not to normal folks because they'd have run you out of town so fast, but—" He paused, putting his hat on and tipping back on his heels. He'd been thinking of his answer on the drive up here. "But did you think I'd care she was Negro? I know what it's like over there."

"I'm sorry."

"Look, Neal, I don't know what's going to happen, but it looks like people are going to hang and here's hoping I've got no part in that and all I have to do is turn my head and you know that I love you like a brother, but I'm not going to step in front of a noose for you. If Seamus thinks you're helping your father, God help you."

After he left, I locked the door and kept the rock beside me while I sat in the dark for a long time wondering if I'd have any more visitors tonight. I reached into my boot and pulled out the check Clyde sent me. I didn't know why he'd given it to me, a man he could barely stand, but I did know the check was the only leverage I had. It might have been better for everyone if I had burned it. The truth was that by that night I knew my uncle wasn't the same man as the one I'd loved as a child, the man who'd taken me in after Jesse left. Even after the war, he'd still been good to me, finding me work during those dark days after Lorraine died. He'd been kind to me, in his own way, for my entire life and maybe he would have looked on me with Christian charity and let Tillie and I leave town on our volition, yet, call it intuition, call it fear, but I didn't believe he'd let us go without a price, because he felt betrayed and that was something a man like him couldn't abide because he'd always been loyal and righteous and he remained that way right up until the moment I shot him dead.

PART TWO

The Handsome Man

—13—

O'Leary's blood still stained the jailhouse floor, while a cadre of Pinkertons dressed in miner's garb—sooted trousers and charcoaled hats and muddy boots—stood around the Sheriff's desk doing some sort of arts and crafts project with rope. It took me a moment to understand they were tying nooses.

"Where is she?" I asked.

Jacob led me past the cells teeming with near-silent miners, all the way to the back, where my sister sat on the bunk of her cell, reading the *Eagle*. She wore a simple blue dress and her hair framed her face in a way that made her seem like one of those fallen girls you read about in True Crime novels.

"Give us a minute," I said.

Jacob locked me inside and I sat beside her as she perused through the articles, seemingly oblivious to my presence, and her situation.

"How are you?"

"I've had three hours of sleep and two proposals of marriage. Do you think I'd make a fine miner's wife? I could comb my hair into a bob and start dropping my vowels."

I gave her a cigarette. "This seems like an appropriate time to take up drinking, don't you think?" she asked. "Isn't that what scorned women do in such situations? Of course, it's my uncle and not a lover who's betrayed me. No one writes poems about that."

I tried laughing, but it didn't seem too funny. She held the paper up for me.

"I'm surprised Roosevelt's become so paranoid," she

said, in an easy, matter-of-fact tone. "A conspiracy between Forest and our father to destroy the statue. Can
you imagine? For what possible reason? He might as well
blame Masons."

She waved me closer.

"Now me," she said. "I'd change the headline. Not 'Statue Destroyed,' but instead 'Revolution Begun,' if we're going to be at all politically accurate."

"You're sounding," I said, grimacing. "Like the daughter of Jesse Stephens."

She folded the newspaper, slid it beneath the bunk. "I
have no qualms about our father's methods, although he had
nothing to do with this murder, though I'm sure he takes no
issue with gaining credit for such an act. It makes him seem
even more dangerous and I believe he enjoys the reputation.
No, his means are fine. It's his cause that disturbs me. It's
too Ludditian. Too antiquated. He wants this perfect world
that never existed and never could. Not unless you rid the
world of power, and that, dear brother, won't happen as long
as humans remain the planet's principle masters."

We were talking around the issue like we always had,
but neither of us had time for this now. "Jacob said they've
caught you down in Rahillville, helping the miners. I
thought you were more careful."

"I'm a doctor," she said. "It's my duty to—"

"But Seamus, Tillie. You know how he'd see it. They've
got pictures."

"Pictures? What good are those? They show me going
into homes, but they don't show me helping people. They
don't show the children who can breathe again and the
casts and sutures—"

"And you've seen dad."

"That's not the point," she said. "Listen to me, Neal,
will you? I haven't lost my mind and converted to Marx.
You know I'm not that kind of girl."

"What did you two talk about?"

"Something Clyde had. Something he used to blackmail
Forest."

I didn't ask her what, because I already knew—the check. I stood and went to the bars and looked down the line of cells. I didn't recognize most of the miners, not really. I'd seen them before, but I couldn't name them, just bodies and boots plastered in soot.

"And I didn't kill Clyde," she said. "Neal, I need you to believe me. I need *you* to trust me."

"How'd the files end up in your house then? Tillie, it doesn't make sense."

"I can't say."

"It looks bad."

"Neal, what are we doing?"

I knew she wasn't just talking about the two of us.

"I'll talk to Seamus," I said. "Hear him out."

She bowed and I think she wanted me to go, but I wasn't sure when we'd get to talk again. "Did you read my file?"

Her eyes flared, burned. If I was her last hope, she must have thought she was a dead woman.

"Don't you think it's best to focus on one catastrophe at a time?" she said. "I can't even begin to imagine what you were thinking. It was shell shock, wasn't it? Bedding a Negro is one thing, but marrying one—my god, Neal, you know what they'll do to you."

"I'm sorry."

When I got outside into the parking lot, Jacob was cranking his car engine. Behind me, a Pinkerton with long burnsides climbed a ladder, fixing a rope to the hanging tree. Gertie was supervising. She came over to me and tried to kiss me, but I pushed her back.

"Tsk, tsk," she purred. "You can't blame Gertie for your sister's troubles."

"She didn't kill him and you know it. She's too small to get the drop on him, even if he was a one-eyed drunk."

"You're underestimating our sex again. I once killed a giant with a fork. Put it right in his throat. He had dishonorable intentions toward me."

I pushed past her, toward the car. "I don't care."

—14—

Jacob drove south along Seventh then turned right on Elm, taking a circular route to the museum. He described his morning in Rahillville. Seamus had posted eviction notices: everyone had to leave by sundown. Picketers lined the mine fence, playing chicken with armed militiamen. One nervous kid with a rifle could set the town on fire.

"A fucking disaster," Jacob said. "Over 3,000 men out of work. Be hungry by Christmas if it keeps up. Need a new damn job, that's what I need."

He turned down O'Donohue Avenue, and sped along a short dirt road toward Pioneer Park. In the west, a burst of snow clouds levitated above the Rockies, while the northern sky was dry, blue. I tried convincing myself that it was a beautiful contrast, a stunning kind of light, but the eastern wind punched my face and it smelled like coal smoke.

"See that?" Jacob pointed at a row of lawn signs in front of a stretch of old Victorians. Each called for Forest's head. "You did that."

"Stop it," I said.

"What did you think would happen by tying Forest to Jesse?"

"Dancing."

"You're an asshole. Nothing scares people more than your pa. Pair him with Forest and the whole town cries for blood."

"They'd have done it no matter what I wrote."

He slowed the car, straining to see a militiaman signaling

him to stop. He pulled alongside the soldier, and then laid his badge out on the door for the armed child to inspect.

"What's the holdup, son?" Jacob said. "The Canadians invade?"

"No, sir," the soldier said, a private. "We're just setting up roadblocks."

"On whose orders?"

"The Governor's."

"Oh him," Jacob said. "We'll be on our way then."

The boy waved us along.

"How many did he send in?"

"The governor?" Jacob said. "Heard a hundred, but it's probably more."

"How bad is it going to be? Like Ludlow?"

"Maybe that bad. Maybe worse. It's a good story for you. Has good guys, bad guys, heroism, bloodshed. Get you famous. Get you on that train you keep lusting over."

Paris

In the spring of 1914, I was freshly engaged to Lorraine, when news reached us about the Ludlow Massacre. It made the back pages of the old *Paris Herald*. Nineteen miners killed when the Colorado National Guard invaded a tent city set up by the union. I knew that Jacob, who'd joined the Guard, probably had a hand in it. Lorraine showed me the article.

We'd met for breakfast at a café in the Latin Quarter on one of those cold, rainy mornings where it felt like your suit was pasted to your skin. She had the paper hidden under her raincoat. People talk a lot about how the French don't see race, but that's not true. People looked at us as we sat together, as we held hands, but the difference between France and the States is pretty simple: there was no hanging tree in Paris, at least not for people like us.

"You're from here, aren't you?"

Ludlow is couple hundred miles south of New Sligo, in the high desert country that looks a lot like New Mexico. While they still dig lignite coal down there, most of them were Italian or Mexican, and there wasn't much of a middle class. It was all company town.

"Never been there," I told her. "Hear it's hotter."

"I could use some heat now," she said, looking out at the sopping sidewalks. She liked to say that she didn't care about what happened in America. She was done with that nation. But every morning she read the *Herald*, alongside *Le Monde*, despite the latter being the better paper. I never called her bluff, though. It would have shamed her and there isn't any pleasure in that.

"They fired at the tents," she said. "I don't think they were aiming. They didn't care who they killed."

"It happens that way."

Then I told her, for the first time, who my father was. I told her about Big Hank, about how the man they called "Dynamite Jesse" taught me to read, to ride a horse.

She buttered her baguette. "I already knew that. I was just waiting for you to get around to it."

I don't remember what I said. I probably apologized—it was always my first defense—but I can't say for sure.

"Do you miss him?" She pulled off her shoes, wiping the insoles with a handkerchief.

"No, I hardly remember him anymore."

"Antoinette," she said.

"The Queen?"

"No, for our first daughter."

"Seems like we're bequeathing her a poor fortune with that name."

"Don't be silly," she said. "It was my aunt's name. I always thought it pretty."

"I love you."

"You'd better."

We met Seamus in the grand hall of the museum. It reeked of privilege, with its vaulted entrance, decorative columns, and dollar admission. I didn't have to pay, however, because the museum was dedicated to my mother.

When we came in, my uncle was barking at two Mexicans building a case to display the Shakespeare Quarto. If everything went well, the book would arrive in two days, and in a week the public could look at the oldest copy of *Hamlet*. People would line up and pay good money just to eyeball a damn book cover.

When my uncle saw me, he held up a finger—one minute. A Wells Fargo truck pulled up outside and two men got out and walked in carrying sawed-off shotguns. They guarded a third man, some burly German-looking bastard, carrying a satchel.

"Why so much cash?" I asked. "I thought you liked your bribes off the books?"

"Banks shut off Seamus' credit until the strike ends," Jacob said. "Don't want to bet on anything that ain't for sure."

Even though the museum was open, it was nearly empty, except for another collaborator hiding in the corner, appearing like he cared about some knight's bust melded during the English Revolution.

I went to Roosevelt, took off my hat, and called him a son of a bitch.

"My mother was no princess, if that's your intention, Stephens," he said. "Family lore speculates that at one time she danced burlesque."

"Did you know they'd arrest Tillie?"

"If I'd known your sister was to be handcuffed, I'd have paid money to watch."

"If you weren't a cripple—"

"You'd what? Still get pummeled by me? Now wipe the tears from your gash and pull yourself together for your sister's sake."

"She didn't do it."

"You're always the last to figure things out, aren't you Stephens? We want your father."

"You don't care."

"I care about my pecker, and I might be the only man in town who thinks your sister provides a noble public service. I'm trying to save her neck."

"They'll call her an anarchist."

"Americans are predictable."

A man with a long, waxed moustache interrupted us. You could tell he was a Pinkerton by his vacant eyes and the way his breath smelled like dead children. He was all menace and anonymity, the kind of man who came to your house at night and put a pillow over you face before you had the chance to protest. It was the same Pinkerton who'd been following Forest, the John Wilkes Booth twin.

"Mr. Rahill is ready for you," Pinkerton Booth said.

"Just a second." I wanted to finish my argument with Roosevelt.

Booth, I discovered, valued promptness. He yanked me with the sort of savage gentility common amongst his clan. "We don't have time for games," Booth said. "Now, go."

My uncle's kept a large, debonair office in the back of the museum. It was here, rather than Rahill Coal & Electric, where he did most of his business. He liked being surrounded by the calm of the museum, rather than the bustle and commerce of his corporate confines. But that wasn't his only reason. He once confessed that the Rahill headquarters reminded him of Big Hank and that was a day he'd rather forget.

He filled his office with old British artifacts: royal portraits, family crests, and even a prop skull from the Globe

Theater. Unlike a lot of men back then, he wasn't caught up in the African fads or the obsession with the primitive. He was top-drawer and enjoyed fine cigars and fitted suits, leaving him little interest in the lives of those he considered below him. Behind his desk, he'd hung a portrait of Queen Elizabeth, before she'd been crowned—stern, nubile, and redheaded—a tempting combination. Near the portrait, he'd pasted newspaper articles about my father, a primary history of Jesse's crimes. My uncle's gun rested on top of the Bible. I looked out the window at the Square, where you could see Negroes sweeping up the remains of last night's explosion.

"Take a seat, son," Seamus said. "Roosevelt, close the door."

I lowered my gaze.

"Let's talk honestly, Neal. Can we do that? Without all these rules?"

I wasn't sure what rules he meant.

"We're finding ourselves in a fine quandary here, a real mess as they say. Isn't that right, Neal?"

I lit a cigarette, nodding.

"We're caretakers, just simple guardians of this town and if that's not trial enough for an old man like me, your father's stolen your sister's good sense. You'd think there was a holy bet on my faith."

"I told Jacob I saw him as soon as I did."

"I know," he said. "You've had a series of shocks this last score of years, but you're going to have to be strong for me. We're obliged to care for the people here."

A secretary in a dark dress and dark heels came in and then handed Seamus a piece of paper.

"Sign here?"

"Here, Mr. Rahill."

"It's the final details for the Shakespeare exhibit," Seamus said. "People will travel from hundreds of miles just to see it. Can you imagine? They'll feel like they're near something great, something holy."

Out the window, a pair of militiamen patrolled the square, marching in formation just as they'd been taught in basic training. They'd grown up on tales of war heroics, maybe even seeing some of my pictures, and now here they were, invading the Front Range.

"Do you remember much of my father, Neal?"

"Pardon me?"

"My father. You were just a boy when the Lord took him."

"A little."

"He was a great man, Mr. Rahill," Roosevelt said. "A real pioneer."

Seamus ignored him. "What do you remember?"

"His voice," I said. "How Irish he sounded."

My uncle stood, turning to a photo of my father from a Swiss paper.

"He was illiterate," Seamus said. "He never read a word, not even the Lord's. I know I speak highly of him, and I dare say I must have loved him, but we never understood one another, not even a little. Back then, well, boys didn't speak to their fathers. They listened, obeyed. Not like now where every little scamp swears the Lord's name to his parents. I imagine that's the curse of man, to misunderstand our fathers, to be ignorant of our sons. I saw him as a shameful, violent immigrant and he saw me as dithering, bookish, without the will to lead. I'm sure that's why he loved your father more."

I looked at Roosevelt, hoping for some sort of sign telling me how to work this confession, but my boss was studying his cane.

"I'd never witnessed such joy in him," Seamus went on. "As that day your father asked for Pearl's hand. Like the light in his eyes burnished enough to heat the Earth. He adopted your father as his heir, casting me aside like Cain. Did you know that?"

"No one tells me anything."

"Explained to me how Jesse had the backbone for it, while I was better served manning the abacus like some Jew. It's haunting to be shunned by one's own father. I vowed that if I ever had my own son." He paused, checking his watch. "Well, I never had a son, not until you."

"I've always thought of you that way, uncle."

He laughed and I heard how pliant I sounded.

"No, you don't," Seamus said. "You're angry. I can see the devil in your eyes. You're the angriest man I've ever met. An inheritance from my father, I'm afraid. You've always been more Rahill than Stephens."

"And you? You're angry. Why else—"

"Would I have Tillie jailed?"

I nodded.

"She is more Stephens than Rahill."

"Stop it," I said. "She's your niece."

I stood and I saw, I believe, just a flinch, a slight gesture of my uncle reaching toward his revolver. It sent me back to my chair.

"There's that anger again," Seamus said. "I can see my father in your eyes. You're a lot like him. He also fornicated with Negroes."

He took my file and held it up as if he was about to hand it over, but paused, removing a small photograph, the last surviving image of Lorraine, the one we'd taken on our wedding day. I wanted to reach for it because, even by then, her memory was disappearing. It was the one piece of blackmail I truly desired. But I didn't take it, no matter how much I wanted to, because Seamus was watching me, studying my reaction, so I sat there passively as he struck a match and put it to the paper, and I was obedient as her picture burned in the ashtray.

He took the rest of the file—mostly legal documents and witness testimony—and then slipped it into a desk drawer for safekeeping.

"I understand the damage war does to one's faculties," he said. "We'll talk of this another time. In the meantime, I think we can keep this between us. No need to upset the townspeople—you know how unforgiving they can be."

I thanked him but I knew this wasn't the end of it: he hadn't thrown the file out. It was still there, in his desk, waiting for the right moment to bite.

"Your father nearly killed you last night and that was your lightning strike. Do you understand me?"

"I'll do what you want," I said. "I just want Tillie safe."

Seamus waved at my boss. "Tell him."

Roosevelt leaned against his cane, remembering his lines.

"I've completed a thorough inventory of O'Leary's files. Forest's isn't there. Your sister pleads that she never saw it."

"We need it," Seamus said. "For the good of the town."

No one believed Tillie acted alone, but only as a patsy for my father, who was using her to get to Seamus. They figured Jesse was holding on to the file and they wanted me to steal it. In exchange, Tillie would leave town, forever. I knew I had what they were looking for. But I wasn't ready to give the check to them. Not yet.

"We have a deal?" Seamus said. "We can spit on our palms if you don't trust my word."

It didn't take me long to answer. "Fine."

"And then we'll talk about the Negro," Seamus said. "But first, we'll pray."

We knelt and recited together the Lord's prayer, to consecrate our deal. When we got to "thy will be done," I looked up to see my uncle eyes closed, enraptured. It was then that I began seeing the real difference between us. When I prayed, I expected nothing in return, but when Seamus prayed, he expected fire and brimstone to rain down on the armies of his enemy.

When I got outside, I considered walking right to McGuffey's, but I figured that I'd drink myself into doing something dumb, so I started toward home. The snow had nearly melted away and I felt the sidewalk under my boots. I thought of just heading back in, giving them the check, getting it done with. The thing was, even then, I wasn't sure how the check from my father to Big Hank worked as blackmail. It didn't seem to concern Forest, but I knew my father wanted it as well and that was enough to know its importance. If it got Tillie out, I told myself, then it didn't matter how it all fit together. Still, I needed to think it through.

As I crossed Pioneer Square, I saw, at the end of an alley,

the dents and scratches on the fender of a black Ford, my stolen car. I went to it and saw the keys were in the ignition and the engine was running.

I got in the car and laid my hands on the wheel. For a moment, I felt happy.

The last thing I remember before the rag hit my face was my father saying, "Good morning, Cowboy."

—16—

When I awoke, I was slumped in the passenger seat, my wrists handcuffed to the steering wheel. My tongue tasted of bitter chemicals and my nose felt like it had lost all its hairs and was rubbed bare. My head hurt worse than any hangover I've ever had.

I sat up—Miss Constance was at my feet, thank God.

The car sat on a low hillside overlooking an abandoned mine shaft two miles east of town. I knew the place. A few weeks before my father shot Big Hank, the miners had been digging here when a cave-in killed six, injuring a dozen others, including Clyde, who'd lost his eye. My uncle said it was just bad luck. The temperature whiplashed between hot and cold that winter, as it so often does on the Front Range, and it made the rock brittle.

My father materialized from a nearby ravine. When he came to me, he leaned into the car. "Smells something awful, don't it?"

I reached for his throat, but the handcuffs stopped me.

"You son of a bitch."

"First time I was ethered was back in '82. Sawbones Sam, this old gray doc who'd said he'd been the one to liberate Stonewall Jackson from his arm, well, he came at me one day thinking I'd fancied his horse—a man can get awful testy about his own mare—and he got me, oh, did he ever. Lucky for me, my partner came in just in the nick of time, otherwise I'd be down a limb."

"You could have just asked to talk."

"You'd have turned me in."

"They've got Tillie," I said. "How can you involve your own fucking daughter in this mess?"

"I know, Cowboy. I'm working on that."

I heard the long horn of the train and saw, out to the east, the *Queen of Isles* chugging toward Kansas City.

"You want to be on that train?"

I wasn't going to answer him.

"Wait," I said. "You had a partner in '82?"

"And back then Chester Arthur was really president. Chronology, cowboy. It's all in the order of numbers. Remember that."

"You were already an anarchist?"

"Cowboy, I've been an anarchist since the morning I left my mama's womb. I was an anarchist long before I came here, and I'll be one 'til the day I turn to dirt, when my power and dominion over this world ceases to be."

I don't remember saying anything, not for a while. Maybe it was the shock of knowing my father had always lied about himself, or maybe it was just the raging ether hangover, but I sat there for a long time, his voice harmonizing with the prairie wind.

"You know what dead work is?" he asked. "That's what they were striking over back in '04. We paid them by the pounds of coal each brought up because we figured it made them more efficient, or at least, we extrapolated more from their labor. But we all knew a miner's job isn't just with a pickaxe because you got to maintain the cart tracks and put up the timber in the shafts and make sure the hole is ventilated, otherwise you ain't walking out the same man and that sort of work, the drudgery of keeping the shaft alive, sucks in hours of a man's time, and we weren't paying them a dime for that work because it didn't make us any gold if you know what I mean, but they're dead if they don't do it. The yoke of their labors is really just a noose. But the point is we were getting them the timber and everyone knew it was the cheap sort of lumber you can scrounge from the foothills and it's what brought that mine down, sure of that as I'm sure of anything, and that's what set the whole mess in motion because I'd bought Big Hank for years, giving him coin to keep the union pacified and he did his best to hide the money, but for some reason he sent his boy down there, hoping it made him look like any other man who needed his son's labors to survive, though he didn't because we'd made him a rich man, a damned capitalist himself. Guess seeing his boy hurt like that resurrected the proletarian in him. But, shit, you don't care about that. Not really. That ain't the history you're wanting to hear. What do you want to know, Cowboy?"

I looked down at the valley of the forgotten mine. I had a lot of questions I wanted answered, but sometimes you got to pick the story you want to hear, just in case you never get another chance with the narrator.

"Who is Mattie Longstreet?"

My father pulled a drink from his bottle, and then gave me a sip. It did nothing for my headache. "Alright, Cowboy. I'll tell you. But don't blame me if you don't like the answers."

JESSE

I've always hated dentists, Cowboy. Hate 'em. They're meaner than coppers, more corrupt than bankers, and even lack the generosity of the taxman. Only men of petrified hearts choose to spend their days wrenching teeth from another man's jaw. They find solace in the screams of women. They seek their daily sustenance in children's tears. Their artistry is in the appliance of pain. It's a low profession, one Dante failed to cosign a level because not even corrupters of young virtue tolerate the tooth-puller. Believe me, Cowboy, when I say that if you ever meet a dentist in an alley, run the other way because their intentions are nefarious, their soul's a snake masquerading as a withered vine from the tree of life. Yet in our vanity, our ruthless designs upon perfection, we keep creating these men, believing their trade honorable, necessary, when in fact they steal the very souls from our damned mouths, then seal the wound in gold. You want an example of exploitation: find a dentist.

Well, it started for me the summer of my fifteenth birthday, and I was working shifts as a butcher's assistant in that awful Kansas town, my father casting me out into the world to earn the keep he couldn't harvest from his meager soil, and it was from my perch between two hanging carcasses that I spotted our new tooth-puller riding into town, the infamous Benjamin Straun, a fat-headed sadist known for his clumsy thumbs and his executioner's heart. He, a cretin of gangly mutton-chops, carried his instruments of torture like they were the riches of Solomon, and I understood he'd be trouble, because I knew, despite my poor lot, that it would be I, the magnificent Jesse Stephens, who would become his lifelong nemesis. It was that slithering snot, that fiendish fraud, who'd yanked from my very skull my four back teeth. He used a witch's brew and the grin of a charlatan to seduce me into submitting to his torture and I shan't ever forget the joyous parting of his lips, the guillotine quickness of his tongue, the dandyish cackle of that ivory-haired sadist. Afterwards, blood pouring from my beautiful mouth, my looks irrevocably damaged—and at the time, I was without a doubt the handsomest man in the Americas—I vowed to seek my revenge in the only way a gunless, beautiful boy can. I bedded his wife.

That's right, Cowboy. Mattie was the dentist's wife.

Now, to be the cuckold is a tragedy. It eats at a man, tearing out his guts and drying them for the public to traipse about with glee. But to be the cuckolder, or maybe it's best to say the cuckolding party, or, hell, the man inside the cuckold's wife, is nothing but pure damn anarchy. It cuts at the fabric of our capitalist culture, diluting the slavery of marriage, the illusions of ownership, until there ain't nothing left then what there should be: man and woman entwined. And isn't that a beautiful sight? Now, Cowboy, you got to understand that marriage ain't nothing but servitude, the unwilling selling of your own body to another, and it's even worse for the woman involved. And I know what your God says about it, but it ain't nothing but a way to keep poor folks from reaching their potentials, finding their own notion of self-reliance, realizing their capacity as denizens of this great Earth. At least that's what poor Emma Goldman used to say before we had that falling out over her cocker spaniel.

Yes, I'm getting to the point, Cowboy. Trust me.

Now, imagine it: Decoration Day of '79, the town parading its blues and grays through the main drag at a cripple's pace, while thunderclouds taunt overhead, and locust mate in the fields, and women cry for their lost lovers and amidst all this commotion, all these revisions of capitalist crimes, there she stood, like a rose petal floating in a piss pot, the

Magdalene of my loins, my Mattie. You can't understand what a sight she was, unless you grew up in world without beauty, without art, because Cowboy that was my Kansas, and I imagine that when I saw my raven-haired darling, it was like how Adam felt when Eve erupted from his rib and he understood that the world ain't made for the lonesome. It broke my heart to think of her suffering under the cruel ministrations of that evil tusk-taker and I knew it was my duty as resident gentleman, town arbiter for the care of pretty ladies, to rescue my damsel.

And what did she think of me? Hell, I was Beethoven symphoning off her brassiere, Shakespeare sonneting loose her corset, Caruso tenoring open her knees. Christ, I was the handsomest man she'd ever come across and ever would, a spry buck of a boy who made women shake with concupiscence, for I was the stuff of poor women's fantasies, the Incubus of their dreams, a spectacle worthy of Baudelaire.

She came to me in an alley, cigarette parting her lips.

—Break my heart, she whispered. Keep the good half.
—Yes, ma'am.
—We'll die together, she promised. Just you and me, sailor.
—I'm here to serve, ma'am.
—Now lift my dress.
—Of course, ma'am.
—Like you mean it.

And it ain't hyperbole, Cowboy. Just truth shaded with imagery. You'd know that if you could write a lick.

But you want facts, you say? Well, she'd married that dentist five years before our meeting, just a tender girl of thirteen, lost in a poker game from her father's poor bluff. Her grandfather, the irascible General Longstreet, sought her until his death, but she had a way of disappearing into the world, becoming whatever was needed, except in my arms, where she existed for the present, for me alone. That summer and all the way through the autumn until the last leaf had fallen, until the water turned to ice, we took to meeting in barns, and out in the fields, and hell, any place where we weren't likely to run up against her husband, for men of that age did not look kindly upon being the cuckold, but even as a child I cared not a lick for the rules of man. Cowboy, you got to understand, she called me her shepherd, but it was she who got me to run off, it was Mattie with whom I fled Kansas that Christmas Eve of '79, my darling girl. We left for many reasons, too many to recount, but let me quickly sum it up as this: there wasn't a man or beast in our existence that would have stopped our union, not for long, so we fled toward our Canaan, our salvation, and the dentist chased us with his pliers, but he died long before he could reap his revenge.

We went South into the dusty plains of Indian Territory, then, after the horse came up lame, we hoofed it to Kentucky, through rolling hills of tobacco and starvation, and we walked clear up to New York, dancing into our brave new world, seeking out solitude, finding refuge from our histories, wanting nothing but each other's bodies in that haven of vice and debasement, my beautiful city, the home of my dreams and nightmares.

Were we anarchists, then? Well, in a way, I'd been an anarchist since birth, breaking the bounds of childhood, the social cuffs upon my wrists, the constraints of time and authority. But, no, we weren't anarchists in the classical sense. I'd never read Thoreau or Kropotkin, never laid eyes upon the poetry of Paine. Not until we reached that dark labyrinth of a metropolis and found a home in the basement of a great library and read the words of our betters and understood why our lot was so poor did my mind catch up to my actions. Soon enough we began running with men of our ilk, like-minded Romans and Bavarians and even an itinerant Dubliner, and it was in those early years that I felt the weight of my poverty lifted from my heart, transformed into a piece of revolutionary steel along my trigger finger.

How'd we survive? Well, shit, Cowboy, we stole everything that wasn't nailed down.

We picked pockets, held up bagmen, cracked safes, marked cards, and even hijacked one of Vanderbilt's carriages on a bet. Mattie was my green-eyed second-story girl, a natural thief and gun moll, who'd clean out the crown jewels of his royal highness if she didn't have a preternatural fear of English cuisine. You had to see it, Cowboy. The girl had Mozart's fingers but her instrument wasn't the piano but the lock pick. She was born for it, a prodigy of the dark arts. We did that. We stole. We robbed. We hoisted. But mostly we rolled travelers with the Woman of Easy Virtue scam. Mattie was the lure, our tight-framed, long-legged bait and I was her jealous husband who'd bust into the flophouses just before consummation and I'd demand my reparations as a cuckold, and that poor sap, whomever he was that particular night, always paid. And Mattie and I ate like Turks and drank like Prussians and we made love like Spaniards and we talked, oh, Cowboy, we talked like two people who know nothing of the future talked. We debated Godwin, scoffed at Engels, and fell in love with Bakunin. I get choked up for that lost time. That time of light and gaiety because the dark crashed down upon us so quick, I can barely recollect how it happened.

Though I know it started with Fat Hershel. Now, here's what you need to understand to really know Fat Hershel, a man without irony: he was our fence and tip-off man, but he always fancied Mattie and I knew I shouldn't trust him, but he came to us during a spell in my life where I thought the only good people, the only trustworthy of our kind, were crooks. Anarchist crooks. I believed Fat Hershel when he introduced us to Charming Rudolf, and when he said Rudolf was a crack thief and no turncoat and a man of the cause, I took that word as divined. But you can already guess it wasn't true.

Rudolf robbed banks. He also acted in an anarchist theater troupe, and I should have known to walk away, because actors, like dentists and child buggers, have no conscience, only gravitating toward men to suck them of their marrow. Rudolf planned on cleaning out the Bank of Murray Hill, a despicable business owned by a real cretin named Maynard Smythe, a man responsible for rendering thousands roofless, for filching from the public trust, for being a leach upon humanity. Robbing him and blowing his bank to kingdom come was his punishment, the only form of justice I yet knew how to mete out. Well, Rudolf needed a gun girl and a dynamite man and that was Mattie and me, and since he talked the game well, and had a reputation, according to Fat Hershel, for forthrightness and intelligence, we agreed.

We met the morning of June 12, 1886. I remember the date like it's your birthday. I remember everything about it and you can look it up in the records because that's the day Rudolf murdered a policeman and even though the scribblers say Mattie did it, she didn't. And hell, the date's important because Haymarket happened a month earlier and the coppers were rousting anyone who'd even perused the cover of an anarchist title and things were tight and closing in on us, but we figured one last score and we could lay low for a year and things might get better for our kind.

In the morning, Mattie put my hand to her breast and said that I'd rescued her from purgatory and no matter what happened that I was her savior and she'd love me until the stars burned away their wicks. And I told her to stop foolin' around because we'd be reposing near Brighton Beach by sundown. Shit, Cowboy, if I could go back in time and kick my younger self's ass, I'd beat myself unconscious that day. Wish I didn't remember it so well.

The plan was simple enough: I set off a series of explosions on the roof of the bank, distracting the guards, while Mattie and Rudolf slipped behind the tellers, held up the bank manager, and cleaned out the tills. At a quarter to noon, I'd pull up in front of the bank with three horses, the rest of the dynamite set to explode, and we'd disappear, leaving a crater where that bank once stood. Simple.

We met Rudolf outside of a tavern on Lexington. He took Mattie's arm.

—See you soon my little lamb, she told me.

Her last words for a long time.

I'd like to think I spent some time memorizing her image as she walked away, that I savored every last sight of her, but I didn't think anything of it. Never been good with foresight, Cowboy, but I guess that's in our blood, ain't it?

I won't bore you with the details, Just know that before I even got to the roof, fifteen coppers already lay in waiting outside the bank and bullets were flying like bats at sunset and I found myself hiding beneath a livery cab, sobbing something fierce, when I saw them pull Rudolf's body from the bank and they took Mattie away in handcuffs.

Later, when I found Fat Hershel and put a gun in his mouth, he told me that Rudolf got drunk a night earlier in a beauty of a tavern called The Swill and performed a soliloquy atop a barroom table on how we were going to do the job, complete with a couplet rhyming dynamite and ignite. Well, someone saw it and snitched and that's how Mattie ended up getting a life sentence. Actors, shit, the vermin of humanity.

You know the rest, Cowboy. You know I walked away and started a new life and tried to forget about her, about my complicity in Mattie's poor fate, and you know how hard that complicity is to live with because you do it all day long.

You're like me, Cowboy. You ruined a woman too.

—17—

"You keep telling yourself that," I said.

"Oh, you're a lot more like me then you think."

"I don't know what you're talking about. I'm law-abiding. I got a job."

My wrists were still cuffed and my back and shoulders felt sore. My father leaned into the car and shook his head.

"You can't lie to me like that," he said. "I know your secrets. Wrote that limerick telling you as much."

"You killed O'Leary, didn't you? You killed him for Forest."

"Not that simple."

He put out his cigar and took another pull from the bottle and then gave me a smile that made me want hit him with a bat.

"Not until I can trust you," he said. "Not until you start coming clean about what you did to that poor girl."

I looked to the mineshaft full of rubble, to the bones never found.

"I'm sorry."

"For what?" he asked. "You just throw words around like that and expect it all to be better and I'm sure a lot of folks will nod and forgive you but they're not forgiving you for the right things, because sorry is just a sorry explanation for a lot of wrongs you did and they're forgiving you for things you ain't sorry for, or at least shouldn't be. So what are you sorry for, Cowboy? Careful with your answer, because it's going to tell me a lot about what kind of man you've turned out to be."

"I'm going to kill you." I kicked, aiming for his head, but I was still cuffed to the steering wheel, flailing like a war cripple.

"Let me go so I can fucking strangle you."

"All right, Cowboy." He came around to the other side of the car. "You think hard on this question. We'll talk this over soon."

"I hope they hang you."

He laughed as he pulled the bottle of ether from his coat pocket, and he cackled as he poured the liquid on the rag, and he guffawed as he put it to my mouth, my father, the merry trickster of New Sligo County.

—18—

When I awoke from the ether fog, I found myself in an alley filled with garbage pails and stray dogs, the latter waiting for me to turn cold so they could gnaw me down the bone. Miss Constance lay beside me. On my chest, my father left another limerick:

> "There once was a bastard named Neal
> Who despite his good heart was a heel
> He abandoned the war
> Left his wife like a whore
> So Cowboy that's shame you should feel.
> *¿En qué pararán estes misas, Garatuza? El Guapo.*"

He'd dropped me in the middle of New Sligo, taking my car with him. Yet he'd made a mistake. I was only two blocks from the *Eagle*.

When I marched into Roosevelt's office, he looked up from his copy, and then scowled. "Did you just resurrect yourself?"

I pulled off my boot.

"Fucking hell, Stephens. Letting me bugger you isn't going to get you anywhere."

I gave him the check. "This is what Clyde had on Forest. It's what my father wanted."

Roosevelt looked it over.

"Back in the day, my father was paying Big Hank off and it kept the union in line and I figure it all went south when Clyde lost his eye because Big Hank found a conscience or something or at least he wanted to get back at Jesse, but later on Clyde found the check and put it to Forest, hard. You know how Forest has made Big Hank into this Christ-figure? If it got out that the union's been taking payoffs since at least '04, it would ruin Forest."

Roosevelt sat there massaging his cane in a way that would make a lady blush.

"My father was searching for it. Got to figure he killed Clyde trying to find it. It was all to save the union's face. It's maybe not enough to convict Forest, but it'll lock him up for a couple of weeks."

"I'd heard rumors back in the day," Roosevelt said. "Even asked your uncle once, but he laughed at me. Calling it fantasy. Never gave it a second thought."

"I doubt he knew."

My uncle wasn't a man for subtlety or backroom machinations. He preferred the sledgehammer to the spyglass.

"I'll bring it to him," Roosevelt said. "We'll see if it's enough."

"It's enough to get Tillie out."

—19—

Like most afternoons in those days, I found myself walking the street for hours thinking of nothing but leaving this goddamn town, before giving up and heading to Mc-Guffey's. Yet this time was different. I couldn't remember the last time I'd eaten, and, after finking on Forest, I felt a craven sort of hunger that made me put away a whole liverwurst sandwich, potato chips, boiled beets, and a pickled egg in a sitting. The bar was quiet, nearly empty, just Jacob sitting between Alma and Sam, the latter explaining his theory on why my father had returned.

"Now, I know it seems mighty odd, but I think he's come back to aid the dirt worshipers in their hopes of conquistadoring this here land."

"Dirt worshipers?" Alma asked.

"Indians," Jacob said. "Ignore him."

"Don't be sly with me," Sam said. "If that anarchist wants no land to be held by decent folks, wants no governing body, wants no real God with a book of evidence on his side, then it sounds to me like a dirt worshiper. Am I wrong?"

"Stop it," Jacob said. "He's come back for revenge."

"You really think he's that crazy?" Alma asked. "Won't they hang him?"

"I disagree, Mr. Detective," Sam said. "Why is it that a man who left the prettiest lady this side of Sarah Bernhardt seeking vengeance? Don't make no sense."

"Did she look like Tillie?" Alma said. "Or Neal?"

Sam wheezed. "Missy, those children got the worst of both parents. Cursed they are."

I could hear the whole conversation, but I just kept eating.

Sam went on. "No, Pearl was the prettiest woman this town has ever been fortunate enough to possess. A regular Juliet she was. Her children just poor-looking progeny if you ask me. "

Alma put her hand to her face, her scar highlighted by the flickering candlelight. "She sounds remarkable," she said. "A real dame."

"She was an angel," Sam said. "If things had just gone a bit better for old Sam Bailey, I'd have married her."

Jacob snorted. He was feeling particularly mean, I imagine, because he'd already heard what I'd done to Forest. "Married her. Woman wouldn't let you wash her feet."

"You're wrong there. Wrong. Wrong. Wrong." Sam stood and shook his son.

"Sit down, you old drunk."

"Jesse Stephens killed that woman," Sam said. "Killed her like he put a gun in her very mouth."

"You don't honestly believe that, do you?" Alma said.

"Well, she was doin' just fine after that evil anarchist hightailed it out of here, but then a sickness came over her like none any of us seen, a curse, you see. That anarchist couldn't leave well enough alone and he cursed that poor woman, made her fragile and such and every sort of sickness that could be caught, she did go and caught."

"It was pneumonia," Jacob said.

That was the story we told everyone: a lingering case of pneumonia.

"Curse, I say," Sam cried.

"Happens all the time," Jacob said. "Sometimes you got no choice in some things."

He looked over at me, giving me a hard, accusatory grin. "Other times you've got plenty of choices, but you just choose whatever's easiest for you because you wouldn't want to ruin your reputation as a lazy, worthless, no-good piece of shit because people might start thinking you give a damn about someone else than yourself. Ain't that right, Neal?"

I put out my cigarette on my boot heel, and then lit another.

"It is a shame," Jacob went on. "Tillie said that one's folks are like the clay that shapes the man, but as far as I can tell that's a bunch of horseshit. You're an old drunk and I turned out fine. And Neal there, well, he's got a Pa who was brave and never let no man make him a coward and look at how he turned out—all coward, all the way through. Here's thinking that parentage doesn't mean shit in this world."

Alma came over to me. She put her hand on my shoulder and leaned in, softly, whispering, "You're crying. Why?"

Why was I crying? Christ, where could I begin?

Jacob took his hat and stopped at the coat rack, then turned to Alma and sneered.

"'Cause he's a fink," he said. "Knows he's a fink and finks cry. Christ, Neal, you stupid son of a bitch."

He disappeared up the staircase.

"Nigger Norris," Sam called out. "Let me buy Neal here a beer."

"You don't have enough for the one you're drinking," Lazy Eye said. "Bastard can afford it anyhow."

Lazy Eye, I could tell, already knew what I'd done to Forest and I knew that everyone was going to hate me. "I did it for Tillie."

Lazy Eye threw down his rag. He went to the other side of the bar, muttering something to himself, then came back, looked at me and spit.

"Don't pawn that shit off on me," he said. "I don't give a fuck about your confessions."

"She's my sister. What do you want me to do?"

"Fuck boy, I know what she is, but the best you can do is the shit you pulled? That's all you got, college boy? Give it up to the first cocksucker who winks at you?"

"I'm sorry."

"You a sorry sack of shit is what you are," Lazy Eye said. "Thought you had more sense than that kid. And you know what else? I never liked having Rahills drinking here but I made you the exception 'cause I thought you had some goddamn sense. Guess I'm shit for brains just like you. And you know what else you pasty Irish sheep-fucking piece of—"

"My wife was a Negro."

Maybe it was the alcohol or the food or Lazy Eye's scolding or Sam's kindness or Alma's sympathy, but I think I lost my mind for a moment. Still can't say why. Guess I just stopped being scared.

"She grew up in St. Louis," I said. "Her mother was Negro and her father was Negro and I knew she was Negro and I don't give a damn what you think."

None of them said anything for a long time, just listening to the house band: the hack of the cleaver, the patter of blood from the ceiling. I rubbed my boots against the floor as if I was pacing at a standstill.

Finally, Sam whispered, "What was it like, you know, on the honeymoon?"

"Shit, Sam," Lazy Eye said. "Ain't like nothing you ever felt before. Like tasting steak after living on salt pork your fucking whole life."

"I just always wondered," Sam said. "Is it the same with a Negress? Is it better? It ain't better is it Neal?"

"He's just makin' this shit up," Lazy Eye said. "No Negro with her right mind ever marry a sorry bastard like him. It was the goddamn French who fucked that girl's head."

Only Alma stayed quiet. I figured Swedish opera singers didn't care about miscegenation.

"You goin' to say anything, Neal?" Sam asked. "Got any words?"

I stared down Lazy Eye. "Fuck you."

"About the only sense you made all day," he said. "Come back when you've got your brains right."

—20—

The Rahillville refugees stretched for a half-mile along the highway, pulling mule carts and wagons spilling out with their remaining worldly possessions: pans, coats, and mattresses. Families staggered from their homes, coiling on to the gravel highway, heading west toward a fallow field, a makeshift camp, bought and readied by the union. It was like they'd done at Ludlow.

Alma drove.

"Have you ever seen anything like this?" she asked.

I had. This sort of thing happened a lot back in those days: it was more like a civil rebellion than a modern day strike with organized picketing and lawyered negotiations. The higher-ups—politicians and corporate barons—saw a strike as insurrection rather than a normal labor practice. It was all a lot more rough and tumble. But I'd also watched scenes like this in Europe as well, during the early part of the war, when they'd pushed families out of Belgium toward the south, into France, but they'd only carried enough to last a few weeks because reporters told them that they'd be home by Christmas.

"Were you in Sweden during the war?"

"No," she said. "Belgrade. I was in Belgrade."

She drove carefully, slaloming through the refugees, skirting the militiamen standing guard on the highway's edge. She kept the wheel steady, concentrating on the road, avoiding the perplexed glares of those wondering why in God's name she drove *toward* Rahillville.

I took out Miss Constance.

"Do you mind?"

"Not me," she said. "My manager doesn't like me out of costume. Aim at them."

The wind blew through the prairie grass, scattering flowers and dead soil and the refugees shielded their eyes against the dust devils while maneuvering down the rutted road. There were too many people, too many images to really nail one down. It was confusing and there wasn't a story I could picture, nothing that would be true, I figured. During the war, my camera illuminated death: men went over the top and never returned. That was the story. But here, it wasn't so simple. I tried pointing Miss Constance at some soldiers, but that didn't seem right. They were just working.

I pulled myself up on the windowsill, bracing Miss Constance against the roof of the car, calling out to various men and women, asking them to turn and look. Each posed before Miss Constance's eye: some fixed their hair, others took off their hats, and one tightened his tie. Behind those portraits, the other refugees pushed on, saddled with blankets, food, and coats, but also packed with picture frames, jewelry boxes, china plates, postcards, Bibles, and paintbrushes. One woman walked barefooted in her wedding dress, mud staining the skirt, while her husband wore a tuxedo and carried a glass vase. A calf brushed alongside of them, a bell wrapped around its neck ringing like the call to prayer. A boy pushed a piano down the road, his tendons tensed, his teeth gritted, while a little girl leading a pet pig and holding a bouquet of daisies skipped alongside crying out "Ring around the Rosy."

The occasional scream, the scattered pops of gunfire didn't bother me. I just kept reloading the film. When those folks looked straight at me, when they posed in a manner of their own choosing, I could see a new sort of truth. It was how *they* wanted to be seen. And they didn't want to be victims. Wish I could say the day ended just as triumphantly.

—21—

Forest lived in a brick house with a corrugated tin roof and a single coal stove that heated both rooms. It was like every other shanty in the company town, forlorn and barely habitable. While everyone else seemed to have cleared out, Forest's drapes were still up. Maybe it was a signal to his men, to Seamus, that he'd fight until the end. But I didn't think so. My guess was that his wife had sewn those drapes, hung them herself, and Forest couldn't bear to take them down.

I told Alma to stay in the car and then I went toward the house, stopping at the door when one of the Pennsylvania union men came out, put a gluttonous hand on my chest, and told me to wait.

"We'll be done here soon."

Across the narrow road, Tobias Smith, one of Rahill's few Negro miners, emerged from a house with a potato sack slung over his sunken shoulders. He was followed by a white woman dressed like a gypsy with mismatched, brightly colored clothes, so radiant in the Rahillville grayness, that she seemed like paint splattered on a daguerreotype. She carried a toddler and smiled at me and I felt handsome for a moment until I saw it was just Ruth O'Donnell, a girl I'd been sweet on when she was Ruth Grant and we'd been in school together. I could tell by the easy grins they passed to me that they didn't know what I'd done to Forest. If they had, Tobias would have broken my knees and Ruth would have gouged my eyes.

I steadied the mule cart, while Tobias dropped the potato sack into it. I asked about Tommy O'Donnell, Ruth's husband.

"He got picked up couple hours back," Tobias said. "Pinkertons took him and a couple others over to the jailhouse."

"I'm getting by. Wish we were leaving for somewhere pretty, like California." Ruth covered her child's ears. "And not some goddamn field out by Germantown."

"You're not lying," Tobias said.

Heavy trucks rumbled through a distant part of town, while the intermittent screams of children flew along with the wind. A hog ran by, slopping mud right and left, and Ruth slipped her child over her shoulder, patting his back.

"Wish I was getting on that train today," I said. "Go all the way west to the water and never look back."

Gunfire erupted from the south and all of us jumped a little, but settled back as it trailed off.

"Neal, you look god-awful. All blue and purple, like you've been getting knocked cold from every which way."

"She's right," Tobias said. "I heard Seamus whipped you the other day."

I touched my face and it felt sore. "Not yet," I said. "But it's his turn."

A fire bell rang, and we looked north toward the smoke pluming into the colorless sky. Another bell sounded. It had a sharper ping like a school bell.

"The work bell. Keeps ringing though no one's working," Tobias said. "We better get you going."

"Just a few more things," Ruth said.

The gruff no-neck union men came out of Forest's house. I couldn't tell much by their faces, but they looked around with suspicious glares and I didn't get a charmed feeling about them.

I went over to Forest's house, knocked, and, when no one answered, I went in.

The place was wrecked. I thought at first someone had tossed it, but it was just the habits of a man in mourning. The sofa, the floor, and dining table were swathed by old dishes, leftover food, mostly beans and corn, and strewn, filthy clothes. On a table beside the furnace, there was a picture of Forest's wife, framed and dusted.

Despite the bells and screams and gunshots, the rest of the house felt just as still, nearly as holy. I found him in the bedroom, a cigarette hooked to his lips.

"Stephens is that you?"

"Forest, I'm sorry."

"For what, kid?"

Maybe it was my lack of nerve, but I didn't answer honestly. I pointed at his cigarette. "For getting you started again."

He didn't say anything. I sat by the window and looked out at the rutted, snow damp street.

"They're coming for you."

"Don't I know it. Whole fuckin'—"

"For killing Clyde, Forest," I said. "They've got you for killing Clyde."

The cigarette bobbed from his lips and he seemed to disappear into his head. It looked like guilt shrouding his face, but it was just acceptance. Like I'd told him he had to get a tooth pulled.

"What's the kindness for?" he asked. "Didn't think you cared."

"My father did it, but you're going down unless you make a run for it. I can get you to Denver and from there, you've got trains that can take you anywhere."

"Should I get a disguise? What getup would make a huge Jew fucking blend in? Maybe I could wear a goddamn dress and join the fucking circus?"

Gunfire, closer and crisper, burst a few blocks south. The gray, diffused light draped his face. He lay back on the pillow; the bedsprings breathed and settled.

"They've got the check."

I expected him to look nervous, or at least go pale, but he just sat there and took it.

"Big Hank, that fucking turncoat."

"My father was paying him."

"Until Clyde lost his eye and then Big Hank wanted blood, fucking blood. Probably went to your father's office fixing to kill him but it never went right for Big Hank. Not once in his miserable life did he do a damn thing right. Couldn't even go crooked right. It was always me cleaning up his messes even after he'd died—had to pay Clyde a shit ton to keep it quiet. You know what the boys would think?"

They'd think Forest was in on it. They'd think Forest sold them out. I understood.

"You've got to run."

"Stop it, kid. I'm not fucking leaving."

He put out his cigarette and lit another.

"You know I probably did kill Clyde in a way," he said.

I stuck my hands in my pockets, felt my notebook, but didn't take it out.

"It was me who sent your father up there. Told him not to shoot Clyde like he did. Should have known better."

"How long has my father been working with you?"

"Months," Forest said, his voice quick like a falling cleaver. "Since July, when we figured a strike was coming. He showed up like some crazed St. Nick teeming with bags full of dough saying he'd get us through it."

"And you believed him?" I asked. "Even though he killed Big Hank?"

"Because of that."

"Excuse me?"

"You heard me, kid. Your old man was never right after Hank died. Not at all. It ate at him," he said. "When he came to me in July, I saw he wasn't right in the mind."

"And you trusted him?"

"He was here seeking a pardon. Figured I could use it."

"What about Tillie?"

"Seamus won't hurt her," he said. "He'd never do that to your mother."

"My mother's dead. You've got to run, run until you're across the ocean."

"You feelin' guilty, kid, for that shit you wrote?"

I peered out onto the smoky street, the light dimmed so it seemed like I was standing in the dark. The fire bell rang and rang, gunshots coming quickly.

A caravan of police and militiamen stopped opposite Forest's house: Seamus, Jacob, and a dozen militiamen armed with rifles and holstering Billy clubs. Another car pulled up. Gertie awaited us, her fellow Pinkertons close behind.

"Forest," I said. "Out the back."

Forest tucked in his shirt, then put out his cigarette. "Time I go talk to that Irish bastard."

I followed him onto the dark, simmering street, which smelled of burnt pine and dead animals. The ground shook from the caravan of trucks and the march of refugees. Tobias leaned against the mule cart, while Ruth and her child looked on from beside him. Forest tipped his hat to Seamus.

"Mr. Rahill," he said. "You bring enough thugs?"

"Forest," my uncle said. "Let's not make a fuss over this."

"No, sir. Wouldn't want no fussing."

With his hat pressed low on his forehead, my uncle appeared like a monastic highwayman, but he was out of sorts. Anyone could see that. Sure, he carried a gun, but he was a man more inclined to boardrooms than street fights. This was Forest's turf and my uncle sensed that. It's why he'd brought along so many gunmen.

Seamus glanced at Jacob. "Should you read the warrant aloud?"

"Ain't reading it. Just get this done," Jacob said. "Forest, come on."

Smoke funneled between the houses, the militiamen shielding their eyes behind handkerchiefs like soldiers during that first gas attack. They gripped their rifles, feeling for their triggers. I wrapped Miss Constance's strap around my wrist to keep her from slipping into the mud.

Jacob stepped toward us and Forest glanced at Tobias and the other miners, backing them off. He didn't want to get them killed, not like this. Instead, he stretched out his hands, awaiting Jacob's handcuffs. I raised Miss Constance, then snapped Forest's picture.

As Jacob took Forest to the truck, I swerved toward my uncle, who stood proud, a good distance from his prisoner, but I wasn't interested in Seamus' picture—I had plenty of those on file. Instead, I focused in on the guards, all those boys in uniform, who'd never left home until they'd been hired on to break strikes, and they were from towns no bigger than New Sligo, and now they looked scared during this, their first taste of war. I then trained Miss Constance on Gertie, snapping the lady Pinkerton's picture. Behind her stood her two cohorts—Burnsides and Booth—guns in their palms.

As Jacob helped Forest into the truck, the platoon of militiamen and Pinkertons scattered throughout the street. I went to Tobias. "Get her out of here."

"I was thinking the same," he said. He put Ruth's boy in the cart, and then gave Ruth his hand to help her up. I started moving the rest of her boxes into the cart, under the din of screams and gunshots and boots stomping. I thought of Matheson, the boot baron bragging about beating me up. It already seemed like a long time ago, by then.

It wasn't until the boots were right on me that I bothered to turn around, finding Pinkerton Booth, Billy club raised over his head. I reached out, but I was too slow. The club drove Tobias into the dirt, his limbs sprawled like a man crucified.

I dove into Booth's legs, the Billy club falling into the mud. Booth hit my back, pushing me into a puddle, filling my lungs with coal water. I gasped, heaving him off of me. I got to my knees, wiped the mud from my eyes. Tobias was still, Ruth holding his head.

Booth pulled out a knife. It shined in the firelight.

"Leave him be," Jacob said, pointing his revolver at the Pinkerton. "Get up, the both of you."

The Pinkerton took Gertie's hand, standing.

"What did I say about stabbing people?" Gertie said.

"Can't touch a white woman." Booth still held on to his knife. "Not in this country."

Burnsides dragged Tobias toward the truck, where he lifted,

then pushed the miner in beside Forest. Gertie followed, waving Booth away.

"You're bad," she said. "You stay here. I'll come get you later after you've thought about what you've done."

Booth pulled the mud from his moustache, while studying my throat. "Try that again."

I pointed Miss Constance at him, firing.

"Fuck you," I said.

He gave me his best assassin's smile.

As the truck carried Forest away, I found Alma Lind beside me. She looked on curiously. "You got to stop picking fights, Jack Johnson," she said. "We should go."

She was right. Beneath the volley of intermittent gunfire and within the cascading clouds of smoke, the guards shimmied like scarecrows, their fingers clasping their rifles. Standing in a circle with their backs to one another, they listened to a slow rumble growing louder, as pine ash fell like snow and Rahillville no longer smelled like burnt coal and smelting fumes, but incinerated wood and melting tin.

"Wait a sec," I told her. I raised Miss Constance at a militiaman, a boy with acne running down his cheeks. He couldn't have been more than nineteen. "Son, look over here."

He raised his rifle like an adolescent Pancho Villa, then screamed "Ole!" The other soldiers laughed and a couple of them even raised their own rifles. Everyone had seen too many films, even back then.

More shots fired. A bullet whisked past my shoulder, pinging a tin roof. The bell rang and rang, the fire closing in. The rumble echoed through the cavernous street and I felt it in my boots like the day the French army marched east only to fall prey to my camera. Through the smoke, in all her color, Ruth materialized like a gypsy ghost, petting her son. She seized the cart handle, lifting it onto its wheels, dragging it toward the gate, toward the rumble. Her kerchief fell from her head, disappearing beneath the wagon.

I started toward her, but Alma grabbed my shoulder, stopping me. Her face went hard and she pointed—

From out of the smoke, scores of soot-stained miners stood in soldierly stances gripping makeshift weapons and appearing in a line like medieval knights who'd lost their steeds. Maybe it's the trick of memory, or maybe it's because I've read their obituaries, but it seems like I knew all of them. There was Joey McKinney, a boy of fourteen who was Cleveland McKinney's son, and he wore his white communion gown and carried his mother's hand mirror; and Ray Costas holstered a well handle and wore the same black skullcap he'd got in the Navy for he felt shame over his bald head; and Leon Keenan wore all three of the suit jackets he owned, all brown, all faded at the elbows and he fastened two screwdrivers to his sleeves like he was afraid of falling through thin ice; and the Scott brothers with their identical red beards and their dual cases of consumption held serrated kitchen knives; and Paul Wilkes, at least seventy, the oldest man in the mines, who hadn't the teeth to chew meat anymore, nevertheless held a pickaxe; and it went on and on: hands gripped coal picks and blackjacks, plungers and hammers, logs and stones, until all the names of all the men I had forgotten fused together as one. I raised Miss Constance and snapped a picture.

"Oh my God," Alma said.

A scream sent the miners at the guards and a shot sent me to the dirt. I took Alma down, shielding her. Glass exploded, sending shards to my back, my neck. A shot hit the mud before me, blinding me for a moment. Boys screamed. More shots. Pinkerton Booth fired into Leon Keenan; his jackets dulled the bullet's thump. The acned soldier fell under Joey McKinney's hand mirror, landing hard on his chest like he'd fallen from the sky.

Rahillville burned. Smoke engulfed the street, turning all but the fattest guards invisible, just shapes shifting in the smoke. The fire seemed close enough to skewer my boots. Soldiers fired into the dark, dropping miners and their kin. A guard tripped on Alma, falling on to me, his rifle firing into the sky. I turned him over, punching him in the neck until he couldn't breathe. My fist hurt and my hands shook. My shirt was drenched in mud and blood. I looked about, unable to see Alma's car in the smoke. The fire was closing in from the north. The gates would be manned. I didn't know how I'd get out.

"Al!"

A burst of color materialized from the black smoke and Ruth sat in the dirt, the leg beneath her right knee shredded, her dress soaked in blood and bone and muscle. She cried out for her son as her mule cart lay in three pieces, her husband's clothes scattered about the dirt. Paul Wilkes dropped his pickaxe, and then gripped Ruth under her arms, lifting her. I looked at Alma, her mouth covered in dirt, hair matted with blood. She nodded. I went for Ruth.

I stood, a knee thumping my ear. It all went dark.

The firelight woke me, my back hot. The ground spun and I held on to the mud. I was bleeding, but I wasn't sure how much or from where. Alma pulled me up and I saw that Paul lay atop Ruth's lap and both were limp with their eyes open and plainly dead.

"Neal." Alma pointed behind me.

Ruth's boy, swinging a pan, his face glazed with ash, cried beside the mule cart, so I stood, my balance suspect, Miss Constance's case swinging from my shoulder and I made my way toward him, skirting a dead militiaman, my boots sinking into the mud, and I picked up the child, heavy like a sack of sand, and saw, nearby, Ruth bent in an unnatural way like she'd been broken then reassembled by a blind man, so I turned the boy around, pushing his face into my coat.

"Stephens."

Booth leveled his gun, firing. I fell against the mule cart, my back cracking against something hard and blunt. I held onto the boy, but he felt light and wet. When I raised him, his head hung limp and his guts poured out of him and into my hands, my fingers straining the boy like a sieve. I dropped to the ground, my head clouded and my nose filled with smoke and my ears aflame. I pushed the boy beneath the cart, out of the way, like a dead opossum off the road.

When I turned, the Pinkerton had disappeared behind a shield of wood smoke.

"Neal, hurry." Alma pulled me through the smoke and I lifted her over a dead hog and into Forest's house. She pushed me behind a wall. The window exploded. Glass fell onto her hair. She swept it away, slicing her hand.

I looked at her, trying to speak, but I kept coughing.

Bullets chipped away at the remaining glass. Through the bedroom window, I saw the fire was only a house or two away. My suit was soaked with the child and I tried to wipe it off. Alma held my shoulder. Blood stained her forehead and her dress was torn. I looked up and down her, searching for bullet holes, but saw none.

"Where's your car?" I said.

Another explosion shook the ground, this time from the south. She coughed and wheezed. There was nothing left to breathe. I took off my tie and wrapped it around her mouth. A man fell through the door, cracking a floorboard. One of the Scott brothers. He held his shoulder and cried out, pushing and kicking into the house. A man wearing a black suit stopped in the doorway, and fired a shot into the miner. I jumped the shooter, throwing him to the ground. We rolled across the room, stopping beside the furnace. I reached for a weapon, finding a bowl. It was clay and heavy and I swung it into the man's face and he tumbled off of me. I grabbed his throat and looked in his eyes and saw it was Booth. I squeezed.

Booth's shoulder jutted up; my arm went limp and I fell to my side. He steadied his knife, but hesitated when an explosion sounded in the room. He keeled to his side, dead. Alma stood in the smoke, holding a revolver.

She handed over Miss Constance's case, then led me out the back door. I cranked the car engine, the flames nearly on us, and when it turned over, I got in and she gassed it through the smoke, running over chickens and pot holes and blackjacks and rifles until she was beyond the houses and blood and bullets, past the gates, which were now just a mound of smoldering iron, and onto Cleary Highway where she drove west as fast as that car would take us.

—22—

We dumped her gun in a part of the Platte River that ran deep and slow. I didn't know that section of river existed and I'm sure the gun is still there, rusting into the riverbed. She drove me home; I didn't give her directions; she knew the way. I tore off my shirtsleeve and wrapped my arm, then wrapped the other sleeve across my forehead. Nothing hurt yet, but it was momentary and I'd need a bed soon.

When we got to my house, she reached under her seat and pulled out another gun—she seemed to have a stockpile—then told me to stay put. She went inside and stayed there for a minute, and then came out and said it was safe and she helped me inside and over to the sofa. She went back to her car, returning with a bottle of whiskey, a jug of water, bandages, and a sewing kit. I reached for the whiskey.

"It's for your arm." She poured the alcohol along the gash.

She took out a spool, then thread the needle. "The cut's not too deep."

She sewed my arm and bandaged the cut beneath my eye. She gave me water.

"Thank you."

She went to the phone. "It's dead."

"My father cut the line."

"Damn fool," she said.

"Are you hurt at all?"

"Just a bruise or two," she said. "My ribs are sore, but my head stopped bleeding."

Fire bells rang from town, the sound traveling across the still lake of the prairie. I thought I could hear the talk of

my neighbors, the moans of the wounded, the chants of the
miners like they were all sitting in my kitchen, a hungry,
tired symphony of sorrow, but that was just the knock on
my head because I realize now that I was too far away to
hear anything.

A car rolled up the road. She went to the window, the
shadow of her gun cutting across the floor.

"Is it snowing hard?"

"It's ash," she said. "You can still see the moon."

I pulled myself upright and looked over at her quick,
sure movements and her hard, prisoner eyes and sighed.

"Have you even been to Sweden?"

"Once or twice."

"Is it Madeline or Mattie? I don't want to presume."

"You should sleep."

"You're waiting for my father, aren't you? I waited fifteen years," I said. "Sometimes he doesn't come home.
He'll do that to you someday."

"No, he always comes back to me. And if he doesn't, I
just take him away."

She sat beside me and put the gun on the table. "You
need to sleep, Neal. We can talk about this later."

I sunk into the pillow and the ceiling spun. "My mother
waited."

"I'm sorry about that. I'm sure she was a fine dame."

"She killed herself, you know?"

"Yes."

"No one knows that but me and my uncle. Not even Tillie. We didn't want to tell her and—"

"It's fine, Neal. Go to sleep."

A car pulled up and cut its engine and Mattie went outside. For some reason, I expected gunfire and screams, but
it was just a soft, sad conversation. The last thing I remember before I passed out was a man putting a hand on my
forehead. "Good night, Cowboy."

—23—

When I woke up, it was still dark, but I could see the outline of a woman in a chair across from me. I sat up and waited for the dizziness, but none came.

The woman was thicker than Alma, with shorter hair and worse posture. I reached over to the side table, and turned on the lamp.

Gertie held a knife. She peeled the skin from an apple and looked at me like I was some sort of lost dog, frightened and searching for my way home.

"You want some?" She asked. "They're delicious. You can just pick them off the tree."

I didn't want any food, or, strangely, any booze. I just wanted to settle myself. The knife glimmered in the lamplight, but she didn't seem all that interested in me.

"It's quiet outside," she said. "Almost spooky."

"I'm not good company, right now."

"I'm not looking for love. Just came to say goodbye."

"You getting sentimental?"

"I'm running, Neal. I'm running as fast as I can from this town, this entire mess. You know why? Because I've been through this before, and you know when the big bad happens it's the Pinkerton who does the time, not some rich fools like you or your uncle. I've got no love for the noose."

She bit a slice of her apple. I wondered if she was really nervous or if this was another ruse. I asked her.

"I do get scared, Neal. I have feelings. I get sad, angry, even jealous. I'm human."

I reached up to my shoulder; it felt tender, burnt.

"You think I'm evil, don't you? You think I'm some bo-geyman who wakes you in the dark, but you're just as mean as me and twice as sad."

"Why are you telling me this?"

"Maybe I'm in love with you." She laughed. "I'm sorry. When I'm nervous I joke. It's the only way I keep from cut-ting my own throat."

She kissed my forehead. "Run," she said. "Run back to France. Go find your wife if she's still alive. Your family is awful screwy, Neal."

"She's dead."

"Are you sure?"

"I can't leave Tillie."

"Get her in the morning. They'll let her go. Then get as far away as you can. Listen to me on this. Take the next train out of here."

After she left, I tried sleeping, but, in the early morning's stillness, I got nostalgic. I went to the bookcase and pulled out a photo album, one from my youth. Looking at your first pictures is a lot like revisiting old love letters: you can remember composing them, but they seem like they came from another's mind. And they're embarrassing. I cringed at my ideas of art, but I could see hope in those snapshots, the ambition and passion I no longer had. My father was in a few of them, my mother and sister too. Seamus showed up once in a while, steady in his suit, his face still like granite. Even by then they were historical remnants, artifacts of a forgotten age.

The truth was that the photos narrated an incomplete history because I had none of Lorraine: the pictures I'd tak-en of my wife lost, like so much, to the war. Sometimes, when her face comes to me at night, I wonder if I'm remem-bering her right. If she really looked as I imagine. I've spent so much of my life compiling and cataloguing images, seek-ing the right light, the proper angles to capture the truth of a man, but my most important pictures are gone, their material returned to the soil, and all I was left with was a note she'd written begging me to run away with her. And not even that lasted. Now all I've got left are memories and I don't trust them, not entirely.

This is the last of them.

MEAUX

Unlike most men on the Western Front, I was freelance and could leave as I pleased. I owed no one, but I was at the time bent on self-discipline, and I didn't like leaving the war in case we had a breakthrough and found our way marching toward Berlin and then I'd be the unluckiest photographer in the world. Even in late 1915, I still had faith that the war could be done any day now. The British had named Haig their new commander, and I thought that push, that sort of foresight boded well for our side. Word was Haig wanted to wage a major offensive that would break the German lines. It seemed like the right tactic.

Yet this freedom to leave whenever I wanted, paired with my reluctance to do so, was a constant source of strife with Lorraine. She wanted me to treat the front like a factory job: on at seven, off at five, half-days on Saturdays. She knew it didn't work that way, but she couldn't let the idea go, and I wouldn't compromise. Not about this. So to mend our marital fences, I promised her Christmas.

I hitchhiked down to Meaux, a couple of miles outside Paris, where Lorraine had rented a small house for the holiday. The town sat on the Seine and had been the spot of an epic battle during the Hundred Year's War. The defense of Meaux was led by the aptly named Bastard of Vaurus, who managed to hold out for months, but eventually was overrun by Henry V's forces. Afterwards, the Bastard was decapitated. Not such a bad end. Henry died of dysentery soon after, and let me say, after watching a dozen men die like that, I'll take an axe to the neck anytime.

The reason I'm bringing this up is simple: it started a fight with Lorraine.

"I scrounge together enough dough for a Christmas duck," she started. "I cook it all day long and set a table and hell, I even put on make-up and I don't have a whole lot left and you sit down at my table and talk of dysentery? You're making me sound like my mother."

"I thought it was interesting."

"What the hell makes you think I'd care?"

The spread was nice, as was the house. I told her so.

"Shit, dear, thank you, but how do I look?"

She looked gaunt, tired. The makeup seemed to be hiding her exhaustion.

"You look beautiful, darling," I said. "You always look beautiful."

"You're the bastard of Colorado. How do you like that title?"

The night disintegrated from there. In fact, we were having a hard time speaking at all. I didn't want to tell her about the front and she didn't want to talk about the hospital. We hadn't seen any theater, heard any music, or read any books worth bringing up. A lot of the time we sat silent or we talked about Paris.

"Do you remember that café Rene Philippe ran in the Seventh?" she asked. "Well, I hear his wife burned it down."

"She finally caught him?"

"You knew?"

I took a drink of wine. "I thought everyone did."

She went to the sink and did the dishes. Occasionally she grunted or sighed, but mostly she splashed water and cursed under her breath. I smoked. After a while, I went to my bag and pulled out a gift and gave it to her.

She bit her lip. "I didn't get you anything."

"Don't worry about it."

"I'm a terrible wife."

"You're a doll. Open it."

It was a photo album that I'd scrounged from some old lady near Brussels on a day off. Inside, I pasted a single photo: our wedding portrait. We stood, stone-still, smiling at the camera, trying not to shake or twitch during the long-exposure for that hackneyed photographer. I remember her looking royal, angelic, while I looked roguish and debonair. But maybe I'm remembering it wrong and we looked scared or tired or sad. I can't remember. Seamus burned it before I ever saw it again.

She turned away, drawing her hand to her eyes.

"What is it?" I asked.

"I love you, Snowball."

That night, undressed, Lorraine first saw my missing toe. She sat up in bed and grabbed my foot. She circled her finger around the scar. I hadn't told her I'd lost it.

"What else you been keeping from me?"

"It's not even a necessary toe," I told her, remembering something my sister once told me. "It's vestigial, something we've outgrown. I'm just more evolved now."

"Every part of you is necessary," she said. "I was married to that toe. I loved it."

"I'm sorry."

She shut off the light and turned away from me, slapping her pillow. "Did it hurt?"

Yes, it had. "Not much," I said. "Felt a bit like a paper cut."

After a while, as the wind whirled across the window and we both could hear in the uneven pace of our breath the other's awakeness, she turned to me and touched my face. "Last week, I sat with a boy who asked me to massage his missing leg. I sat there for near two hours and rubbed the air. How is this right?"

By the time I woke up, she was already out of the house. It was like her to leave early, to go buy food or take walks along the river. I remained in bed for a long while as the cold sun trickled between the shades. It had been a long time since I'd had a proper bed and I was intent on enjoying it, but after a while, my back felt sore because of the soft mattress. I rolled over and felt her indentation in the pillow. I could smell her hair.

I made coffee and waited, reading yesterday's newspapers, cleaning Miss Constance, smoking. By the time noon rolled around, I'd gotten worried, so I went searching for her. I figured she'd gone into town to find more food and had gotten lost because of her awful sense of direction. It wouldn't take much time to find her; the town was crowded with the old and the infirm and a black woman stuck out like you could imagine. Yet she wasn't there. I went to the baker, the fishmonger, and the fromagier and still nothing. I couldn't ask anyone if they'd seen her: I had never learned more than a dozen words of French.

Eventually, I followed the river back to the house and there I found her standing outside our place, speaking French to some old couple who had a small white dog with a gray face. It was a skinny little thing, attached to the old woman's leg like a tumor. The dog looked at me with mild indifference.

"Where'd you go?" I asked. "You scared the hell out of me."

"For a walk."

"It's noon."

She shrugged and said something in French to the old couple. All of them laughed.

"What did you say?"

"My husband worries after me like a stray dog."

"I wouldn't put it that way."

"Just when I'm around, that is." She kneeled and the dog licked her hand then tried to jump on her. "I want to take her home."

"I hate dogs."

"You would."

That afternoon we sat around by the fire, reading the newspaper. She brought me the *Paris Herald* while she read *Le Monde*. She traced her finger along the lines and furrowed her eyes like she was imagining the inner lives of the story's subjects.

"I'm sorry," I said. "If you want a dog, we can have a dog. I can get used to a dog."

I kissed her cheek, then started rubbing her shoulders. She shrugged.

"What is it?" I asked. "I was just worried about you. You get lost so easy."

"No, it's not that."

She put the paper in front of me.

"You know I can't read it."

She pointed at a headline. I didn't recognize the other words, just the name—Jesse Stephens. I asked her what my father had done now.

"Destroyed a bank in London."

"Figures."

"His girl was killed in the process. A woman named Madeline Longstreet."

"He probably got bored of her."

"Neal, please. He killed her on accident. It's got to be awful for him."

"He did it to himself."

"How can you say that?"

I didn't want to fight. We only had a day and I wanted to enjoy our time and that meant not talking about my father and his mistress. I drifted toward the icebox.

"Do you want a drink?"

The next morning a knock woke us just after sunrise and I sat up and thought I was being shelled again. Lorraine grabbed my shoulder and tried to relax me.

"You're having a dream," she said. "Go back to sleep."

Another knock startled her.

"Stay here." I dressed and opened the door to find three British soldiers, their topcoats unbuttoned, their eyes reddened, and their breath smelling like wine. The closest one had bright blond hair and red cheeks. He held a rifle fixed with a bayonet, as did the others.

"We're here to commandeer your supplies," the blond soldier said. The other two hung back. Across the street, the old couple stood in their robes, while soldiers ransacked their house.

"Don't you speak English? *Vous faire parle l'anglais?*"

"We haven't got any supplies for you. Go away."

Lorraine came up behind me.

The soldier stepped back, eyes widened.

"I'll commandeer the Zulu or are you paid through the day?"

I stepped on to the porch and tried closing the door behind me, but Lorraine held it open.

"She's no whore and you need to leave now."

"Is that so? Then what is she?"

"I'm an American photographer with credentials. You take another step and I'll talk to your lieutenant and you'll be the first over the top come next week."

"Neal," Lorraine said.

I waved her away. "And another thing," I said. "If you don't leave that couple alone and stop rousting civilians, I'll call the RMP's and have you dragged out for court martial, Private. You've got no authority."

"Neal."

She was pointing at the old couple weeping as they watched a soldier holding up his rifle, the little dog impaled on the bayonet.

"Christ," I said. I fetched Miss Constance. When I came back, the soldier was twirling the dead dog like a flag. I slipped passed Lorraine and raised Miss Constance and snapped a picture.

"Run away, Private," I said.

When I got back to the house, Lorraine sat on the sofa. She poured wine.

"Did you get a good picture?"

"Stop it," I said. "I wanted to scare them off."

"How much will you sell it for?"

"I'm going back to bed."

Lorraine stayed in the kitchen. I looked over at my bag: she'd gone through it.

"What were you looking for?"

"A gun," she called out.

We didn't say much that day. There seemed to be a fog in the house and we mostly stayed in separate corners, reading books, newspapers, anything we could get our hands on. For dinner, she cracked a couple of eggs, fried them quickly, and then put them on the table.

"Eat."

I figured the soldiers upset her. They'd frightened her, ruining our last afternoon together. I didn't want the evening broken as well.

"I can't believe those kids waking us like that."

She chewed.

"You'd think British soldiers would be better disciplined, more behaved."

"Why?" she asked.

"Excuse me?"

"Why would they be better behaved? They kill people all day long. They kill and kill and kill and what's a dog to them? What's a woman to them?"

"You're acting crazy."

She flung her plate across the room and it crashed into the wall and you could see how shocked she was, and regretful.

"A woman dies and you act like it doesn't matter."

"What are you talking about?"

"Don't go back tomorrow."

"Stop it."

"Neal, please."

She went to the kitchen and came back with a broom. I grabbed her and pulled her to me. "It's almost over," I said. "Just a little while longer. Just give me a little more time. I promise."

"You make a lot of promises."

In the morning, I dressed silently. I had bread and cold coffee and drank a little wine and put my bag on the stoop. I'd found a ride north where I'd follow a battalion entrenched by the Somme River. I wanted to get a picture of Haig at the front and I'd heard he'd be nearby, surveying the men.

I went back to our room. She lay asleep, quiet as a graveyard. Her hair covered the body of her pillow and the blanket was up to her chin. I sat on the floor and wrote her a note and left it on the nightstand. I told her I'd see her soon.

I stood above her for a beat or two, trying to memorize her face, before I shouldered my pack and walked out the door.

PART THREE

When Will These Masses End, Garatuza?

—24—

By the time I got out to the jailhouse, Forest was already dead. They'd hung him at sunrise and when I pulled up they were cutting him down from the oak. There were four or five other bodies nearby, a pyramid of flesh, and I saw Tobias among them, along with Ruth's husband, who was better off dead. I could tell you what Forest looked like: his distended eyes and stretched neck and flailing tongue, but you can imagine it just fine. After the Pinkertons cut him down, they dragged him over to the other bodies and left him there and then went to find a can of gasoline.

With my boots caked in Rahillville ash, I went into the jailhouse, stopping on O'Leary's bloodstain, then looked at my uncle. He sat at the desk, his hat on the table, and he wrote out reports like some insurance man. There were nearly a dozen Pinkertons mulling about but I didn't see Jacob and I was relieved. I walked toward my uncle but I was stopped by a couple of men I recognized: the no-neck Pennsylvania union men. It took me a moment to figure out why they were here, and, more importantly, why they weren't upset. They'd been in on it. Forest was a liability for them, not only because of Clyde's check, but because Forest was mostly honest and that did them no good.

"I came for Tillie."

Seamus kept working on his papers. "Sit down, Neal, just for a moment. There's so much paperwork."

"Have one of your thugs unlock her. I don't care who does it."

He looked up, glancing surprise.

"The world doesn't stop for you," Seamus said. "There are letters to the Governor, the county commissioner—"

"Give me the keys. I'll do it myself."

He put down his pen and waved at a Pinkerton wearing a Garibaldi coat to fetch my sister.

"I know seeing dead men is hard, Neal."

It was a silly thing to say to me.

"Just know that we're better off now," he went on. "You've spent too much time out in the world away from your people. You've come home with these ideas, this kind of infection, and you apply them without thought, but that doesn't work here. Out here is the border between savagery and civilization. You should know that by now."

I bent toward him, whispering, "Out there, what you did, isn't just and isn't Christian."

His eyes went wide and he slapped me across the head like a dog. Before I got my bearings, I felt a gun against my back and saw the Pinkertons crowd in on me. My uncle looked at his hand, surprised, as if it was another man's palm. His face slackened and he turned toward my sister slumping down the hall.

"Tillie," he said. "You understand, right?"

She turned away. I went to my sister and took her hand and pushed through the Pinkertons to the doorway.

"The both of you," Seamus said. "Leave here and don't come back."

"I'll go when I'm ready," I said.

"If you help your father." He came around the desk and the Pinkertons parted for him and he stopped in front of me and looked at me with his Victorian solemnity. "Well, just know, we aren't family after that. No forgiveness."

Garibaldi pulled me out the door and I stumbled into the parking lot, my sister close behind, and I saw Jacob leaning against his car watching as Pinkerton Burnsides struck a match and threw it on to a piece of man: fire flared then receded into a slow burn that cooked the dead.

Garibaldi laughed, then yelled, "Use enough gas there, Ralph?"

Jacob looked at me and I lowered my eyes until he'd cranked his car engine, got it started, and drove off.

Tillie took my arm, her eyes trained on the fire. I looked over at my car. My father had left it when he'd come for Mattie and I'd been grateful to have it back, but now, seeing it in the light of the fire, I remembered it wasn't my car. Seamus had given it to me when I'd first come home from Europe and I don't remember having any papers saying it was mine. I took Miss Constance from the car's floor and slung the camera around my shoulder. I left the keys in the ignition.

—25—

We walked the road to New Sligo like a pair of soldiers
returning from Appomattox, keen on every noise and
every odor besieging us. We straggled side by side with
burnt-smelling clothing and muddy shoes within the tracks
laid down by militia trucks and mule carts. Our bodies
were warmed by the dying coals of Rahillville, which was
a mess of iron and tin simmering above weary flames. The
wind dissipated and the air felt as still as a tar pit and all
that could be heard were our own footsteps along the mud
and the gravel. The road seemed like a steeple race, as we
hurdled over scores of dead animals: cattle, hogs, goats,
mules, cocks, sheep, and alpacas. But mostly dogs. Some
soldier had taken to shooting everyone in his path and a
mess of hounds were piled along the roadside in a dune of
limp tongues and wet fur. Beneath a turned-over wagon,
a burro lay with twin bullet holes adorning its forehead.
In a pond off the road, a pair of kittens floated limp and
buoyant atop a poorly bound satchel. Scavengers circled
overhead. We would have covered our mouths because the
stench in the static air was unbearable, but our kerchiefs
were useless because they were doused in the ashes of dead
men and it seemed like we'd never lose the smell of them.

Tillie stopped in the road, above a dead raccoon, and
then vomited. I held her blouse as she convulsed, her whipping ribs plain against my hand. A crow squawked above
the carcass of a dead horse, its beak stained in the mare's
entrails. When Tillie finished, when she'd wiped her mouth
and regained her balance, we trudged on.

At the western edge of Germantown, in a long abandoned field poisoned by smelting fumes and coal dust, a refugee city arose from the dead soil. Thousands of tents lined the land. Cooking fires burned in oil drums. Men dug latrines. The colorless refugees seemed dressed in mourning, but it was ash staining their clothes. Militia trucks sat along the roadside, their occupants becoming men overnight, trading their freshness for newly sprouted beards. Their rifles had lost their sheen, dulled by the repetition of firing. A few old miners, men with hunched backs and no hair, sat on crates beside the road, watching us pass. I remember wondering if they knew about Forest. Did they know it was my doing? I couldn't look at them, only giving a vacant nod toward town.

Once beneath the railroad steeple, we entered the merchant neighborhood lined with Victorian homes set behind cement sidewalks and fresh cut lawns and the only odor of death came from our own clothes. Tillie turned to the railroad track. "I'm getting on that train."

"Denver?"

"Somewhere farther. Somewhere else."

"I can't go with you."

"You shouldn't," she said. "I need to be alone."

I took her hand and led her along the sidewalk into downtown New Sligo.

"You know they tortured him," she said. "Forest, they tortured him."

"Why?"

"Because that's how they were raised, how they're bred. They kept asking about our mother though. I don't know why. I couldn't hear everything, just his screaming and our mother's name over and over again. It's like every phobia I ever had came to me in a dream."

The wind blew east from the mountains and cut through our clothes to our skin and I wrapped my arm around her.

"It wasn't dirty," I said. "I loved her and I'm not sorry I married her, only sorry it ended as it did."

"I don't care, anymore," she said. "We're no better than dogs. Any of us."

When we got to her home, she stopped me at the door and told me not to come in because she wanted to be alone, to wash the day off of her before she left New Sligo. She'd write me when she settled somewhere.

"I was with our father the night O'Leary died." She paused in the doorway. "He didn't kill him. You need to know that. I don't know who killed him but it wasn't Dad."

"Alright."

"You can trust him," she said. "If you need to. He may be a madman, but he's mostly a good man."

"He didn't come for you or me."

"He's not God," she said. "He can only do so much."

She leaned across the doorway and kissed my forehead. Her hair brushed across my cheek, the strands smelling of burnt skin. She closed her eyes and shut the door.

—26—

That afternoon, I drifted through town, past familiar haunts and shuttered storefronts. I bought cigarettes from an Arapahoe tobacconist, and then smoked three in quick succession. I stared for a long time at a flock of southbound Canadian geese, contemplating the merits of nature photography. I wandered the empty streets, quiet like a snowstorm, reliving the week's events. The papers would call Forest a murderer who had been justly executed. They'd call Seamus a western hero. Historians would tell that story. I was responsible for those lies.

Before I knew it, I found myself roaming Pioneer Park. I stopped at the pond's western edge, studying my warped reflection, which projected a man with two fat eyes, a swollen jaw, a crooked nose, and an uneven beard. But it wasn't a distortion. That's what I looked like: grotesque. I turned down the path, walking for a spell, until I saw Roosevelt smoking a pipe on the bench, looking no worse for wear, probably concocting an elaborate scenario by which Forest's death was a sort of political suicide, rather than an old fashioned western lynching. Hell, maybe he'd accuse Forest of dying while trying to escape. We printed shit like that a lot back then.

But I was wrong.

As Roosevelt let loose a sadistic grin of carnivalesque proportions, a young couple picnicked not ten feet away atop a bed of dead leaves, eating sandwiches and drinking pop with the delight of their blonde youth painted across the clear canvases of their Hollywood faces.

Roosevelt, with the bravado of a ringmaster, swung his cane into the air then pointed it at me.

"You lived to walk another fucking day," he hollered. "Bravo. I thought those cocksuckers had broken you like a raped mule."

The boy left his mouth agape in rehearsed shock. He clasped his sweetheart's ears, and then whispered to the old scribbler.

Roosevelt revealed a full set of teeth grinding beneath his moustache, and then hobbled toward the couple, whacking his cane on their blanket, splattering mustard across dead leaves.

"Unless you want me to bugger you with your love watching, you'll hold that tone before me. Now toddle off before I drop my trousers and show your lady what Shakespeare meant by a brave new world."

As Roosevelt yanked loose his suspenders, the park flooded with the squawking of sparrows and blue jays, while hundreds of red leaves rained upon the couple as if Roosevelt's curses had summoned a sort of tree god. Quickly, the girl abandoned her perch, while the boy trailed behind, dragging his blanket like a child sent to bed.

"Sons of bitches," Roosevelt said. "I curse you both with chlamydia."

He returned to his bench, exhausted from his fit of righteous taunting.

"I just can't stand happiness," he said. "It's like summering in an asylum."

I slid in beside him.

"How can anyone exude joy in such times?" Roosevelt struck a match to his pipe. "It's a type of syphilitic insanity. That's what it is. Like man has become so enamored in the self, like he's so infatuated with his own id or ego or whatever those alienist sheenies are saying that he fails to acknowledge the storm thundering over his own head. Just bloody balls-up bullshit if you ask me. By the way, you smell like death."

I did. Even drenched within the odors of autumn, I couldn't shake it.

"That's fine. I can speak for both of us," he said. "I quit the *Eagle*. Gave my notice, unfurled my pecker and pissed clear across my own desk for the next bastard to clean up."

"You've been there twenty years."

"And I'll die before I'm there another twenty minutes. See. Speaking isn't that much of a chore, young Stephens. Just open your mouth and let your tongue do the work."

"Forest died in a bad way, Rosy."

"I know. I know. Seamus bragged to me. Just laughing gleefully like the bog-trotting Irish cunt he is. I couldn't stand it. I couldn't. I've covered up enough for that leprechaun and I won't do it anymore."

"But you're out a job."

"Maybe I'll go into the blackmail business. O'Leary seemed to do well by it."

"Except for getting murdered."

"Yes, there's that."

"I take it he hasn't nabbed my father?"

"Not even close. People have been sighting Jesse all over town and even as far south as Santa Fe. Your uncle thinks Jesse's here to kill him."

"You don't think so?"

"No," Roosevelt said. "I think he's here to burn the lot of us down. He can have my matches."

"I don't understand. If he hasn't caught my father, why was he happy?"

"Perhaps because the chase is still on. Perhaps killing men gives his cock a jiggle. In either case, he's pissed at you. He said you're an ingrate and a Benedict Arnold and that you've been helping Jesse the whole time and I told him it wasn't true because you haven't a damn principle in that 90 proof body of yours. In any case, Stephens, you'll need to find new work."

The last rays of sunlight dripped through the trees and spilled upon the pond, crisscrossing shadows atop the leaves like a spider web. But the connections were tenuous, blurred, and imaginary.

"Maybe you're right," I said. "Once it gets out about

Lorraine, that I lied, I'm fucked. No one will hire me."

"There'll be new lies. You're still a young man," he said. "You're not quite aware of what being really fucked feels like. Makes you walk with a cane."

I told him my plan to move to the mountains and live as a hermit, take up nature photography.

"It's not as bad as that, Stephens. I took your file out back to the jakes and read it over again with clear eyes and all you did was marry a Negro, and in France no less, which is nothing any honest man, or at least scoundrels like us, wouldn't do, and it certainly isn't worth too much blackmail or ruin or social shame as far as I'm concerned, not for men who work in such a low profession as we do, so I gave it the justice it deserved and crapped all over it, then left it to fester in the hole with the rest of the turds. You got to remember, Stephens. We're in a new age, a new world. There I go again with the imperialist talk, but it's a truism like a modern day Song of Songs. In some circles you'd be hailed a hero. Hell, you might consider turning red. Easy snatch and cheap rent."

"I didn't make up the *Trench Angel*. All the other shit was lies, but Rosy, that was real. It was on my camera. All I did was develop it. I don't remember taking it, but it was on my camera."

"Do you really think it was your wife?"

"I don't know."

"Do you believe it was her?"

"I'm not so sure anymore," I said. "I don't think I know what's true about that day."

"She's dead and you're mourning her still."

"I think so. I was sure then, but now I'm having a hard time remembering why."

I lit a cigarette and gave him one.

"Where do you think my father is?"

"Just walk around long enough," he said. "I'm sure he'll find you."

I had something else to do first.

—27—

It was near sundown by the time I got to the cemetery. I buttoned my coat while an army of clouds marched down from the mountains and a cold wind led the charge. At the foot of the graveyard, I bought flowers from a Chinese boy—he might be the only one who made a fortune during that week of funerals—and trudged up the hill through rows of Irish surnames until I found the Rahill plot erected in the heart of the dead. Although we only numbered three—my grandfather, my grandmother, and my mother—our headstones were the largest, the bone yard's center of gravity, as was Seamus' wish.

I sank to my knees, laying the flowers beside my mother's stone in the silence of the early cold. We'd buried her ten years earlier, but the calendar is a poor gauge of time. Some decades slip by like a passing car, their impressions fleeting, forgettable. Other decades seem like a long exposure in dim light, forever ingrained upon the celluloid of your mind. The ten years after her death were the longest of my life, yet, even remembering all that occurred, I couldn't recall much of my mother's final year. I'd seen her at Christmas, but I was away at school when she finally passed, only discovering how she died after a nighttime confession by Seamus; she'd left a note of apology, sending her love to Tillie and I, but she could no longer bear her abandonment by my father.

Seamus told me she'd been peaceful on her last day, going up to bed early after supper, taking all of her laudanum in a single glass. But he told the town—and our priest—it was pneumonia. Seamus struggled with the lie, knowing God would judge him, but he wanted her buried here.

I prayed.

Mattie Longstreet, my father's woman, waited for me at the gates of the graveyard, her hands in coat pockets, no doubt massaging a pistol butt. I lowered my hat and walked past her, but she strode alongside me.

"You like graveyards?" she asked.

"Yes."

"Me too," she said. "Every time I'm in a new city, I first visit the cemetery. I can get a feeling for the people that way."

"Well, we've got that in common," I said. "Should I call you Ma now?"

"Men have said worse."

We walked through empty Pioneer Square. My grandfather's statue had been swept away, and now there was just the stump of a pedestal in the middle of the circle.

"I'm glad you blew it up," I said. "I hated that statue."

The Square was empty and there wasn't even a militiaman on the street, just some stray dogs. "It's like the whole town's gone and died."

"Now you're being melodramatic," she said. "People will lift their heads up in a few days. That's how it usually works."

She stopped by a park bench and she figured I'd stop with her. When I didn't, she pulled out a bottle and offered it to me.

"Feels like I should be buying you a drink." I took the bottle. "You did save my life, but I guess that's why you've been following me."

"Consider it a peace offering."

"I never asked how you resurrected yourself. The newspapers said you were dead."

"I was," she said. "I mean I still am dead, legally at least in England, and I think Italy, but I'd have to check on that. They keep such poor records there. But that was ages ago, and now I've been back for nearly two years, the longest spell, well, in a long time."

"Since prison."

"No need to be so pointed," she said. "That was a life-time ago."

"It was," I said. "My mother's."

"I'm sorry over that, but you're not angry at me or your father." She took a drink. "It's strange to think of him as a father."

"You know he named his horse after you."

"He always was a bastard."

The first flurries began falling. A milk truck drove by and I looked around the streets, wondering if we were really alone.

She took the bottle from me. "Your father wants to talk to you, but—"

"Then he can come get me. I won't turn him in. Not if Seamus puts a gun in my mouth."

"Keep your head down," she said. "I'd hate for you to have to live up to that promise. It's no fun having a gun in your mouth. Awful for the teeth, my husband used to say."

"I'll be fine."

"No, your uncle has got a couple of Pinkertons looking to drag you out of town and I don't think they care if you're alive or not, because whatever you said to him made him nuts, so take me seriously. This is no fat shoemaker."

—28—

I walked south on Dartry, and turned west on 11th, a road lined with seamstress' shops and shoe cobblers. The snow piled up on my coat, while the wind stabbed my eyes and I shielded my face with my hat. My boots cut into the thin, muddy snow and I felt well balanced, like I was more in control of my body than anytime since the war. The soreness in my limbs and torso dissipated in the cold as if I'd been numbed by morphine. A car approached. I kneeled and flicked my lighter as if I was about to smoke, only standing as the car disappeared around the bend.

I surveyed the deserted street. There was nothing obviously menacing, just the same street that had been here since I was a boy. But I felt eyes on me. Pinkertons didn't sound the bugle before the charge. I walked on and then began to jog, and finally, after I spotted another set of approaching headlights, I ran. I cut north into an alley between Garavogue and MacManus, slaloming between garbage cans in the night lit by a faint moon diffused through the storm clouds. At the end of the alley on 12th street, I listened, but I heard nothing. I stepped into the street, but a turned over milk crate sent me running into another alley. I figured it was just a cat or a coyote, but I couldn't be sure. I ran until I was out of breath and coughing and spitting down my chin, and I kept running, until finally I reached the cobblestone alley that led to McGuffey's.

I donned a slicker, and then entered the speakeasy, which was awash in miners and old drunks. I figured they might look at me different, take a swing at me for Forest, so when

I stepped into the bar, I braced myself, but instead I was greeted with raised glasses. They were a sad lot to be sure, the horde of unwashed commemorating their fallen leader in hushed revelry and open displays of weeping, yet they seemed happy to see me. I bee-lined toward the bar, nervously sandwiching myself between Jacob and Sam, then took a pint from Lazy Eye.

"On the house," Lazy Eye said. "All night long."

I lifted the beer, smelling it.

"Ain't poisoned kid," he said. "If I wanted you dead, you'd be holding your throat closed."

"Then why?"

"Pinkerton killers drink free," he said. "Them are the house rules."

A miner I barely knew, a guy named Éamon Magee, recounted to the whole of McGuffey's how I'd killed Pinkerton Booth down in Rahillville. Said I'd plugged him twice in the face.

"Said you tried to save Ruth and her kid," Lazy Eye said. "Said it went down ugly, fucking cocksuckers."

I should have corrected him—it was dishonest not too—but I couldn't put Mattie's name out there, and, hell, if it made them all like me a little better, I'd let it lie.

But I didn't know if my newfound reputation would ease Jacob's anger. He stared at the blood-damp bar as if he was reading it, while Sam jostled next to me and I bought him a beer.

"That's awfully kind of you, Neal," Sam said. "I'm sorry about your mama."

"I know, Sam. Can I ask you something?"

"As long as it ain't about my Betty."

"No, it's not about her," I said. "Do you remember my father, you know, before Big Hank?"

In the teetering candlelight, I could nearly see the thin man's heart sigh. "Them were dark years, real dark. Started believin' the world was coming to Rapture but now I know this is just the test of men's faith."

"I only knew him as a son," I went on. "And I was wondering

what you thought of him before, before everything. Was he like Seamus?"

"I don't know, Neal. I don't. For the life of me, I can't say I ever understood your father and that's a shame for a me because I once believed I knew the hearts of all my fellow man. Now, I'm not so sure. Not after Betty. Perhaps, it's true that only the Lord can see into another man's heart. Only thing for sure is he's no longer a good man."

"Shut it, you old drunk," Jacob said. "Ain't you one to talk about being a good man."

We turned to the fat detective. "Don't matter anyhow," Jacob said. "Just don't care anymore."

"Then don't be telling me to shut it, Mr. Detective," Sam said. "I can still put you over the knee as is the God-given right of any father."

"Ain't no father," Jacob said. "And I ain't no detective, not anymore." He threw his badge on the ground and moved to get up, to make a scene, I imagine, but he sat back down. He was drunk or tired or both.

"Shit, your old man is good," Jacob said. "Man stood up, didn't put up with no guff. Can't say the same for any of us and what does it mean to be good man but to stand up and say to the rest of us to go fuck a pig and not care what happens after? But all of us just scared. Scared of Seamus, scared of O'Leary. Just a bunch of cowards, all of us."

Jacob grabbed my shoulder and shook it and I felt the force of his doughboy rage in his palm.

"Fuck you," he said. "You two-bit propaganda hack."

"Fuck you," I said. "You pig cocksucker."

"Fine."

"Fine."

Amidst the ordered chaos of McGuffey's, where the men wept for the dead, where a detective pondered his guilt, where an old preacher sang sad, silent songs to his departed wife, where a one-eyed barkeep kept watch like a centurion, the bar noise picked up and a Saturday night raucousness overtook the crowd. Festivity blazed through the basement, as everyone reached that perfect state of drunkenness, that feeling after melancholy and before anger, a sort of inebriated crescendo that never lasted longer than a single round, and its resulting merriment could be seen in the suave way a pair of miners threw craps against the back wall, and it could be felt in the shake of Swift Mickey's crutch when he dropped three Queens during a Poker game, and it could be heard in the beautiful voice of New Sligo's oldest whore, the fifty-six-year-old patriot Daisy Fisher, who wore garters decorated in the Stars and Stripes. Everyone joined her when she stood upon a table and sang, "When Irish Eyes are Smiling."

I turned to Sam and wanted to say something sweet and meaningful to the old preacher, but he lay upon the bar asleep, so I stuck a rag beneath his head, then pulled out my own wallet and dropped a ten-dollar bill upon the bar and told Lazy Eye that Sam could sleep for the week.

Lazy Eye took the money and nodded toward the crowd.

"Fucking Irish," he said. "Pie-eyed at a funeral."

He was right. It was a funeral, an Irish wake for a dead Jew.

I put my arm around Jacob. "I love you, you corrupt son of a bitch."

"You're just drunk."

"No," I said. "I really love you."

"Thanks," he said. "Been awful lonesome lately."

The crowd kept on with their mirth, only pausing, only shutting up when they all heard a sharp bell ringing from behind the bar. Everyone turned toward Lazy Eye, who held a double-barrel shotgun like he'd been carrying it all day long.

Two sets of footsteps descended the rickety stairs. The light was dim, just strings of shadow and light dancing across the dirt, but I could see that the pair of men wore black suits.

Pinkertons Burnsides and Garibaldi stopped in the middle of the crowd and glared at the men to give them space. Burnsides took out a sheet of paper. "Tommy Corrigan, Raylen Hewitt, and Neal Stephens," he said. "They here?"

Blood puttered from the ceiling. Sam wheezed. I looked over at Tommy and Raylen standing against the dartboard, their eyes fixed on the Pinkertons.

"We want no trouble," Burnsides said. "Just them and we'll leave you boys be."

I picked up Miss Constance's case because I'd already decided no one else was going to die because of me. I stood but something heavy and cold pushed me back. I turned. Lazy Eye's shotgun rested on my shoulder. I wanted to say something noble, but Lazy Eye took that choice from me. I looked around: slowly, almost imperceptibly, a score of miners inched, hobbled, and limped their way in front of me, so that I could hardly see the Pinkertons. As the blood dripped onto the miner's slickers like a symphony of tapping fingers, the Pinkertons whispered to one another, figuring on what to do.

Burnsides coughed, then pulled his hands from his pockets, revealing a revolver. "I don't want no trouble from you, nigger. This ain't your business."

A gun fired into the dark. I pulled Sam to the ground as more shots were traded. A miner tumbled over me. I covered the old preacher's head with my body and looked out as feet shuffled through the blood and I tried to catch of sight of who was shooting whom, but all I saw were boots, as was my lot in life.

The mirror behind the bar exploded sending glass to my back, and Sam, awoken from his dreams of parishioners and lost wives, squirmed beneath me and screamed, "Red Sea. I'm drowning in the Red Sea."

The gunfire stopped and a humming sang in my ear and Jacob stood in the orange light holding a revolver, with two Pinkertons splayed at his feet.

Lazy Eye laid his shotgun on the bar. "Everyone alive?" he hollered. "Check yourselves for holes."

I turned to the miner who'd tripped over me—Lyle Macarthur—but he was fine, only falling because of his bum knee. I helped him up, and then walked over to the Pinkertons, their blood mixing with that of the animals. I reached into Burnside's coat and pulled out his billfold and handed it to Lazy Eye.

"You didn't have to—"

"Shoot your uncle's Pinkertons?" Lazy Eye said. "Shit, I'd do that for free."

Lazy Eye pointed at Jacob. "Take them upstairs and feed them to the hogs. Can't be stepping over dead Pinkerton all night."

Jacob hoisted Burnsides over his shoulder, while another miner followed with the remains of Garibaldi.

"Now you." Lazy Eye pointed at me. "Back here."

We walked into the storeroom where Lazy Eye handed me a candle, then stooped over trunk, removing a gun and pushing it into my palm.

"Your father came by earlier," he said. "Said to give this to you if I thought you'd need it. I think you do."

It was a .36 caliber Colt revolver.

"Whatever your old man has planned, I think he could use your help." His eyes glanced upstairs.

I retreated to the bar to fetch Miss Constance's case, but when I picked her up, I heard the grating of glass and I bent over and felt sick and knew she was dead and I was again a photographer without a camera. I imagine I was crying when I laid the case on the bar, taking her out of her home, piece by piece.

I took out the film and Lazy Eye dropped Miss Constance into the trash can. It can end that quickly.

I walked up to Rochelle Street. At the corner, I examined the line of cars. An engine turned over and a car's lamps illuminated. I walked toward it and stepped onto the road and opened the passenger door of my old car, the one I'd left at the jailhouse. My father was in the driver's seat.

I sat beside him and the old anarchist drove east toward the plains. I felt my gun. I hadn't owned one since Belgium, and, like that time, this gun belonged to another man.

BELGIUM

It was during my third day of searching for Lorraine that I came across the farmhouse with the two dead women in the vegetable garden. The farm stood alone on a short plain enclosed between two hills. At one time, the farmhouse had been painted bright red, but now it seemed rusted in the dusk light, like a locomotive abandoned in the desert. I paused on a hill and took out Miss Constance. The camera's stout metal frame made a poor weapon. For the first time since I'd followed the French army east during that joyous summer in 1914, I wished I carried a gun.

Beneath the salvo of the German and English cannons and the rifle volley of the men rooted in trenches, a breeze rustled the short spring grass and crows squawked from tree limbs like a shrill chorus; that those limbs appeared aflame as they eclipsed the sun setting into the Somme River Valley; that I'd seen an old man hanging from a similar limb a mile back; that I only had a vague idea of my location gave me pause, but I knew then that guns would always fire, and trees would always burn, and men would always hang, so I walked on because I figured Lorraine might be inside the farmhouse.

Both women had been shot in the head. They lay encased in mud with their knees buckled and stiff as frozen soil. I could see that they'd been kneeling when the shot came. Their blouses—torn at the breast—had been soiled by the constant rains. Their skin was frosted in flies; their eyes hollowed, pecked clean. I covered my face with a handkerchief, and then kneeled in the mud. It was clear that they were mother and daughter. The eldest had the blanched, translucent skin and brittle hair of a woman accustomed to chronic hunger. The youngest looked no older than sixteen: her cheeks blazed with youth and shame, her dress and fingernails stained in blood. I stood, and then wiped the mud from my trousers. I raised Miss Constance and fired.

I stepped onto the porch and pulled at the window shutters, before pressing my ear against the door. Silence. I hesitated, imagining what awaited me on the other side, but the only food I'd seen in three days had been a patch of blackberries that smelled like gas. I couldn't walk for another night without food, without sleep. Lorraine would wait for me: she'd promised. I opened the door.

An old man sat at the table eating soup.

He held his spoon just below his lips, looking at me like he expected, or maybe hoped, for his own bullet to the head. He wore a mud-caked shirt, with his sleeves rolled up above the elbows. Even in the dim room lit by a lamp, the old man's eyes were a deep blue shaded by black lids like a lake inside a volcano. He looked at his soup, and then pointed his spoon toward the pot on the counter. I ladled some broth and carrots into a bowl, and then sat across from him. We ate.

The soldiers had ransacked the house. Copper pots lay strewn across the kitchen floor and pillow feathers tumbled and settled on glass shards from shattered picture frames. Only the upright piano seemed to have escaped the barrage. At one time the house must have been cozy and quaint, the kind of home merchants maintained in the country for their summer holidays. But now it looked like the rest of Belgium, crippled.

The man had tried to clean. He'd swept the glass off of the long Persian rug, which dominated the middle of the room as if the house had been built around it, but you could see that he struggled to survive alone. The lukewarm soup tasted sandy and putrid and the spoon and bowl were caked in dry food. The draft through the old floorboards rustled his limp white hair, and he smelled of piss and dirt.

"You're an American," he said. He spoke English with an easy, educated grace. "You were here to steal from me?"

"You can't steal from the dead." I waited for the old man's reaction, but none came.

"Were they English or German or French?" I pointed at the front door.

"I know what you're referring to," the old man said. "They were Germans."

"Were you here?"

The old man picked up his bowl and took it to the kitchen, leaving it in the sink with a score of other similarly dirty dishes.

"No." He dipped his hands in a glass bowl filled with water. "I was in town."

We smoked outside. The old man led me to a grassy field twenty yards behind the house, stopping at two mud patches, nearly six feet long and two feet wide, but only an inch or two deep and pooled with rainwater.

"Every morning I dig," he said. "I dig for two hours, then my back hurts and I go inside and it rains and all my work is gone."

"Where's the shovel?" The old man's fingernails looked like scorched beef.

He looked out to the west at the fading sunlight, which mixed with the smoke of the Somme and turned the sky orange. Gray storm clouds hung behind the light like a cape. "They took it. To dig graves for their soldiers. They took all my tools. My pick, my axe, my hoe."

I dipped my hand into the mud. It strained through my fingers. The old man laid his hand on my back.

"In the morning," he said. "Better left for the morning."

He returned to the house, while I finished my cigarette. I listened to the pounding guns, miles away, and considered leaving. She was heading north and I hoped to catch up to her, but it was near dark and in a storm I'd lose my way.

The old man's name was Albert. Before the war he'd taught ancient history at a college in Brussels. The farm had belonged to his wife's family for generations and they'd come here in the first days of the war, after his university had sent all its students to the front. He didn't know how to farm, but his wife did, and they got by on the little they managed to grow. Three days earlier he'd left the farm, walking two miles into town in order to buy medicine for his wife. It was then that the Germans arrived.

"How do you know they were German?" It wasn't an innocent question. I wasn't exactly sure who controlled this parcel. It was a gray zone, a borderland. If Lorraine fell in with the English or French, she might be fine. Then again, she might not. But if it were the Germans, she'd have no chance.

We sat at the dining table, a candle burning between us. Albert reached into his pocket and removed an army medal: The Iron Cross.

"Do you think he'll come back for it?" I asked. "I'm sure he'll miss this."

Albert shrugged, his old shoulders cracking and popping with the movement. "Perhaps he thinks he left it on another woman," he said. "Perhaps he is already dead."

"Do you have any arms?"

Albert paused, studying the floor. He still feared that I was a thief.

"I had a rifle when the war started, but the English took it," Albert said. "I have an old gun my father-in-law left in the house, but what good would it do against monsters?"

"David had a slingshot."

"David had a God," Albert said. "Do you have a gun in there?" He pointed at Miss Constance's case.

"Just a camera. I'm a correspondent for an American newspaper."

"Are you lost?"

"I'm looking for my wife."

"She is missing?"

"Yes. She's walking north to the sea."

Albert pulled off a splinter from the dining table, then stuck it between his teeth, picking. "You're sure?"

"That's what she said she'd do."

Albert nodded then stared off at the candle flame, silent. I remember not minding his disbelief. I understood his lack of faith. But it didn't matter, because I knew Lorraine and I knew she wasn't dead. I'd have seen her.

• • •

The rain shook the roof. It surprised me: I hadn't spent a night indoors for months. The guns quieted for an hour, then began again, as familiar as a sparrow's chirp. Albert stoked the fire. He rubbed his hands together and held them up to warm near the flame.

"Take off your boots."

"Thank you." It felt like I had to amputate them from my feet.

"Do you want a drink?"

"Yes."

Albert kneeled in the middle of the room, then turned the rug on its side, revealing a trap door with an iron latch. He opened it. It was a small dugout, no more than three feet deep, but from what I could see, there was enough room to fit three people.

Albert reached in, then handed me a bottle of French brandy. I dusted off the bottle and saw that it was half full. He hesitated above the dugout, before pulling out a large painting. He stood, holding the painting outstretched, then he blew the dust from it and hung it above the piano.

"It is my most beautiful possession," he said. "It is called *Girl with Yellow Flower on her Day of Marriage.*"

The painting showed a young girl wearing a blue blouse buttoned to the throat, her brown hair tightly bound above her head. She gazed at the floor, her blue eyes vacant, devoid of passion, while holding a yellow flower to her breast. She appeared constricted, like the act of sitting for an artist suffocated her. She sat in front of a large window, behind which lay a city with long, gray canals. Except for the flower, the colors were muddy, dull. The painting was dreadful.

"It was painted by Robert O'Shaughnessy, an Irishman who'd fled Galway for Amsterdam. He painted for the aristocracy and this is his final portrait, during the summer Napoleon entered Amsterdam."

Albert began to cry.

"I can't remember last summer."

"Everyone got sick," I said. "The flies were awful."

I poured drinks, and then sat at the piano. My fingers rested on the keys for a long time, while I gazed at the sheet music before me. I couldn't read it—to my mother's eternal chagrin—but I thought back to all the songs I'd memorized as a child. Most were American standards or Negro spirituals. I hadn't touched a piano since the war had begun and none of the old songs seemed quite right, right then.

"Play your wife's favorite song," Albert said. "That which would give her comfort."

I played an old blues tune. I couldn't remember all of the lyrics, just the chorus. "When your way gets dark/turn the lights up."

My fingers felt stiff, creaky. Albert tapped his foot against the old floorboards.

When I finished, I turned to the old man who was still crying. "She grew up in St. Louis. In the middle of America," I said. "They sang a lot of songs like that there."

"Is your wife colored Negro?"

I hesitated.

"Yes, she is."

"I've studied the Negro," he said. "In books."

I didn't say anything. It seemed like a silly thing to study.

"You cannot go back to America, can you?" he asked.

I looked down at my hands. They were cut in nearly a dozen different places. Pieces of skin peeled off like I was shedding. Lorraine liked my hands, liked how I played the piano with them.

"Not with her."

"Your family will not accept her?"

"No."

"But you still search for her?"

It was another silly question, yet I had trouble answering it. "She's waiting for me."

"That is a sin of pride."

This was the last thing I needed. If it hadn't been such a piss-soaker out, I'd have left Albert to fend for himself. He was old and European and couldn't understand.

"When I was a boy, the nuns told me that lust was the worst of all sins. God hates the lusting man. Fools. Pride is worse." He finished his drink and poured another. He leaned against the piano and his expression was sorrowful and patronizing and it made me cold. "Take your wife home with you. Let fate decide."

"I'll go to jail. They'll do worse to her."

"So you stayed in Belgium to avoid pain?"

"Yes."

"You're either a liar or a fool."

I looked at the keys and repeated the song. I felt Albert's gaze, but I couldn't return it. When I began playing the song a third time, he laid his glass on the piano and walked into his bedroom and closed the door.

● ● ●

While the rain poured against the house, I tried to sleep on Albert's sofa. When I closed my eyes, light, like from a prism, slapped the darkness. I felt horrible for resting, for pausing even for a night. Although Lorraine had promised to walk north, I worried she might have wandered off and could be heading toward the Germans. She'd never had a great sense of direction—always asking which way was west—but I hoped she'd been clever enough to head the right way.

Although Albert didn't believe me, I was certain Lorraine was still alive, because when I'd abandoned my unit, I'd run toward her, but an explosion sent me into an irrigation ditch. When I woke, I couldn't tell whether it was day or night. Smoke smothered the sky and I could neither remember how I landed in the ditch, nor how long ago it had happened. Miss Constance had fallen out of her case, and I had to search for her amidst the rubble, and, after I found her, I climbed to flat ground, bracing myself against a telegraph pole. My legs wobbled and I tasted blood. Above me, a body hung suspended from the telegraph, its arms knotted in the wires, its skin burned away with smoke emanating from the coals. A pair of boots lay below the corpse. I picked them up—saw they were too small—then walked on.

I searched the rest of the day for the hospital tent, circling over and over again the place it should have been, but there was only the wreckage wrought by an explosion—bodies, burned and maimed, lay strewn throughout an enormous crater—and it wasn't for hours, my head keening, until I realized it was her tent I circled. I dropped to my knees. There must have been nearly forty corpses, most burned to the bone. A shell had lit the tent and sent a fireball down upon the wounded and their caretakers.

What I did next wasn't a conscious choice. It was mechanical and passive.

I went to the first corpse, a stiff, single coal. Whether it was a man or woman, I couldn't tell. I took its charred left hand and counted the fingers. Five. From the smallest I looked over to the next finger and saw that it didn't have a ring.

I went to the next and did the same. Repeat.

A few wore rings, but they were gold bands melted into the corpse's hand. None were silver. None were Lorraine's.

I am sure of this.

•   •   •

The rain continued. Lightning struck like cannon shells along the hillside. I didn't have a book to read and I had no paper to write on, so I pitched a tent in the middle of Albert's living room and developed my last roll of film—at the front, I found, you could build a makeshift darkroom nearly anywhere. As expected, I had a lot of boot pictures. I also had a lot of negatives of men looking right at me: eventually I'd print them and send them to their wives and mothers. But I also had one frame that made no sense. It was a man on fire, levitating.

I can't remember anymore what I thought of that photo. It's tinged with so many other memories by now—seeing it in newspapers and on recruitment posters—that it seems like something separate from me, its own entity. I'm not even sure I connected it with the image of an angel. Yet, I'm certain that I hadn't tied it to Lorraine. Not in Albert's house. It was only later, after I'd gone back to America, when I threw all my war photos across the floor that I began to construct the story of *The Trench Angel*.

• • •

In the morning, I found a bucket and dug into the mud. It had rained all night long and the mud was heavy like concrete. The sun was warm, but a breeze cooled my neck. The wind blew from the south and the air smelled like smoke. The first hole took over an hour. When I was three feet deep, I climbed out of the grave and dusted off. I walked to the front of the house, to the well and pulled a drink of water. Two vultures, perched on the porch railing, scouted the dead women. I clapped. The birds flew away.

I dug the second hole. Afterwards, I walked inside the house. The bedroom door remained closed. I found two old blankets in the linen closet. I wrapped each woman in a blanket and carried them, one at a time, behind the house. I dropped them into their graves.

When I returned to the house, Albert was at the stove, making tea.

"Do you want to step out and say a few words?"

Albert stood above the graves, but he didn't speak. Their bodies were hidden, wrapped in the blankets. Only their feet remained visible, rain swollen and blue. He dropped a handful of dirt onto his wife, then another onto his daughter.

"Thank you." He shook my hand. "Take what you need."

The vultures squawked from behind the graves as Albert walked toward the house. When he shut the door, I picked up the bucket. I was wasting time, I thought. I should let the old man finish the job. They were his dead, not mine. Lorraine needed me.

A gun fired inside the house. I dropped the bucket and closed my eyes and the farm went quiet.

I dug a third grave.

By the time I'd finished burying Albert and his family, it was past noon. I washed myself off in the house. I ate the remains of the soup and scavenged the last of the food from the cupboard and placed them in my pack. I went through the family's drawers and closets.

I looked inside the dugout. It was empty. I climbed inside and pulled the trapdoor down. I listened. I heard the breeze blow against the windowpanes and the tree branches bending and the grass rustling and the guns firing. I heard everything clearly as if I was standing on the front porch.

I stepped into the bedroom. On the bed where Albert shot himself, below the bloodstain on the pillow, lay the pistol. It was an old single-action French revolver. It had been recently cleaned. I picked it up and swung open the cylinder. Three chambers were empty.

For a long time, I stood over that bed. Out the window I could see three muddy graves. I put the revolver in my pocket, and then hoisted my pack over my shoulder. I checked through the living room one more time, finding nothing of value. I hesitated in the doorway, then went to the piano and looked at the painting. In the daylight, the painting seemed even worse than at night, yet I began to see Albert's fascination with it. The colors were muddied, the composition sloppy, but I no longer saw vacancy in the girl's expression. Just hopelessness. I looked at the window behind her and saw past the cityscape and into the sky, where a plume of smoke rose to the heavens, a symptom of an anticipated defeat.

I walked out of the house and over the hill into a new valley where a stream snaked toward the sea. I followed it. About a mile from Albert's farm, I slipped into a bog and had to pull myself out. Exhausted, I rested beneath a tree.

I searched Miss Constance's case. I had a single package of film left, a change of clothes, and a Bible. My mother's old Bible. I opened it, flipping through the pages until I stopped at the Book of Matthew, where my ticket acted as a bookmark. I didn't know if the steamship line was running anymore. Maybe all those ships had been sunk. It didn't matter. What mattered was this: I hadn't torn it up, even after Lorraine made me promise to never return to America. She'd never forgive me.

I walked on, toward the sea. I remember considering what I'd do when I found Lorraine, how I'd feel when I discovered what had been done to her by men, how I'd explain my shame for not keeping my promise during that sad time of our lives, how I was just as culpable as any man, for the sins of fathers and husbands run deep in our memories, but then I sighed, knowing she was already dead, and I was relieved.

—29—

We drove off into the plains along a scraggly dirt road, cratered from the remnants of old prairie dog colonies, rutted from spring floods. Along the roadside, through the scattering snow, the green eyes of coyotes stared at our passing car. I lit a cigarette to keep warm. The snowflakes slipped into the cab and settled on my trousers. Even though the landscape was familiar, the darkness of the night, the quiet of the snowfall, the foreignness of the road, made it seem like my father was taking me somewhere secret and important, toward a world that only those who choose to live on the borderlands, the outsiders and anarchists, dared to tread.

"You cold?" he asked.

"A little."

"Tired?"

"I think so."

"That's the worst kind of tired," Jesse said. "The kind you're only a little aware of. Mattie and I once walked clear to Kentucky with maybe a day's sleep. Never been so tired in my life, but we couldn't stop, so it was like I wasn't tired, but I didn't feel alive either. Like I was a ghost in some shit dime novel."

"You told me that story, yesterday."

"You get old, you repeat yourself."

"Mattie's a sharp woman."

"She a good old broad."

I felt the absence of Miss Constance on my lap, and the outline of the gun in my coat pocket. It was heavy, solid, and loaded.

"You upset at me?"

"No," I said. "Why?"

"Mattie?"

"No." I wasn't, not anymore.

At a crossroads, Jesse steered into the grassland, and then motored up a snowy slope, stopping atop a hill just before the road descended further into the plains. He shut off the car, then rubbed his hands together and blew into them, his breath blending with the smoke. The car rocked back and forth. The moon split the clouds and cast a white beam along the grasslands like a lighthouse shining upon a frozen bay. Across the valley, a train gunned its engine south toward Denver.

"I saw something awful today," I said. "I don't know how to feel about it, what to say."

"I know."

"What do you know?"

Jesse squeezed the steering wheel, his old hands strong like they could still climb a rope or strangle a man. "I know you helped pin that O'Leary boy's death on Forest and you were wrong to do that even if it was to save your sister, but that's not what killed Forest because the Pope could have decreed Forest a damned archangel and Seamus still would have strung him up because that's who Seamus is."

"He could have run. Man didn't seem scared at all."

"Don't make him a saint, Cowboy," Jesse said. "He's not. He was a tough man and knew what he was doing and what Seamus might do to him, but he took his chances because he thought it right, but it wasn't like he walked on water or nothing."

"He said he didn't kill O'Leary. I believe him."

"You're probably right. But Forest would have if he had thought it had done any good, because he'd done in scabs and backstabbers, so what's the difference between those men and someone like Big Hank's boy who was no good? Just don't go romanticizing anyone. Not me and certainly not Forest. I don't care what the leftists are going to say. He was a hard man. Killed plenty of scabs. Beat them with pipes. Just poor bastards, so desperate, so hungry, they'd do anything to feed their kids. That's the problem, Cowboy. It ain't union versus baron. It's pain versus pain. It's this exploitive system that sets the whole cycle up, and you did what you did because you thought saving your sister would set all the other things right, but it didn't because saving her won't absolve you."

"I loved her."

"Your wife?"

"Lorraine." My mouth felt tight like tetanus. "I know it looks bad what I did, but I really loved her."

"I know, Cowboy. I believe you."

"It's like it was another person who married her then. I didn't mean to lie about it."

"You're lying again."

"It doesn't matter. It wasn't who she was."

"Shit," Jesse said. "You grow up Negro in America, Cowboy, it matters more than anything in the world."

I shut my eyes.

"I never saw her body," I said. "Or maybe I did and I just don't know. Hell, maybe I just convinced myself she'd have been better off alone."

"Or you'd be better off running away."

I stomped my boots and blew into my hands. I lit another cigarette.

"Cowboy?"

"You hear those stories of girls finding their husbands in hospitals years later and you think it's possible and it nags at you but I think she would have found me if she was still alive. She'd at least sent a letter telling me to go to hell."

"That's a lot of faith there, Cowboy. A lot of faith."

We sat until the windshield was covered with snow and we couldn't see the prairie anymore.

"I used to come out here often, when you were a boy. Escape to this spot, just for a moment. Cleared my head."

My father was getting at it, working his way toward the answer I'd imagined for a long time. I had to make sure he got there. "What happened? What made you go?"

"It's a fair question." Jesse said, pulling a drink from a bottle and then offering me some. "A real fair question."

"You've had to have thought about it, thought about what you'd say if you saw me again, or didn't you think you'd ever see me again?"

He took another drink. "I wasn't sure. Not ever. Figured I might, but then I thought someone might kill me before I got to. Then I heard you were in the trenches and I figured you'd be the one to get killed and I, well, I had a hard time with that because I blamed myself for you going there."

"Why'd you go?"

"Glory and adventure, like Robinson Crusoe."

"You're lying." I said.

Jesse closed his eyes and mumbled.

"Go on."

JESSE

I've always despised the prairie dog, Cowboy. Hated them.
It is, beyond a shadow of doubt, the most filthy, vile, in-
cestual, disease-ridden, polygamist creature that has ever
traversed this green Earth, having within it morals little
better than your common Mormon, not that I oppose the
idea of free love because Emma G. in her less batty years
argued persuasively on its behalf. But prairie dogs, Cowboy, prairie dogs. They've tortured me since boyhood. As
soon I could crawl, I'd be chasing them around my Daddy's
farm with a sawed off broom handle. I'd be chasing after
them screaming for them to get off our land—ruined our
crops, you see. Those rodents were much more vexing than
those poor wolves the government exterminated in such a
horrible fashion. How they could kill a beast of such mag-
nificence by feeding it broken glass, I cannot explain.

Even in manhood, they kept after me. That day I left so
long ago, that terrible autumn morning when I fled, that
day I know you pain to hear me speak of, that day I rode
east into Kansas, my old Palomino snapped her ankle on
a prairie dog hole and I had to put her down right there.
Mattie was waiting for me in Kansas City. You should know
that, Cowboy. I had dreams of riding toward the rising sun,
and instead I ended up walking into Kansas City with wet
boots. Humiliating, Cowboy. To fancy myself a great man,
yet to reunite with my lifelong love like some downtrodden
hobo. I can't tell you how bad I felt. Utterly dejected.

I know you don't care, Cowboy. But listen.

Even with my long history with that certain rodent and

despite my complete disdain of its habits, when I gaze upon a colony of them, I can't help but have the metaphor shoot through my guts like an arrow shot from Apollo's bow. In this industrialized world, where shysters and robber barons endanger every decent freedom, parcel and imprison in barbed wire every sweet slice of soil, the prairie dog, nevertheless, survives. And do you know why, Cowboy? Well, it's simple.

The prairie dog is the anarchist of the animal kingdom.

It's true, Cowboy. It's a truth as apparent as the Earth's roundness. It's a truth as obvious as the imperial corruption of the capitalist system. Truth exists. And the truth is that the prairie dog is a lower form of anarchist like the ape is a lower form of man. That is not a judgment. Just evolution. Someday the prairie dog may dynamite his own oppressor's castles, but for now he exists in the animal kingdom and the animal kingdom does not have the requisite thumbs to detonate nitroglycerin. Let me explain. The prairie dog cares none for the trappings of civilized life—our fences, our churches, and our factories. He knows them for what they are: artificial constructions of a moneyed class that seeks to subsume nature to further the basest of sins and that sin is avarice. He refuses to partake, unwilling to be shackled into domestication. He is a mustang that won't be broken. Like those New England pilgrims who braved the rough Atlantic three hundred years ago, the prairie dog is a separatist, forming its own egalitarian society, ignoring the artificial rights of property owners, living as one body, yet preserving the rights of each individual prairie dog to choose his own path.

Pure damn anarchy.

And like the anarchist, the prairie dog has been under siege for the last century. With every industrial advancement, the prairie dog is attacked. With every natural or man-made disaster, the prairie dog's sought out for extermination. He is blamed for drought and flood, for fire and tornado. The propagandists laid the blame upon his dirt doorstep for the discontent of the populists and the violence of Bleeding Kansas. Hell, if they could have blamed him for corrupting old

John Wilkes Booth, they'd have done so. Yet like the anarchist, the prairie dog survives. When the men with guns seek him out with malicious intent, the prairie dog barks his alert and saves his kin. He burrows deep underground, and before long reemerges smarter and stronger with a keen sense of his enemies and a desire to seek retribution through sheer survival. Just like the anarchist.

I know, I know. The point. I'm getting there, Cowboy. Just be patient.

Now, this happens for a number of reasons. The prairie dog adapts to his surroundings. He builds where he can, when he can. But he is no coward. He does not seek shelter in the remotest field, hidden from modern life. No, the prairie dog is courageous and bombastic. He'll thumb his nose at the usurpers whenever possible. He builds his colony in the middle of the town if he can find a way. He does not rely on the past for a crutch, but instead learns the lessons of the history to build for the future. He is not a romantic. He is a pragmatist. Which of nature's creature defines anarchy better? A prairie dog, Cowboy. That's who.

I came to this conclusion a few days back as I lounged on my stomach staring out at the New Sligo Jailhouse. An adjacent cornfield provided me cover. I relaxed beside a colony, where a half dozen prairie dogs gazed down upon my speculating. But did they sound their alarm? Of course not. No, they recognized me as a fellow of their sorts. If the animal kingdom had jails and if the prairie dog thumbs, he'd be the best at busting his kin out of captivity. No, Cowboy, they observed me, seeking to learn the proper technique to perform one of life's great joys: the jailbreak. You see, most practitioners of the jailbreak over-intellectualize it. They give too much credit to their captors. Hence, they seek out convolution when simplicity is the sword in the stone. Too many folks have taken Dumas as a textbook, when really there is little need to sneak into a body bag meant for someone else. And few occasions ever call for tunneling. No, Cowboy, sheer will suffices. Maybe some dynamite, occasionally a well-placed bribe, but those are ancillary.

You see, prison guards expect tunneling. They expect high stakes breaks. What they don't expect is simplicity.

But during that cool night just a few days ago, after I had scouted the jailhouse for a full two weeks, learning the movements of the guards, memorizing their routines like I was a pupil and they were my multiplication table—you remember when I taught you to multiply?—I knew I was ready to strike, so after the day guard departed, I loaded my Colt, and then waited for the last of the sun to disappear behind the Rockies. The night smelled of cold iron and dust, while mosquitoes nibbled at my arms and a praying mantis observed me from the middle of a cornhusk. The mantis might also be considered an anarchist, if it weren't for their unequal sex relations. I ate a jar of nuts for strength and waited for the night guard to extinguish the jail cell lights.

I strode across the lot beneath that evil tree, right up to the jailhouse door, and then turned the knob. Locked. But that was fine. I'd planned on a locked door. Expected it. So I knocked, a dainty, ladylike knock using a single knuckle and bouncing it off that old wood door to a sweet Scott Joplin beat. I knocked twice like that, then stepped back to await my prey. Hardly a moment passed, when a voice whispered through the wood.

—Who there?
—Seamus Rahill, I said in my most corrupt falsetto.
—All right then.

The door opened. Standing on the other side was a young Cyclops. Based upon his sunken jowls, poor hygiene, and lack of depth perception, I recognized his lineage. He was an O'Leary and I figured him for young Clyde. His father had been a man of low moral character and substandard intelligence, yet he'd also been a man of great courage and my own part in his early exit from this world haunts me to this day and I'll explain why momentarily.

As I looked upon young O'Leary, I observed two things I hadn't planned on. First, he was without his gun. Fine. A little easy, sure. Takes a bit of the fun out of it. Not nearly as romantic. No one writes home about busting into a jail with an unarmed guard, but needless to say, it's not a terrible obstacle to overcome. Second and more troubling, he wore neither shirt, nor trouser. This was embarrassing. An unarmed guard was one thing; an unclothed guard was simply humiliating. My sense of importance, my own grandly romantic image of myself, was greatly diminished. So staring at the young O'Leary, unarmed, unclothed, I decided that killing him, letting the world know he was offed without his britches to shield him from the vermin, was in poor taste. So I asked myself a simple question: what would a prairie dog do?

I introduced my revolver to his forehead.

He took to the floor.

I walked inside with a cheap victory.

The room was lit by a teetering lamp. On my right was a wall of wanted posters—I recognized my likeness in one—and before me stood an empty desk. To my left lay a Mexican girl, her hands bound to the bars of a jail cell. She lay there still as cement, naked and crying and cut up and bleeding. It turned my guts to see a girl so young in such a state and I thought of Tillie, my own sweet daughter, and I felt shamed because I had been a poor father. Inside another cell were a couple of Mexican fellows. I hadn't any connection to those boys. The jailbreak was just a ruse, a way to disguise my real intentions, because, as you know, what got me really hopped up were them files, but first I had to take care of the prisoners to make said ruse work.

I pulled out a pocketknife, and then cut the ropes binding the naked girl. She lay still, hesitant of me. I tried to calm her, speaking in a quiet tone.

—*Soy el Jesse Stephens magnífico. El hombre mas guapo en el mundo.*
—*Como?*
—*Soy el Jesse Stephens magnífico.*

I wanted to check her over. Once she felt the gentleness

of my touch, she relaxed. I saw that the wounds were neither light, nor deep, but somewhere in the middle where only infection could take your life, but pain was the obvious intent. Once freed, she cried something awful, then grabbed hold of one of the men in the adjacent cell. Her brother, I later discovered. It was just awful, Cowboy. And I was filled with the sort of righteousness I'm rarely prone to. But I didn't have much time so I turned to the Mexican and asked her where the keys were.

—*Su cinturón.*

I walked over Clyde, still unconscious, and searched to his britches, unfastening the keys from his belt. As I looked at the young O'Leary, my righteousness got the better of me. He lay face down on the floor. I raised my Colt to the back of his skull. He'd raped that girl before her brother, tortured her for play, but after I pulled back the hammer, after I massaged the gun against his cranium, I found that I didn't have it in me to take him like that. Perhaps I've mellowed in my old age, but more likely I couldn't do unto the son as I had done unto the father.

I turned toward the man, the brother.

—What are you in for? I said, but in Spanish.
—Stole a horse, he said.
—Horse thief, hmm. Whose horse?
—Senor Rahill's.
—Good work.

I unlocked him and his compatriots. His sister fell into him and she was plainly ill. I told him I'd get her to a doctor, a good one. I turned to O'Leary and looked down at that poor seed of a failed man. The boy, for I could only see him as a boy, lay naked on his belly, his backside taking in the air. I searched the jailhouse for some rope. When I found some, I dragged O'Leary to the desk and tied up his arms and legs. I wrote a quick limerick—the preferred poetic form of the anarchist—signing it *"¿En qué pararán estes misas, Garatuza? El Guapo."* Mighty odd the police never found it. My hunch is the real killer didn't know what to make of my fine verse and decided to dispose of it.

You don't speak a lick of Spanish do you, Cowboy? Well, it means "When Will These Masses End, Garatuza?" It's from an old Mexican trickster who conned the country into believing he was a priest. One of the world's first anarchists. Figured it apt in these days of holy frauds.

Then I told the kids to hang on for a minute as I searched through the desk for them files. After a quick tossing of the jailhouse, I realized that despite the O'Leary boy's carelessness in regards to his visitation policy, he had been careful enough to place those files, his livelihood, in a place not so easily discovered. So I went to him and woke him with a couple of quick slaps and he looked up at me with that awful eye and wouldn't speak, so I gave him a hard tug of his pecker and asked if he knew the story of Alcibiades and when he said he didn't I gave him an abridged history lesson on the ancient origins of love and he quickly pointed to a hollow wall panel where I found the files. Forest had been covering up for Big Hank, and, well, me for a long time and it was always going to be the ruin of him and for that I'm sorry. That's the lesson in sanctifying your leaders, Cowboy. We all got demons. Every last one of us.

Well, I shoved all the files in my briefcase and I figured there might be something useful for later on, yet I couldn't help it when my eyes fell upon an envelope with your mother's name. It wasn't like the others, not in the way it was blackmailing her. It was pictures of her body after she'd died and it broke my heart to see her in such a state, how she'd become so sickly in the years since my departure and the pictures showed that she had been on dope when she passed. There was also a letter and it said, "Forgive me lord, for I have sinned." She'd taken her own life and if it's because of me, I'm sorry. I wanted her to live on, but she couldn't. She'd killed herself and that little bastard had a file that said so. What he planned on doing with it, I couldn't say.

I followed the Mexican girl and her compatriots out into the lot, leaving the door open, hoping, somewhere deep down, that O'Leary might die of exposure. As I left he called out asking who I was. I went back to the door and lowered my hat.

—I am the magnificent Jesse Stephens, the handsomest man in the world.

But I want you to know Cowboy that I left him alive. Someone else shot him. I assure you, it was not I.

My hideout was in an abandoned building in the heart of Germantown. It had these old water worn ceilings and broken windows that froze the joint on those cool autumn days, but it was good enough because there wasn't anyone living nearby for almost half a mile. So when I kidnapped your sister in the middle of the night, she was surprised by where I was driving her.

—Why here? she asked.
—Who would look for me here?
—The police, tomorrow, when I tell them.
—I should have blindfolded you.

I threw my cigar out the window and it gave her chance to climb up on to her soapbox, an opportunity she'd been wanting on for a long while.

—You know you might burn down the whole town doing that.
—You nag me like your mother, I said. How do you know I won't kill you? I am, after all, what did the papers call me, the greatest criminal mastermind of the 20th century.

She laughed, Cowboy. She really chuckled.

—You wouldn't, she told me. My death would have no ideological ends. And you are, after all, an ideological animal.

She'd gotten smart in the years since I last saw her, even if some of her smartness is of the loony kind.

—You're a property owner and Seamus Rahill's niece, I said. Why shouldn't I kill you?
—Because you love me.
—Perhaps, I told her.

And I did. I really did. Cowboy, you and your sister have turned out so beautiful, so amazing. I well up just looking at the both of you and it makes me sad to think of all that time apart. I went to your sister because I was desperate, but I also felt somewhere inside me that she wouldn't fink on me. That she'd find some benevolence to help out that poor girl because she'd been healing the sick in Rahillville and that is an act of charity that esteems her in my old eyes.

Well, when we got to my hideout, I opened the basement shutters, and then followed Tillie down into the lamp-lit room. The Mexican girl was holding her shoulder and sweating something fierce. Her brother sat vigil beside her. And this is when I figured the trouble would start, because right then out of the backroom came Mattie.

Your sister, sharp as she is, knew right off what the story was.

—So you're the other woman.
—I was here first.

Mattie's sensitive to a fault, Cowboy, but she knew not to let my daughter push her around.

—You look like your father.
—Can't help that, now can I?
—Thanks for coming and not snitching. It's a kindness.
—I'm a regular Florence Nightingale.
—Ladies, we can save this for later, I told them. I'm awful tired after my heroics and I think this poor girl could use some help.

—Is he always so cocksure? your sister asked.

—Like a regular Buffalo Bill.

After that they got on swell. Can't say I wasn't nervous, but as long as you channel a woman's scorn toward something other than your own woman, it all comes out right as rain.

Tillie placed her doctoring bag down by the bedside and took hold of the girl's body. She looked her over carefully, and then said something I should tell you.

—You haven't dragged poor, helpless, lost, misbegotten Neal into your messes? He'll just get himself killed.

I think she meant it in a kind way. I really do, Cowboy.

—No, I told her. He doesn't know anything.

I hadn't planned, originally, on telling either of you of my arrival. I hadn't planned on staying into November, but then things changed and I couldn't get at Seamus quite like I wanted until tonight and then it seemed best to stick around to see what mischief I could make in the meantime.

As the sun rose, the girl lay asleep and healed beside her brother. Tillie had stitched up the girl with expert care and I was pleased about her finding such a noble calling. I know you have no children, Cowboy, so you can't understand what that kind of pride feels like but it's something fierce and exhausting. After I drove Tillie back to her house, I followed her into her home to use her toilet. Afterwards, I saw her crying and I remembered I'd left the files in my satchel and she'd gone through it and seen your mother had died the way she had and I felt evil for letting her find it. I held her and told her I was sorry and I was because I felt like a widow, and I had no right to that feeling.

But I felt it.

And I realized what I had done so many years ago, fleeing like I did because I was ashamed of shooting Big Hank, but it wasn't the only reason, because I was no good as a father anymore and I truly believe that—even if you don't—and I was never much of a husband to a woman like Pearl who had a certain idea of how a man should be and I couldn't masquerade as that sort of man anymore. Because before I met your mother I was an anarchist, me and Mattie, but she got pinched for what seemed like life and I needed to move on and become someone new and that's why I fell in with your mother and her ilk. Pearl was a good woman but she never knew who I was and I couldn't tell her because that meant jail. I've been an anarchist since the day I was born and I found Mattie and she made me right and when she went to jail I was never really right again, not until she showed up in New Sligo a few months before Big Hank died and while I told her to go away, she kept pestering me because she knew I was acting. I was different with your mother. It's confusing. What I mean is, well, I believed I was an upstanding man at that time. I really did, but I wasn't. I was the same man who'd robbed banks with Mattie, but I was playing another man and I believed it and I liked it because it was comfortable and safe and I liked the money and the horses and the power.

What about Big Hank? I'm getting there.

So when Big Hank came into the office that day, I believed I was a very different man than before I knew your mother.

No, Big Hank didn't have a gun. We planted that. The newspapers had a lot of stories about what happened, but it wasn't quite right because Big Hank didn't go mad, but was as calm as a Lutheran when he dropped a thick envelope on Seamus' desk and said he knew all our secrets and he wanted more money. He knew about Mattie. He knew Seamus had gotten cheap ditch pine to put up in the mines and it had killed a lot of men and maimed Clyde and that if the miners found out, he'd be hanging from a post in Pioneer Square by sundown. I never knew how he knew it. He said we were bad men and he knew he could ruin us so all he asked for was a good contract and more bribe money, but that was just the beginning, because it meant he owned us, and neither Seamus nor I could abide that. So after I wrote a check and gave it to that son of a bitch, Seamus pulled a little pistol from his desk, but he was as slow as a train going uphill, so him and Big Hank struggled over the gun. And what did I do?

Nothing, not a damn thing.

Just stood there and watched because I knew if either got killed it would be better for me, so when the gun went off and Seamus fell back with a bloody shoulder and then screams 'shoot him' and I knew I had to do something to keep my fortune, to keep my secrets and family intact, so I knocked that big son of a bitch to the ground and took his gun and shot him in the head just so I could keep myself in soft suits and a big house, so I could keep riding fine horses and drinking good whiskey, but I might as well have put a second bullet in my own head for all the good it did.

The epiphany I spoke of happened partly then and it happened partly when I saw your sister and I realized that I had been wrong abandoning Mattie because it was her I owed my allegiance, but I'd been too scared to bust her out, or too unsure of myself, or too afraid to just live like a monk and wait, and I knew if I stayed in this town I'd die without being happy, or at least living a just life, and all I'd do was be a bad husband and a bad father. When I saw your sister days ago, I realized I'd been right. I doubted myself over the years, but I was right to leave you all.

What am I back for?

I'm here to make it right. Seamus has got something that needs to go to the men, a fortune that needs to be returned to the people, money made of men turned into slaves and now it's time to be returned. He's imprisoned a fortune and I'm here to liberate it.

—30—

The car trembled in the wind. I closed my coat and wrapped my arms around my body. "Are you going to kill Seamus?"

"Not unless I have to," my father said. I wasn't sure if he was lying, but I thought he might be. "No, I'm going to take what he holds dear."

My father drove back to town with care, leaning over the steering wheel, peering out at the slippery road.

The streets appeared abandoned, the stores bolted, the horses put away, and the cars stowed in auto barns. Jesse drove down Tenth until he parked beside an old, decaying storefront that had once housed a candlemaker.

"You sure you want to do this?" he asked. "I can let you out here. You can't turn back once you're with me."

"I'm sure."

The front door swung open and Mattie strode out into the snow. She wore a black coat with a black hood and she seemed sure and happy.

"Neal's going to come along for the night."

"Good to hear," she said. "We finally got some luck. The Militia's blocking all the roads out of town."

"How's that good luck?" I asked.

"Means they ain't at the museum, Cowboy."

—31—

I hid behind the car, holding a crate of dynamite, counting the steps of the museum guard, counting my own breath, because you can't understand the fear that comes with larceny until you've done it once or twice. I looked up at the museum—granite walls and ornate columns and my mother's name under the dedication—and it looked the same it always had, but now I noticed the cracks in the granite, the fading of the paint. Seamus wanted it to last centuries, but I already had the feeling it wouldn't make it through the night.

In snow lit by the dull streetlight, Mattie danced up to the security guard and Jesse had the ether on the boy's mouth before he could even say "Evening, ma'am." He slipped to the ground and Jesse pulled the boy's keys and opened the door, dragging the ethered guard inside.

"Come on, Cowboy. Don't be meandering."

I walked the dynamite across the street, taking care not to slip.

"Hurry it up," he said. "We've got ten minutes tops."

I wasn't going to rush this: dropping nitroglycerin wasn't how my story should end. I looked down at the crate, then back up at the museum. There were maybe twenty sticks of dynamite inside. "I don't think it's enough to take the building down."

Mattie laughed. "It's not for the building, honey."

We stopped in the grand hall. Mattie locked the doors while Jesse dragged the security guard behind a kiosk.

"Get a load of this place," Mattie said. "Who'd think a two-bit cow-town could afford these digs."

"It's a fucking grift," Jesse said. "Skimming dimes from those poor bastards underground to build a goddamn collection of false idols to Royal buggery."

Mattie put a finger to his lips. "Language, dear."

The grand hall's vaulted ceilings rose to a skylight covered in snow. On clear days you could tell the time based on how the sun dripped into the room, but now the museum seemed like a relic.

"Christ, I hate this place," Jesse said. "It has the stench of corruption seeping through its walls."

He knocked on a wall and the noise echoed throughout the hall. "Reminds me of the first time I broke into Versailles. Had to spend two days hiding from some Parisian detective who fancied himself a regular Auguste Dupin. Once I got clear, I bathed myself three times a day for a week to get that filth off my skin."

"So if we're not dynamiting it, what the hell are we doing?" I asked.

Jesse smiled. "Like I said, liberation."

The museum had a few important items—a couple of old Renaissance paintings, a Knight's armor, some old Bibles, and even a few Celtic artifacts from the Pagan ages—but nothing that struck me as particularly meaningful, nothing so symbolic it seemed worth losing my life over. And then I saw it: overhead a banner advertised the *Shakespeare Quarto*. My uncle's prized possession, worth nearly a hundred grand, an artifact he'd been craving for years.

"Shit," I said.

"What is it, Cowboy?"

"I don't think it's here yet." I pointed at the banner. "Tomorrow, I think. Hamlet's being delivered tomorrow."

Jesse and Mattie exchanged glances: I was missing the point.

"What do I want with some cribbed copy of a too-long play about a spoiled rich kid?" Jesse said. "Not like I could fence it."

"I like that play," Mattie said. "It's funny."

"All right, Ophelia," Jesse said. "There's a guard in the west gallery. You know what to do."

Mattie pulled out a gun and disappeared into the dark halls of the museum.

"Come with me, Cowboy."

I followed with the dynamite, taking care to watch my step. He headed toward the backrooms and I tried to stay close, but he moved quick, like a cat or a leopard or some other damn animal instinctively suited for hunting at night.

"If we're not stealing the book," I said. "What the hell are we doing here?"

"Quiet."

I pressed myself against a wall, besides a painting of Napoleon at Waterloo. The General looked worried.

We waited. I lowered the dynamite to the floor and reached for my gun.

Footsteps came around the back. My father took out the ether, dampening the rag. A guard walked by; my father put the rag to the guard's face; he held on as the guard's arms flailed, but eventually the guard's legs went slack and his weight fell on Jesse; the two of them collapsed to the ground, but even as he fell, my father had a grace about him, a sort of sureness, and, though I could see he was scared, somehow he pushed through, concentrating on the details.

"Poor bastard," Jesse said. "He's gonna have a hangover not even Tom Paine could imagine."

"I know."

"Stay here," he said. "If he wakes up, knock him on the forehead with your gun."

He started toward the back offices and I grabbed his coat. "Where are you going?"

"Relax, Cowboy. Don't do anything brave."

He disappeared toward the museum's guts, while I leaned against the wall and lowered my hat and tried to look tough without spewing on my shoes. I could hear my own breath, so I paid attention to it like some sort of Buddhist, and, after a while, I just held my breath because the loudest place in the world is that space where you're trying to be absolutely silent. I could hear the patter of snow against glass and the gasping of the walls and the doped wheeze of the unconscious guard. The kid was no more than twenty years old and it didn't seem fair to knock him out, but he carried a gun for a dollar an hour and he was probably proud of his power and he'd grow old telling stories of how Jesse Stephens tanned him.

The wind slapped the museum and the bricks creaked and sighed. A cry behind a pedestal made me reach for my gun, but it was just a field mouse abandoning its hideout.

"Calm the fuck down." I hummed the Marseillaise, a trick I'd learned that first winter on the front.

The only noise left was the sound of my pacing boot heals: Mattie and my father stalked like ghosts through the building's bowels. The boy began to stir. His breathing quickened and you could hear a little groan, the beginnings of a cough. I turned the gun around; the butt facing his forehead. I aimed, rocking back and forth, like a batter awaiting his first pitch.

"Stop it," said a voice in the dark.

I scampered across the floor.

Mattie put her finger to her lips. "He's just dreaming," she said. "Relax. We're almost done."

She took out a pair of handcuffs and a handkerchief from her handbag and then bound and gagged the boy.

A knock at the front door sent us behind a pedestal. I looked through the Grand Hall, but could only see a shadowy figure on the other side of the glass door. A relief guard? A Pinkerton? My uncle? I couldn't tell, not in the dark. I knew, though, if someone didn't open the door, the stranger would call the cops. And our car was out front.

"Why's our getaway car, out front?" I asked. "That's ridiculous. Shouldn't we have hid it in the back or behind some hedges or—"

She put her hand to my forehead, and then swept it through my hair. She was petting me like some Schnauzer. It did, however, calm me.

Jesse snuck behind us. "Found it," he said. "Just two sticks."

Mattie pointed her gun at the door. "Visitors."

"If he hasn't opened it yet," Jesse said. "It buys us about five minutes."

Jesse grabbed two sticks of dynamite and told me to leave the rest—no use carrying it anymore—and we followed him into the back, the click of his heels leading us through the dark maze of halls and dust, and into Seamus' office, where my uncle sat handcuffed to his desk chair, bleeding from his mouth.

"Old Seamus here," Jesse started. "Burning the midnight oil trying to catch me and all he had to do was look up and there I was, the magnificent Jesse Stephens, in the flesh."

Seamus tried to say something to me, but he couldn't find the words. I bent toward him.

"You shouldn't have killed all those men," I said.

"Yep, you old bastard, and now we're going to pay you back," Jesse said, patting my uncle's tensing shoulder. "Old Seamus here put up a little bit of a struggle, but he was always a hundred pound man masquerading in a two hundred pound body."

"You're going to hang," Seamus said. "All of you."

My father pulled off the wall a painting of Queen Elizabeth, revealing a safe. "It's an old model," he said. "Won't take much."

"What's in there?" I asked. "Treasure? Secrets?"

"Something like that, Cowboy."

"If you steal—" Seamus said.

"Why are we blowing it?" I asked. "Why not just get the combination from him?"

"I wouldn't tell you if you put in a gun in my mouth."

"We could try," I said.

"Ain't a road we need to walk down yet," Jesse said. "Besides, I stole all this dynamite and it would be a shame not to use it."

Mattie coughed. "Who stole it?"

"I meant the collective I, as in you and me form one I."

"Sure you did." Mattie kneeled before a display case and

pointed at a painting of Thomas More, who was shown with wide, protruding eyes, the eyes of someone realizing the imminence of his own execution.

"I think I knew him," she said. "I think he tried to make love to me once."

"So this is your whore?" Seamus asked.

I looked at my father, but he didn't seem to hear it, or at least care.

"I prefer mistress," Mattie said. "It's got a much more sophisticated ring to it."

Jesse smirked. "Tape," he called out.

Mattie tossed him a roll and Jesse fastened the dynamite to the safe's combination lock. He backed away. "Should do it."

"You think?" Mattie asked. "Might need another one. Remember Budapest."

"Don't you ever forget anything?" Jesse said. "That wasn't my fault."

"I said you needed another one, but no, you didn't believe me."

"Fine," Jesse said. "Cowboy, go get another stick of dynamite."

"Neal," Seamus said. "If you do this, there isn't a road back home."

I went down the hall, careful to retrace my steps. I found the dynamite where I'd left it and saw that the guard was still asleep. I grabbed a stick and felt its lightness and I realized that even though I'd grown up around miners, I'd never held dynamite before.

When I got there, I looked around, but didn't see anything until I slipped around the corner and looked at the door and saw a half-dozen men on the street. They seemed to be waiting for the man with the key and I knew it wouldn't take but another minute for them to get in and they'd see the knocked-out guards and know it was us and we'd be cooked beneath the hanging tree by sunrise; so, knowing what was at stake and unwilling to consider second thoughts, I took out my lighter and lit the fuse on a stick of dynamite until the wick caught and sparked and I threw it at the door, and then I lit another and did the same and they both rolled to a stop about five feet from the door and I thought of running up and pushing them closer but I wasn't that damned foolish. Instead, I threw a third, which landed perfect, nestled up against the door's hinges.

I grabbed another stick for the safe and ran back to my uncle's office and when I got there, my father had a queer look on his face.

"You get lost?"

The explosion shook the museum and I found myself on the floor.

"Fucking Pinkertons," Jesse said. "Using goddamn dynamite in a fucking museum. The shame of it."

Mattie looked over at me and she knew what I'd done. "Yeah," she said. "You two are kin."

"What did you do, Neal?" Seamus called out. "This is your mother's museum."

"There were six of them," I said. "It'll hold them off."

"Or let them in," Mattie said. She brushed off her coat and then took out her gun. "I'll go."

She disappeared down the hall and my father got up and taped the third stick of dynamite to the safe then lit the fuses. He rolled Seamus out into the hall and shut the door and we ran down the hall and ducked.

"Oh, God," Seamus said, lowering his head. It looked like he was praying, but I could see that he was just cursing us.

Gunfire erupted from the Grand Hall and I felt sick with myself because they'd been generous bringing me along and all I'd done was ruin their heist.

"I'm sorry," I said to my father.

"Ah, don't worry," Jesse said. "She'll be fine. Can't fault you for blowing up Pinkertons. It's inherited, like eye color or flat feet."

The explosion blew the office door out into the hall.

"You hear that, you old sheep fucker?" Jesse said. "The sounds of revolution. The walls are coming down and you're looking at Joshua right here."

"You fools," Seamus said. "It's mine. It's mine. You haven't got the right."

We made our way through the smoke and ash and into the office. The desk was covered in steel chips and the paintings were on fire.

"This will bugger that cranky old bastard," Jesse said. He went to the safe and pulled out a bag and it seemed intact, which amazed me but I guess he'd been doing this long enough to know how to avoid burning the loot.

"What's in there?" I asked.

"Christmas oranges for orphans, doctors for whores: dreams, Cowboy. There are dreams in this bag."

I shook my head. "What?"

"About a hundred, hundred and twenty grand, Cowboy."

The money for the Shakespeare Quarto.

Seamus rolled into the door way and I could see he was near crying as he looked over the wreckage of his office and saw our hands in his loot.

"Neal, please, you can't do this. I've worked and earned and protected you and this town and now you're stealing—"

"You want a peek?" Jesse asked.

I went to the bag and looked inside and saw, over and over again like some hallucination, the portrait of an old patriot in a suit, next to the number 500.

"Who the hell is that?"

"John Marshall," Jesse said. "Chief Justice and a real son of a bitch. You can blame him for a whole host of crimes, but you can trade his face for gold and that's all that matters to rich bastards like your uncle."

"And anarchists," I said.

"What you getting at, Cowboy?"

"You're just a thief."

"He is," Seamus said. "A red thief and a rapist and a murderer."

More gunfire in the Grand Hall. My knees shook and I looked toward my uncle, whose face, flushed and wilting, stared lust at the cash. Was he right? Was my father just an old crook? Was that it all along?

"Now," Jesse said. He bent down to my uncle's eyes. "You're doing that again. Just because a man holds certain political beliefs that countervail the common norms doesn't mean he breaks the sins of decency. That's reserved for old child buggers like you and Vanderbilt and Hearst. Me, I'm just a revolutionary with sticky fingers. But I ain't keeping the money. Old men like you are thieves. You're nothing but a pickpocket. I'm Robin Hood."

"You took my virgin sister," Seamus said. "You soiled her and abandoned her like a whore."

"Your time's done, old man," Jesse said. "There ain't going to be no more hanging trees."

Mattie stopped in the doorway and reloaded her gun. "Should hold them off for a while." She looked at me. "You blew the whole entrance up. It's like Pompeii in there."

"Dear Lord," Seamus said.

"We should go," Jesse said.

I looked at my uncle, his eyes lit like a gas lamp.

"Good luck, you old bastard," Jesse said. "Sure we'll be haunting each other in the next life."

I went toward the Grand Hall, but my father grabbed me and pushed me the other way. "Down the corridor, Cowboy."

Mattie led us through the dark reaches of the museum and into a janitor's closet that had a backdoor. We emerged into the eye of the snowstorm. I shut my eyes and the cold swept over me. It took me a moment to get my bearings— we were in a back alley between the museum and Miss Ida's gallery. I looked up at the gallery window, but I couldn't see my pictures.

Mattie walked west behind the gallery and over to a small auto barn. She raised her gun, firing. The lock split open and we went inside.

"Which one are we going to steal?" I asked, but they looked at me with shrugs and I realized, once again, I had no idea what I was doing. I followed them to the back of the lot, where, nestled between a Model T and a Packard, awaited my uncle's two stolen appaloosas, saddled and reined.

"You're kidding," I said. "It's a damned blizzard out."

"Never stopped Chief Joseph," Jesse said. "Rode these beauts through Montana in January and Montana in January's a whole lot colder than this drizzle. Come on, Cowboy—you still remember how to ride?"

It had been a very long time.

Mattie shared Jesse's steed as we rode down the snow-drenched alley into the dark of the abandoned town. We slowly marched along side streets, while I kept my eye out for cars and Pinkertons and my uncle. Shuttered windows hid crouched families awaiting word of the militia's next move, while the occasional oil lamp illuminated a lone reader unable to feign sleep. We turned east and trotted through Pioneer Park. All of the animals hibernated and it seemed like we were the only life left on the emptied world.

"Where are we going?" I asked.

"Train station," Jesse said.

The militia had roadblocks in all directions and I figured they'd also have men at the train station. I was about to tell him this, but I realized he knew it and he had another plan. They rode ahead of me: Mattie held on to my father, resting her head on his back, while the snow coated her shoulders and hair.

"Used to be, in the old days," Jesse started. "We'd blow the building and march off and think we'd won some sort of battle, but then the banks and the barons just go and build another and pay men poor wages and it didn't seem to do much good and then this time in Vienna—"

"Munich," Mattie said.

"That's right, Munich," Jesse said. "Well, we got in this bank in Munich and I was rigging charges along the beams, set to bring the big bastard down, when I realized I was short a few sticks and I was awful upset by this because you know how I'm a perfectionist about my work, but then I saw, out of the corner of my eye that steel vault and it cried out to me, "blow me up, blow me up" and so I did and we took near two hundred thousand marks and hightailed it to Berlin where we gave it all away, minus traveling expenses, mostly to some poor Jews and they started a paper and a dance hall and Mattie even taught them how to make their own bourbon, and so, what I'm getting at is we found that liberating the ill-gotten purses of the overlords had better rewards than simple symbolism. Though I still like dynamiting shit."

"He does," Mattie said. "It gets awful loud at home."

We took the back trails, old paths carved by Arapahos, toward the New Sligo railway station. The appaloosa— sturdy as my father promised—seemed to drive itself as if he was navigating by a compass passed down from its sire. The snow began to pick up again and I felt the cold in my hands and my nose. To the south, smoke funneled out of Rahillville. It was nearly burned clear through and smelled of wood and tin.

I checked my watch when I heard the first blow of the nearing *Lady of San Francisco* coming up from Denver. It was almost midnight.

"Let's pick up the pace, Cowboy."

I got my horse cantering along the snowy trail and we ducked under a railroad trestle and came up on a long stretch of road that we galloped down. The horse moved fluidly, sure-footed and I felt the old muscles from my early century youth tightening and yawning as we spurred the horses on toward the station. The *Lady* cried out in the white night as she pulled into the station. We cut south then east, coming around the back of the station as I heard the familiar sounds of the train coming to a halt. We ran those horses the last thousand yards and the wind in my face cooled my sweat and I felt, for the first time all night, the joy Mattie and my father shared. I'd spend my life searching for that feeling again.

"Over here," my father called out.

The east gate, which was usually crowded with men moving coal, was abandoned. We got off the horses and my father smacked each on the ass.

"Get on," he called out and the appaloosas galloped out on to the prairie and disappeared into the shroud of snow.

We ducked under a gap in the gate—one my father had cut himself—and slipped passed some sleeping cargo loaders toward the back end of the train, where a row of freight cars awaited coal that they'd never see. The cars were vandalized by old signatures and drawings from before the war and as the *Lady* cried out for her departure, my father took out a pen and wrote "El Guapo" on the door.

"You're such a ham," Mattie said.

My father and I boosted Mattie on to the train as the sound of a speeding auto and its accompanying siren came around toward the East gate.

"Hell," Jesse said. "Thought they'd take longer."

From the low rise of the track, I could see it was Jacob's car parking at the gate. He got out and Seamus joined him.

"They know we're here, don't they?" I said.

"Well, shit, Cowboy. What do you think?"

"How?"

"Well, I imagine someone spotted three people atop two horses running away from the museum. But that's just a guess. Come on."

The train edged slowly away from the station. My father pulled himself on to the freight and I handed him the bundle of cash. He reached out his hand.

I didn't take it.

"They'll stop the train," I said.

"We've got guns, Cowboy."

"They'll have more."

"Grab my hand."

On the west side of the track, a radio usually stood unmanned this time of night. It didn't have much distance, but it was enough to call a train back if it was within a mile or two of the station. But once out of reach, the *Lady* wouldn't stop until Grand Junction, which gave a fleeing couple over two hundred miles to jump to the safe anonymity of the Rocky Mountains.

I turned and saw Jacob and Seamus making their way toward us. Each was armed.

"Go on," I said. "I'll hold them off."

"You don't have to."

"I do."

My father turned to Mattie. She shrugged. "He's your son," she said. "He'll do what he wants."

As the train pulled away, my father lowered his hat and smiled. "If they try to hang you, Cowboy," he said. "I'll bust you out. I promise."

I stopped walking and watched my father and his gun girl disappear around the bend and into the snowy night toward their next escape. It was only when they were passed me that I began doubting my plan.

By the time the sound of the train disappeared into the dark, Seamus and Jacob were on me. The fat detective put a gun to my back, and then frisked me, patting the gun in my pocket, before pushing me toward the station.

"I told you he'd leave you, again," my uncle said.

"Shouldn't we chase them?" Jacob said.

The question didn't seem serious, though. Jacob put his revolver in his pocket, then pulled a cigarette from his pack, lighting it, before offering the pack to me.

"No," Seamus said.

We followed him up to the station, which lay empty and fallow, abandoned except for the breathing pile of cripples huddling together beneath the clock tower. The militia was gone, driving off to the museum when word of a robbery arrived.

It was just a minute past midnight.

Ten minutes, I told myself. Ten minutes and they'll be out of range.

"Your father has my money?" Seamus asked.

I didn't say anything.

"You're going to hang, you know that, don't you?" Seamus said. "No more forgiveness."

Seamus got to the radio room but it was locked. He fired two shots into the door, unhinging it.

"All this," he said, waving his arms about and staring swift justice at me. "All this is because of you. You, Neal. This is your fault. If you'd kept your nose out and done what I said, none of this—hell—I just wanted Pearl to rest in peace. That's all, but you wouldn't let her."

And then it became clear to me: the mystery that had begun it all, the crime that had triggered this mess. I finally had a truth, a single truth. It was Seamus' truth and it was one rich in binaries, dualities, blacks and whites. It was all notions of honor and Manifest Destiny. In his mind, Seamus had built his own city on the hill, where right and wrong was as clear as the rivers before coal. It was a world with its own version of history. In it, my mother hadn't killed herself and anyone who questioned this had to die. After dim Clyde O'Leary had discovered my mother's suicide, he had put the screws on Seamus. So when Seamus found poor O'Leary, bound and naked, Seamus changed history: erasing any trace of my mother's suicide.

"My father didn't kill O'Leary," I said. "But he did steal the files the night O'Leary was executed."

Seven minutes.

"What did you say, Neal?"

"Jesse was there the night O'Leary was killed. He busted into the jail to get the files for Forest. That part was right. He tied O'Leary up, but he didn't kill him."

"Then it was Forest himself or some other Jew or Negro or whomever he hired," Seamus said. "It doesn't matter anymore, Neal."

"But you shot him, Seamus."

My uncle froze.

"Stop it, Neal," he said. "You've really gone mad like your father. After all I've done for you."

"O'Leary was blackmailing you," I said. "He knew my mother killed herself, but she couldn't stay buried Catholic if it came out and you couldn't let her be put away like some sort of heathen, not with the whole town watching you."

"Jesse killed your mother." Seamus flipped on the radio and it began warming up.

"It makes sense," Jacob said, his voice even, mildly curious like he was talking about the ball game. "You had a motive, Seamus."

"What motive?"

"Vengeance," Jacob said. "Biblical reason if I've ever heard one and I'm a preacher's son."

"You'll hang too."

"You found him tied and naked," I said. "Even had a note on him, from El Guapo, and you knew that was my father and O'Leary let him get away and he had my mother's file. O'Leary had put a play on you because that was the type of man he was, so you shot him because that's the type of man you are, then you hung Forest for it. It took care of everything. It would make things right for you, but it isn't right, Seamus. It isn't."

"Your father murdered Pearl." Seamus reached for the receiver. "And you've helped her killer and I'll sit there and watch you hang."

I raised my revolver. Five more minutes.

"Sit down, Seamus. You're not calling anyone. Not until they get clear."

Seamus grunted like I'd sold him out to the Romans. He looked at Jacob. "Aren't you going to do anything?"

"Don't see anything worth doing." Jacob slipped his hands into his pockets. "Just a man exercising his right to bear arms."

"Sit," I said.

Seamus raised the receiver to his ear, and dropped his other hand toward his gun, unfastening his holster. Four minutes.

"Sit."

"Son, put it down," Seamus said. "Do it for your mother."

"Sit."

Seamus tugged at his gun lifting it as far as his hip before I squeezed the revolver twice and it jumped in my hand and Seamus fell, crashing into the radio and collapsing into a heap of train schedules.

I stopped above him. The old man's gray eyes were dry, and blood poured from his chest and his throat and made a sound like a whistle. He still clutched his gun, but he was dead.

I looked down and saw my boots were steeped in blood and snow. Dizzy, I bent over and dropped my gun and felt tired. I loosened my tie and yanked my collar and pulled up my sleeves and wanted to get out of my clothes until Jacob stopped beside me and picked up the gun, and then offered me his flask.

I waved him away.

He went to the radio, putting the receiver to his ear. He changed the frequency.

"New Sligo Police," he said.

I crouched beside Seamus and touched the old man's face. I'd done this and I mourned him, but the ten minutes were nearly up and it was for some kind of good. I took the old man's hand and said I was sorry for how his life turned out and I was because I wished events hadn't built up like they had so that it made sense for me to shoot him.

"Yeah, it's Detective Bailey. Mr. Rahill's dead. Up at the train station," he said. "Yes. Shot."

I met Jacob's gaze.

"Jesse Stephens," Jacob said. "Jesse shot him. Get the militia to set roadblocks out toward the south. Stole a car and headed toward Denver. Yeah, I saw him."

After a while, I found myself on the platform. I looked over at the war cripples and sighed and I made my way to the tracks and watched the snow melt on the rails. The station was silent, but I knew trucks full of kids with rifles were on their way, and those kids had ideas about the world that led to the sort of disasters that repeated themselves every generation or so. Yet, for that moment, on that platform, everything seemed silent.

Beyond the station, across town, smoke plumed from the museum. It burned to the ground that night, the columns, arches, and art turning to rubble and ash. They never replaced it. Instead, they turned the lot into a shrine for my uncle, erecting a statue of his likeness, and, on its pedestal, they placed a placard chronicling his heroic life and his tragic death at the hand of my father. It's still there today, but not much else remains of that time: Rahill Coal

& Electric was long sold to a Pittsburgh interest, who had their own strikes, their own version of Rahillville.

On that platform, I was the last of the Rahills, our power disappearing overnight. I can't say what was lost because of Seamus' death, perhaps just a sense of historical proportion, a connection to our founding, but I know, no matter how much I deny it, his life and death live within me. Him and Jesse Stephens.

Jacob approached, his coat glazed in snow. He stood beside me like he would for a long time after that day, after we fled New Sligo.

"When's the next train?" Jacob asked.

"Six thirty-five to Kansas City."

"Good," he said.

"There are some things I've got to take care of out there," I told him. "I've got to make sure she's dead."

"Alright."

"I think she is, but I want to be sure."

"And if she's not?"

I didn't have an answer, then. I'd have to go searching for it and I did and of course I never found her and that's a pain that has stayed with me long after the pictures yellowed and the letters crumbled. I still mourn her. Yet, in the end, searching for her gave me a purpose. It led me back into the world, to the places I saw, to the photographs I took.

But that doesn't absolve me.

Sometimes at night, when I can't sleep and I've run out of prayers to make or pictures to develop, I imagine Lorraine alive, not as she once was, not as young and vital and beautiful, but instead the woman she would have become if she'd made it out of that nearly-forgotten war. I imagine her growing old and growing gray, living in a big house somewhere in Lisbon, children and grandchildren at her feet, and I like to think that she occasionally sees a man with a camera and remembers me, remembers Paris, and even if she's cursing me under her breath, I hope she remembers our stories.

THE TRENCH ANGEL

As I waited on the militia, I went down to the track and my boots sunk into the snow and I laid my hand on the rail, feeling the warmth of the steel and its possibilities. From there, I looked west toward the mountains, toward California, toward the end of the white horizon, as the snow made invisible the tracks laid by the anarchist.

A SELECTIVE BIBLIOGRAPHY

I'm particularly indebted to the works of Patricia Limerick, Richard White, and Donald Worster, along with the archivists at the Colorado Historical Society who walked me through the myriad of old letters, diaries, and newspaper articles that made this book possible.

Killing for Coal: America's Deadliest Labor War. Thomas G. Andrews. Harvard University Press, Cambridge, 2010.

First World War Photographers. Jane Carmichael. Routledge, New York, 1990.

Nature's Metropolis: Chicago and the Great West. William Cronon. W.W. Norton & Company, New York, 1992.

A Cloud of Witnesses. Anna De Koven. E.P. Dutton, New York, 1920.

Intimate Matters: A History of Sexuality in America. John D' Emilio and Estelle B. Freedman. University of Chicago Press, Chicago, 1998.

Rites of Spring: The Great War and the Birth of the Modern Age. Modris Eksteins. Mariner, Boston, 2000.

The Great War and Modern Memory. Paul Fussell. Oxford University Press, New York, 1975.

An Overland Journey from New York to San Francisco in the Summer of 1859. Horace Greeley. C.M. Saxton, Barker & Co., San Francisco, 1860.

The Culture of Time and Space, 1880-1918. Stephen Kern. Harvard University Press, Cambridge. 2003.

No Place of Grace: Antimodernism and the Transformation of American Culture, 1880-1920. T.J. Jackson Lears. University of Chicago Press, Chicago, 1994.

The Legacy of Conquest: The Unbroken Past of the American West. Patricia Limerick. W.W. Norton, New York, 1987.

The Eye that Never Sleeps: A History of the Pinkerton National Detective Agency. Frank Morn. Indiana University Press, Bloomington, 1982.

The French in Love and War: Popular Culture in the Era of the World Wars. Charles Rearick. Yale University Press, New Haven, CT, 1997.

Low Life. Luc Sante. Farrar, Straus and Giroux, New York, 2003.

Colorado Mining: A Photgraphic History. Duane A. Smith. University of New Mexico Press, Albuquerque, 1977.

The First World War. Hew Strachan. Penguin Books, New York, 2005

The Contested Plains: Indians, Goldseekers, and the Rush to Colorado. Elliot West. University Press of Kansas, Lawrence KS, 1998.

"It's Your Misfortune and None of My Own": A New History of the American West. Richard White. University of Oklahoma Press, Norman, OK, 1993.

The Experience of World War I. J.M. Winter. Oxford University Press, New York, 1989.

Rivers of Empire: Water, Aridity, and the Growth of the American West. Donald Worster. Oxford University Press, New York, 1992.

Acknowledgments

After eight years of working on this beast, there are far more people to thank than I could possibly list. But here goes. . . .

At Leapfrog, thank you Lisa Graziano for believing in this project, Ann Weinstock for the badass cover, and Laura Hess and Rebeca Schwab for your advice.

Thank you Eleanor Jackson for your counsel and dedication.

Thank you to the University of New Hampshire's MFA program for supporting me, educating me. There are too many folks in snowy Durham who heard me out and offered me rides home and told me when a specific line was off-key to properly recognize, but particular gratitude goes out to the critical eyes of Ann Williams, Elise Juska, MRB Chelko, Kate Megear, Dylan Walsh, Tim Horvath, Nate Graziano, Clark Knowles, Amy VanHaren, Sara Erdmann, Sue Hertz, and Leah Williams. Thank you Nicola Imbrascio and Abby Knoblauch for being my confidants.

Thanks to the librarians at the Colorado Historical Society, the New York Public Library, and the University of New Hampshire. You're truly doing God's work.

At the University of Massachusetts, Heather Cox-Richardson, Noel Hudson, and Shane Brennan encouraged me and gave me confidence. At the University of Miami, Andrew Green and Gina Maranto welcomed me and taught me how to survive Florida. In Houston, Willie and Mabel were my inspiration. At the University of North Carolina, Melissa Geil has been my friend and work wife.

Thank you to my mother Julie Gutierrez and my sister Laura Lee Harlan. No man could ask for a better pair of women to raise and nurture him. Eileen Ulrich gave me my first books and set me on this course. The Iselins have provided me love, support, and a second family.

Joe Lewis, despite our wives and your children, you'll always be my life partner.

Brian Wilkins, you've taken my calls during both coffee and bourbon hours, kept up my swagger, and read far more of these pages than I had the right to ask of you. This book is as much you as me.

Alex Parsons, you're the mentor all young writers dream of. You gave me the talk during my second draft that pushed me to my tenth. I'd have quit long ago without you. Someday, for you, I'll learn how to pronounce my last name correctly.

Finally, Jessica, darling, I love you. Anytime you and the Sue want to get in the car and drive off for parts unknown, just know I'll be right beside you, always.

THE AUTHOR

Michael Keenan Gutierrez earned degrees from UCLA, the University of Massachusetts, and the University of New Hampshire. His work has been published in *Scarab*, *The Pisgah Review*, *Untoward*, *The Boiler*, *Crossborder*, and *LA Weekly*. His screenplay, *The Granite State*, was a finalist at the Austin Film Festival and he has received fellowships from The University of Houston and the New York Public Library. He lives with his wife in Chapel Hill, where he teaches writing at the University of North Carolina.

About the Type

This book was set using the Bauer Bodoni™ typeface. Giambattista Bodoni (1740-1813) was called the King of Printers and the Bodoni font owes its creation in 1767 to his masterful cutting techniques.

The Bodoni font embodies the rational thinking of the Enlightenment and was the most popular typeface until the mid-19th century.

Bauer Bodoni™ appeared in 1926 with the Bauer font foundry. It was designed by typeface designer and book binder, Heinrich Jost (1889-1949), the artistic director of the foundry from 1922 until 1948. The forms are closely related to those of the original font and they are more delicate and elegant than many other Bodoni interpretations.

Composed at JTC Imagineering, Santa Maria, CA
Designed by John Taylor-Convery